Liberty, Fidelity, Eternity by Jill Stengl
Justine Didier's father wishes her to wed a man she despises when her heart belongs to Émile Girardeau, a family servant and Justine's lifelong friend. As turmoil begins in revolutionary Paris, Justine is trapped and hopeless. A masquerade ball offers an opportunity of escape—and much danger. Only when Justine learns to trust God with her future can she and Émile find safety and a life together.

A Duplicitous Façade by Tamela Hancock Murray
In obedience to her father, Melodia Stuart agrees to marry Sir Rolf, a man she has never met. She is certain her life is over until she falls in love with the godly knight. But when a mysterious woman flirts with Rolf at the masquerade ball to celebrate the marriage, Melodia suspects she has more enemies than friends. Is Rolf who he claims to be? Or are they both trapped in *a duplicitous façade*?

Love's Unmasking by Bonnie Blythe
Viscount Matthew Leighton is certain a godly girl does not exist among London's money-grubbing debutantes. He imitates a fop at society functions to repel them, but his own ruse traps him in an engagement with Amaryllis Sinclair. As they work together to find the truth behind a murder, will they discover the truth under each of their masks?

Moonlight Masquerade by Pamela Griffin
Letitia, an unassuming lady's companion to her cousin, quickly finds herself the focus of attention from two mysterious men. Edward, a servant, saves her from being trampled; then the marquis, who is entertaining her cousin's party, singles her out. But who can she trust when she overhears a conversation and discovers a terrible crime?

MASQUERADE

One Mask Cannot Disguise Love
in Four Romantic Adventures

BONNIE BLYTHE=PAMELA GRIFFIN
TAMELA HANCOCK MURRAY=JILL STENGL

ISBN 1-59310-836-2

All scripture quotations are taken from the King James Version of the Bible.

Interior Art by Mari Goering

Published by Barbour Publishing, Inc., P.O. Box 719, Uhrichsville, Ohio 44683, www.barbourbooks.com

Our mission is to publish and distribute inspirational products offering exceptional value and biblical encouragement to the masses.

Printed in the United States of America.
5 4 3 2 1

MASQUERADE

Liberty, Fidelity, Eternity

by Jill Stengl

Dedication

With love to Sally, Pamela, and Tamela,
three talented ladies and *trois cheres amies.*

Let us hold fast the profession of our faith without wavering;
(for he is faithful that promised).
HEBREWS 10:23

Chapter 1

Paris—August 29, 1792

Émile carried a serving tray upstairs and along the upper hall, warped floorboards squeaking beneath his feet. He knocked before entering mademoiselle's bedchamber, on the unlikely chance she might have arisen early. Stripes of sunlight on the carpet shifted as a breeze ruffled the draperies. Émile placed the tray on a table, dared a glance at the four-poster bed's occupant, and smiled grudgingly. An Egyptian mummy could be no more entangled in its shroud than was Justine Didier in her bedclothes.

By long habit, he focused on his duties. "*Bonjour, mademoiselle.* The morning is half spent, and you have plans for the day." He pushed open the draperies. Sudden brightness made him squint.

Fabric rustled and popped as she kicked her way to freedom. "Plans?" she moaned. "What plans? Why must the sun be so bright?" From the corner of his eye he saw her sit up in bed and embrace a coverlet in startled modesty. "Why are you in my chamber, Émile? Where is Berthe?"

"Monsieur—your father—mentioned plans for a carriage ride."

She gave another, more heartfelt groan. "*Oui,* I remember now."

Émile poured steaming chocolate into a china cup. "Berthe found a position in the household of Madame Evrard, who lured her with the promise of double pay. Cook's lumbago keeps her downstairs, so I brought up the trays. Your father studies in his sitting room. Do you take sugar?"

Justine flopped back on her pillows. "Another maid lost. Émile, why do they leave us? Am I so difficult to please? Does Papa insult them? Ever since we arrived in Paris, the story is the same. Papa hires them, they work a week or two, then poof! Off they flit to greener pastures." She sighed. "Of course I take sugar. And plenty of cream. This is most irregular—and awkward. Will you please bring my dressing gown from the back of that chair?"

Émile bowed and fetched the lace-trimmed garment. While she donned it, he busied himself stirring sugar into her chocolate. Seeing his hand tremble, he willed it back under control.

"I am ready now, Émile. You may bring the tray."

He placed it across her lap and backed away. "Anything else this morning?"

"Oui, I require much more. Émile, why do you avoid my gaze? If I did not know better, I would think you conceal a shameful secret. I have prayed for an opportunity to speak with you, and God has provided." She tasted the chocolate.

"Perfect. Berthe never prepared it so well."

He dared to offer a brief smile and immediately regretted it. The lips pursed to blow upon her hot drink changed to an answering smile. Leaning back against her mounded pillows, Justine was like an exotic flower amid the snowy disarray of her bedclothes. However, worry shaded her eyes.

Émile fought to keep affection and concern for a Christian sister foremost in his thoughts. "What troubles you, mademoiselle?" he asked.

"I am in a quandary. I need guidance. The future looks bleak, and I haven't a true friend in the world. Otherwise, all is well." She sipped her chocolate as if to demonstrate nonchalance, but her furtive glance in his direction spoiled the effect.

"What frightens you?"

"Everything." She dropped the sarcasm. "I feel terribly. . . alone. Émile, since our mothers died, no one but you advises me about spiritual matters. Yet since I returned from school, barriers exist between us—barriers of position and of propriety, I suppose—yet. . .I miss the friendship we once shared." Her voice sounded small. "I am so very homesick."

"I, too." His admission came out in a squawk. He took a step back and glanced toward the open door. How much of this conversation could her father hear?

"Do not leave me alone, please! Almost I begin to question the beliefs dearest to my heart. Papa and his enlightened friends deny the existence of God and ridicule the redemption of Christ. Sometimes I fear I have placed my faith in a sweetly devised tale."

Émile heard near-hysterical anxiety in her tone. "To the

lost, the cross is foolishness." His chest felt tight—almost as tight as his cryptic answer. He could imagine which of the "enlightened" friends mocked Justine's faith.

Her eyelids flickered. "To me, the cross of Christ is life itself. Oh, Émile, I would die before I denied my Lord. The alternative is. . .unthinkable. Yet I find myself tempted to join their elite group under false colors. You must think me vain and frivolous, allowing flattery to turn my head."

She paused, but Émile held his tongue. A laugh, half sob, escaped her. She set her cup back on the tray. "And you are right to think so. But it isn't vanity alone. Papa attended school with Monsieur Boniface's father long ago. The plan of a marriage alliance between the families has long been dear to Papa's heart."

His brain and body seemed wooden, yet a mannequin could never feel such pain.

"You will not advise me? Yet I know the truth for myself. Why do I annoy you with my petty trials? Henri Boniface is charming and clever; everyone says so. He is near your age, is he not, Émile? I recall following you both around when we were children. He says I was an adorable pest. I could not have been more than seven when he went away to school. I do not remember him clearly, though I think he liked to tease me."

Émile dared not refresh her memory. He glanced back at the doorway again. Justine sat up straight. "Please wait, Émile. If you will not help me, I don't know what I'll do."

Her plea and her outstretched hand caught his full attention. "Justine, the Lord is your unfailing source of comfort and wisdom, not I." A cough from the sitting room across the hall spurred him to action. Bowing deeply, he excused himself.

When he collected Monsieur Didier's breakfast tray, the master acknowledged his presence with a nod. His gray eyes expressed disapproval, though he said nothing.

As Émile stepped into the hallway, sobs and sniffs from Justine's chamber seared his heart like a branding iron. *Why, God? Why must it be this way? You must comfort her, for I cannot.*

Chapter 2

Tilting her head to listen, Justine followed Émile's progress down the creaking stairs. Another quivering sigh ended in a sob. She pushed tears from her cheeks with the back of one hand.

Although he alone remained of all the family servants her father had brought with them from Normandy to Paris, Émile seldom crossed Justine's path. This rental house was small compared to *la Maison d'Arbre de Cerise*—Cherry Tree House, her childhood home in Normandy. She should bump into Émile regularly. Actually, she often searched the house for him in hopes of creating such a chance meeting. Where did he spend his time?

Suspicions filled her heart and produced another rush of tears. "I will not think of it," she muttered, then set aside her breakfast tray and rolled out of bed. She had wasted enough of the morning already. Henri would soon arrive to take her for the planned carriage ride; he must not find her unprepared. His time was valuable.

She dressed quickly and brushed out her hair at her dressing table. Unskilled in the art of arranging hair, she settled for a simple chignon. Glaring at her reflection in the mirror, she again forbade herself to think of Adrienne. Her former maid would have arranged Justine's abundant hair in an elegant cadogan, chattering all the while about. . .

Bits of conversation darted into memory before Justine could stop them. She pressed her hands over her ears. "Stop it! Stop torturing yourself, you stupid girl. He loves her, and you can do nothing about it."

Sickening jealousy brought her to her knees. Hands clasped over her heart, she prayed aloud. "*Jésus de seigneur, m'aider!* Émile is so right that You alone are my help and my strength. Why must my heart cling to him so? Please remove this. . .this *thorn* from me and help me to face the future alone, if need be."

"Justine?"

Still kneeling, she turned to see her father's black-clad figure in the doorway. "Papa, I did not know. . . ." She scrambled to rise, stepped on her petticoat, and stumbled to her feet.

A frown creased his broad forehead. "Do you wish to speak with me, *ma fille*? It saddens me to hear you weep so. Had your mother lived. . ." He heaved a deep sigh. "Speeches I give every day, yet before my own daughter I am stricken dumb. The plans I make for your future are meant to bring you happiness and security, Justine, not sorrow. Long have I known of your unfortunate attachment to Émile Girardeau, a good and intelligent man yet your inferior in every other respect. A woman needs a husband with a promising future, especially during these turbulent times."

"I know you have my best interests at heart, Papa, but I cannot love and trust Henri Boniface. Papa, he. . .he does not honor me with the respect a woman desires from her future husband."

Papa approached, took her hand, and patted it. "*Mon cher enfant,* ride with young Boniface today and hear his proposals. I disapprove of many of his ideas, and I know he gives free rein to his passions at times, but he is young; he will learn. If you remain unmoved by his ardor and eloquence, I shall not press you to accept his suit. There will be other suitors for one as beautiful as you, *ma petite Justine.*"

Encouraged by his affectionate expressions, she dared to confront him. "Papa, was not the Republic set up for the purpose of establishing liberty, equality, and fraternity for all?" When he nodded warily, she reached one hand out to straighten his cravat. "If Émile and I wished to marry, surely you would give us your blessing. Already we are equal in God's sight."

Storm clouds gathered on her father's brow. "You speak of equality in simplistic terms. Leave such matters to men, and trust your father to decide if a man is worthy of your affections. This childish attachment to a servant will pass soon enough. I hoped the fellow would move on to new employment when we arrived in Paris, but to my disgust he is the one servant who remained when all the others deserted us. I would suspect him of maneuvering to avoid military conscription if the true reason were not evident."

"If you imagine I am the reason he remained with us, you are mistaken. To me, he behaves like a brother. He taught me to follow the Lord Christ, as Maman did." Justine squeezed her father's hand. "Maman believed that you would accept Christ's salvation someday."

He stepped away and swore. "This religion of blood and guilt and mystical *bêtise* has addled your brain. I forbid you to indulge such fancies any longer!"

"It is truth, Papa, not foolishness. I suspect that if Émile were a rampaging *sans-culotte* instead of a meek Christian, you might approve him as suitor for your daughter. How charming is this *liberté*—freedom to choose only one choice!"

He lowered his bleak gaze and backed away. "I hear Henri's carriage at the door."

Justine collected her hat and her red scarf. She descended the stairs just as Émile admitted Henri Boniface. Henri, trim and debonair in his fitted jacket and long trousers, towered over Émile. "*Non,* I'll be leaving again shortly," he said when Émile offered to take his hat and gloves.

Then Henri caught sight of Justine. His eyes widened. "Such beauty is seldom seen in this old city, *cherie*. And the patriotic theme," he grinned, "lends the finishing touch to your perfection."

Justine smoothed her blue-and-white-striped redingote jacket and touched the red bow adorning the filmy white *fichu-menteau* wrapped around her shoulders. "My bow matches your cap, Monsieur Boniface." Pausing before the hall mirror, she pinned her bonnet of ribbon and red ostrich plumes into place. "Émile, have you seen my gloves? I cannot find them."

"Here, mademoiselle." He picked them off a hall table and offered them with a little bow.

Henri looked Émile up and down, focusing with evident scorn on the servant's knee breeches. "Still wearing culottes, eh? Some embrace liberty and equality while others wallow in subjugation. I recognize this servant as the boy with whom you and I played long ago, Justine, whenever my family came to visit yours." He chuckled. "As I recall, he was always weak. Remember the time I brought my bow and shot a cat in your mother's garden? Non? Well, you were young. This fellow was fat back then, with the roundest cheeks ever seen. He cried like a baby over that cat. I cannot recall a time I've laughed harder."

Justine looked at Émile's stolid face, then back at Henri, who winked as if to share a joke.

"My mother loved her cats. I imagine Émile was not alone in mourning the animal's death." She drew on her gloves, approached the door, and waited for him to open it. "I am ready."

Henri apparently put the incident from his mind, for he was a jovial companion during the ride. Justine tried to encourage his pleasant mood by admiring the river, the horses, Henri's driving, and anything else that came to mind, yet a cloud of gloom hung over her spirit, much like the dreary midday haze that shrouded the city. The lovely Tuileries gardens brought to her only visions of the recent ransacking of the Tuileries palace. Papa tried to shield her as much as possible from the details of that violent day, but Henri felt no such concern for her sensibilities.

They lunched at a café near the gardens. While Henri downed a quantity of burgundy and discoursed about recent events in the Assemblies, Justine picked at her food, her thoughts far away. If she were to suggest marriage to Émile, a union based on mutual esteem and spiritual harmony, how would he react? With all kindness he would explain the impossibility of the scheme, pointing out her father's disapprobation and his own engaged affections, and her heart would quietly break.

"I had hoped to speak with you today about our future

together, but your humor seems unpromising," Henri observed as he assisted her to the seat of his yellow phaeton. His groom, a boy of no more than ten years, climbed to a precarious perch in back.

Once Henri seated himself beside her, Justine granted him a wan smile. He held the reins with one hand and reached to grasp her wrist. "Even in silence, your company is golden," he said. "And the vision of your features in pensive repose inspires my soul with an agony of bliss. But I will not annoy you with expressions of passion today, though they crowd my heart every moment, demanding release in spoken word or"—his hand traveled up her forearm—"in physical touch."

The man was gifted with a silver tongue, she mused, yet his flattering speeches left her heart unmoved. Her only reaction to his touch was a sense of gratitude for her long sleeves and his gloves. Evidently displeased by her lack of response, he snapped the reins and clucked to his chestnut pair.

As they drove along one crowded street, Justine read a poster nailed to a wall: TO ARMS, CITIZENS! THE ENEMY IS AT OUR GATES. She spoke her thoughts aloud. "Are we truly in danger of attack? Everywhere I see citizens bearing arms. Sometimes I wish to return to the country."

"You would not escape danger by running. France is liberated from the curse of monarchy, but we are under attack from evil oppressors like Prussia and Austria. Also, within this city abound traitors who would undermine our cause and set the former king back upon the throne. Many of these have already been imprisoned, yet we fear the Republic's enemies may find a way to free them before justice can be served. Keep your eyes and ears open for any sign of treachery. Even you, a tender young woman, must be vigilant in support of the *patrie*."

"Do they not expect you in the assembly today?" she asked as Henri drove into unfamiliar parts of the city. "I thought you had already assumed your new duties as a Parisian delegate."

"Soon." He licked his lips, his eyes alight. "The assembly's tone must change with the times, Justine. I shall be honored to represent my section at all cost."

Donkey carts laden with rotting fruit or freshly killed poultry rumbled past; one fat driver nodded at Henri and called out a greeting. Yet elsewhere Justine saw desperate faces and ragged clothing. Raucous music drifted from a tavern doorway. A woman screamed. Men laughed.

"Do you know where we are?" Justine asked.

"I know this section of the *faubourg* well. Never fear; you are safe with me. I brought you here for a purpose. I do not believe you take our cause enough to heart, Justine. Look around." He waved one arm. "Here you see evidence of abject poverty caused by the evil excesses of royalty, nobility, and clergy. Soon we will eradicate all such parasites—already we have purged Paris of many enemies, and the former tyrant is imprisoned. Only when he is dead will this suffering *canaille* rise to its proper place in a liberated France. Keep the horror you see fresh in your mind. Let it feed your hatred in days to come." Feverish excitement throbbed in his voice.

A fetid mist rose from the cobblestones. Justine covered her nose with a handkerchief and inhaled as little as possible. Shaking her head, she tried to deny her constant sense of dread.

At last she began to recognize her surroundings. Modest row houses faced the street on either side. A few shop signs swung overhead. Henri drew up his horses and leaped from the seat. Justine accepted his help down and let him walk her to the front door, where she turned to face him. "Thank you for the ride and for luncheon, Monsieur Boniface."

He spoke in a smiling undertone. "If you take me inside, I'll make every attempt to increase your enjoyment of the day, Justine."

She extricated her hand from his grasp. "I must refuse your kind offer today, monsieur, but perhaps another time Papa will invite you to dine with us."

He placed his hand on her waist and drew close. "You increase my anticipation, *ma belle cherie*, but I cannot wait forever. I wish to present you with a gift—a costume for the grand masked ball. You must plan to attend. Madame Perotine would be insulted if you missed it. Everyone will be there to celebrate our freedom from tyranny."

"We shall be there." Her father had not yet agreed to attend, but she couldn't imagine him missing such an event. As a deputy in the assembly, he felt obligated to take part in major social events.

Henri's eyes flickered dark fire. "You will accept and wear my gift?"

"Merci." She saw no reason to arouse his anger by refusing. "I've never been to a *bal masqué* and have no idea what would be proper to wear."

A satisfied smile spread across his face. "You will be the most beautiful creature ever seen."

Chapter 3

While Émile shoveled ashes from the parlor hearth, the front door closed. He paused, hearing rustling sounds as Justine removed her bonnet and gloves. Heavy steps descended the staircase.

"*Bonsoir,* Papa. You are home? No meetings today?"

"I met with Monsieur Danton at noon. Did Boniface propose marriage?"

"*Non.* He offered to procure me a costume for Madame Perotine's bal masqué. I trust we plan to attend. I haven't yet responded to the invitation for it is weeks away."

"But of course we must attend." A pause. "This is good. I am grateful you did not anger Boniface at this time, Justine. He has the ear of the *sans-culottes.*"

Monsieur's quiet reference to the aroused rabble of Paris chilled Émile's blood. Justine must have felt it, too, for she paused before asking, "Did your meeting today go well, Papa?"

"Not as well as I'd hoped." Discouragement weighted Monsieur Didier's voice. "Several prominent citizens encourage the populace to. . .But do not trouble your pretty head, *ma fille;* I am certain all will soon be resolved." Émile heard him climb the stairs.

Returning to his duties with a start, Émile rose and picked up the heavy bucket. His shovel clattered to the hearth. Justine's skirts rustled as she hurried into the room. "Here you are. How can you work with so little light? Did Monsieur Danton come to this house to meet with Papa?"

"He did."

"That man frightens me, as does Henri—Monsieur Boniface. When I listen to them, I think they must be right even while they say things I know to be false." She sat upon the settle near the hearth and patted the empty space beside her. "Come talk with me?"

He set down the bucket and brushed his hands on his breeches. "I am covered in ashes."

"It matters little. My gown is dusty after that carriage ride. Please, Émile, I must talk with you."

He found himself sliding into the seat. Glossy curls spilled over her shoulder, her eyes glistened, and high color filled her cheeks. Always a fervent little creature, at the moment she appeared ready to burst with pent-up emotion.

"You. . .enjoyed your luncheon?" His inane question dimmed her glow. She played with the bow on her *fichu*.

"Émile, as a child I looked forward to being grown up so I could wear beautiful clothes and attend thrilling parties. Life seemed a lovely thing then, full of joy. Now that I am grown I find that life is frightening. I see fear even in my father's face, though he would conceal it from me. This world is evil." She looked squarely into his eyes. "Except for you. I look at you and see goodness, freedom, and hope."

"You see Jesus in me, mademoiselle."

"Oui, yet I see Him nowhere else."

"He has other servants in this city," he said.

"I can scarce believe it. Where are they?"

"Many currently languish in the prisons, yet a few carry on His work in secret." He stood up. "I must dally here no longer."

She rose with him and pointed at the bucket. "Émile, this is menial work, far beneath your abilities. You could find employment at any smithy in the city. Why do you remain in my father's service as a household drudge? To avoid military conscription?"

"Is that what you believe?"

"Non. You're no coward. I believe you stay because I. . .*we* could not survive without you. Am I correct?" Her direct stare confronted him.

He slowly nodded, and her sparkle returned. "I would hear more about these servants of God, dear Émile, but I will not keep you from your labors. Tomorrow?"

Again he nodded.

Dieu, m'aider—God, help me! You know I stay also because I could not survive without her.

The following morning when Émile delivered Monsieur Didier's tray, the master sat reading in his sitting room. "*Merci,* Émile. I expect to hire a maid today so you need no longer perform this role." He lifted one brow. "Although your humble service is commendable, do not imagine me blind to your motives.

My daughter will never be yours."

Émile finished pouring the chocolate without spilling a drop. "I know this, monsieur. She and I share only friendship." He added sugar but no cream and stirred.

Didier snorted. "Do you think me a fool?"

"Far from it, monsieur." Émile knew his face was scarlet, yet he met his master's cold stare. "You correctly identify my affection for your daughter. However, you misread my intent. I would die before I betrayed her trust. She views me as an older brother, and that is the role I shall play as long as God grants me opportunity."

M. Didier rubbed one hand over his mouth. "I see. 'Affection,' eh? In my day, we used more accurate terms. I can conceive of only one reason a fine smith like you would carry trays when he could make a good living at the forge. I'll blind myself to your lecherous yearnings no longer. Begone from this house. Make no attempt to see my daughter again. Return on the thirty-first for your due wages."

Fury built in Émile's chest and hissed from between his teeth. "Monsieur, I've served you faithfully since I was old enough to help my father in the forge on your estate. Not once in twenty years have I betrayed your trust. What right have you to accuse me of evil intent toward your daughter and turn me out like a criminal?"

"The right of a protective father." Monsieur Didier looked away, sullen yet determined.

"Then you protect your daughter from the wrong man. *Adieu,* monsieur." Émile bowed stiffly and stepped into the dark hallway. Justine's chamber door stood ajar. Humiliation rolled over him. She must have heard. Shoulders bowed, he descended the stairs and headed down the back hall.

Surprised to hear voices, he paused outside the kitchen door.

"—Better than having a man in your *boudoir.*" That was Cook's wheezing voice. "I trust the master will soon hire a new maid so you won't be bothered again. I'd take your tray up myself except I can't manage those steep stairs."

"I understand, and you needn't apologize," said Justine. "Émile is the soul of discretion at all times. Any other man might embarrass me, but never Émile. He sees me as a sister, not as a woman."

So Justine had not overheard her father's accusations. Émile straightened his shoulders, entered the kitchen, and picked up his shoulder bag.

"Bonjour." Justine welcomed him with her brilliant smile. "Today, you see, you needn't carry up my tray, for I am determined to become an early riser." She lifted her cup.

Sorrow weighted his heart. He could not say good-bye; better to leave with her smile fresh in his memory.

Leaving her chocolate on the worktable, she followed him into the hallway. "My day is free of engagements. After Papa leaves for the assembly, I'll help you work. I can be good company, Émile. You will see."

He stopped to look at her in wonderment. Why would she sound hopeful? What did she want from him?

"Tell me what is wrong, Émile." She spoke in a squeaking whisper. "You are leaving. I knew as soon as I saw you in the kitchen, but I did not want to believe it. How could you think of leaving without speaking to me? You promised to talk with me, to tell me about God's other servants in Paris! Émile, you cannot leave! What would I do?"

Crazy ideas spun through his head—ideas sparked by her nearness, her need. . .his need. Yet responsibility and conscience tempered his longings. "Come with me to meet some faithful servants."

She blinked. "Now? So early? Shall I order a carriage?"

"We must go now, on foot, if you still choose to come. Afterward I shall escort you home."

"I choose to come."

Chapter 4

Justine clutched Émile's arm and gazed about at the milling crowds. At this early hour, most people in the streets were ordinary citizens going about their business, but she spotted many jaunty red caps amid the throng. The sight of dirty, hard-faced men bearing pikes made her shiver. Several loitered in doorways or gathered in knots, but others marched along the street in crooked formation, assorted weapons propped on their shoulders. "They look almost like children playing soldier," she said.

"If only they were that," Émile said quietly.

One burly man with rotting teeth addressed Justine. She scarcely understood his harsh dialect, but his tone sent a bolt of fear through her.

Émile pushed Justine behind himself. "Do not insult a patriotic woman." His voice, usually reedy and soft, carried sharply above the street clamor.

The man grinned, lifted his open hands toward Émile, and took a step back. "My mistake, young cockerel. I mean no offense to a good daughter of the Republic."

Émile wrapped his arm around Justine's shoulders and hurried her away. Trying not to gasp for breath, she let him guide her along a back alley and up stone steps between half-timbered buildings. He turned a corner and stopped to look around. A cart rolled along a crossroad; the donkey's clopping hoofbeats echoed between the walls. A tall stone wall lined the street's far side. Émile hustled her across the road and inside a crumbling, ivy-draped arch in the thick wall. An iron-braced oak door blocked the opening.

Thump! Thump! His fist struck the door near Justine's head. She spun to face him and found herself bracketed between his arms as he braced himself against the door. Panting, she stared up at him. "Wh–where are we?"

"Hush." Removing one hand from the door, he held his finger before her lips. She looked into his eyes and nodded.

A rattle at the latch warned them to step away before the door opened.

"Émile." A man drew them inside and closed the door. "We did not expect you today."

"Frére Martin."

The men gripped each other by the shoulders, and then the gray-haired stranger turned to Justine. "You are welcome." His eyes revealed a keen intellect.

"This is Mademoiselle Didier, daughter of Sébastien Didier."

"The Girondist assemblyman." Frére Martin nodded sagely. "Blessings upon you, *mon enfant*."

He spoke like a priest yet wore the garb of the *bourgeoisie*, the layman. Justine nodded and curtsied, uncertain how to address him. "Monsieur."

He turned back to Émile. "When you have a free moment, I wish to speak with you. *S'il vous plaît m'excuser, mademoiselle.*" He bowed then opened a door in the wall opposite. As he stepped inside, she glimpsed a book-lined chamber.

"Come." Émile beckoned.

"What is this place?"

"The remains of an abbey."

She followed him along a stone hallway lighted by breaks in the walls and ceiling. He paused at a door and knocked, then pushed it open.

Small cots lined a narrow chamber. Windows high in one wall allowed thin daylight within, but the children occupying the room seemed pale and gray.

"I've brought Mademoiselle Didier to meet you," Émile said quietly. "Mademoiselle, these are my little friends. Frére Martin Marron and his sister, Sarah, have taken them off the streets and endeavor to feed and house them here until better homes can be found."

The children observed her cautiously. Justine noticed one with a drooping eyelid and another with a withered leg. All were thin. "Bonjour," she said.

They each repeated her greeting. "Do you like babies?" the droopy-eyed girl asked. No hint of a smile lightened her face.

"I think so. I've seldom seen a baby," Justine answered honestly.

"We have babies. Come."

The girl took Justine's hand and headed for the door. Émile remained behind with the other children.

"What is your name?" Justine asked the girl.

"Marie-Louise. I am seven. How old are you?"

"I am eighteen. When I was seven, Émile was my best friend. My only friend. You have many friends here."

Marie-Louise pushed open the next door in the hall. They entered a smaller room holding four cots. A child occupied each one, asleep except for one boy who lay sucking his thumb. Marie-Louise climbed onto his cot and pulled him into her lap. "This is my brother, David."

"Bonjour, David." Justine sat on the cot beside them and leaned against the wall. The beds and floors were neat. The children smelled clean, although their clothing looked worn.

The smallest baby stirred and lifted his head. Justine knelt beside his cot. Wide dark eyes stared up at her. He seemed to be deciding whether or not to cry. "Enh?"

"Did you sleep well? Are you hungry?" she asked, uncertain how to address an infant.

The baby dropped his head suddenly, then turned his face to the side, peeked up at Justine, and smiled. Her heart melted into a puddle.

"That is Luc," Marie-Louise explained. "He eats mush and milk."

The door opened, and a woman entered. Graying hair dangled around her gaunt face, yet her eyes were kind. "You must be Mademoiselle Didier," she said. "I am Sarah Marron. If you will change Luc's cloths, I would be grateful." She handed over a bundle of clean rags. "I shall return shortly."

After Sarah left, Justine looked blankly at Luc, then at Marie-Louise.

"He is wet," the child said. "Unwrap him, then wrap him

in clean rags. You truly know nothing about babies."

Justine gingerly rolled the baby over and followed Marie-Louise's instructions. Luc cooed, kicked, and at last began to fuss before she finished changing him. His tiny legs kicked surprisingly hard. In an effort to quiet him, she cuddled him close. The wiry little body relaxed against her. He gripped a fistful of her hair.

After Sarah demonstrated how to feed the baby, Justine took a turn at the messy task, then changed his cloths again. When Luc reached for her from Sarah's arms, delight filled her soul. "Would you like to hold him?" Sarah asked.

"*Oui, beaucoup.*"

Sometime later Justine realized she was being watched. Without pausing her rocking of baby Luc, she looked at Émile in the doorway. "Can you see if he is awake?"

"His eyes are open, barely." He went down on one knee beside her.

Justine continued her rocking motion and patted the baby's back. "Tell me about the children, Émile. Are they orphans? Why is the church not caring for them?"

"Religion now belongs to the state, and the state cares nothing for foundlings. Martin and Sarah care for these children with their own dwindling resources. I give what I can, and so do a few others."

"Is Frére Martin a monk?"

"Non, but he is a minister to God's people." Émile's tone closed the subject.

"He looks tired."

"I know. He and Sarah remain in the city for the children."

Recalling Frére Martin's aristocratic features and Sarah's refined voice, Justine wondered if they might be poor members of the nobility. Better not to ask. She pressed her cheek against the baby's head. "Tell me about Luc."

"Someone left him in the street beside the wall. He is older than he seems. Sarah loves the children, but she lacks time to cuddle them all. Last year, many died in a smallpox outbreak. The survivors bear scars. Most people prefer to let such children die since they have no family."

"It is tragic, Émile. But you are right; I do see Jesus in your friends." She hid her face in Luc's wispy hair and felt tears burn her throat. "I want to take Luc home with me. Back to Normandy where he can have a happy childhood."

"He is one among hundreds in the city."

"But if. . .if I could help even one. . ."

Émile patted Luc's back. "Remember what Jesus said about 'doing unto the least of these'?"

"When I hug and kiss baby Luc, I hug and kiss Jesus." Tears clogged her voice. "Émile, there must be a way to remove these children from the city. They need a garden to play in like we had. They need country air and good food."

Émile just looked at her, his great brown eyes revealing tender affection.

"Do you think Frére Martin and Sarah would take the children from the city if they had a place to go? I might convince Papa to purchase a small farm for the purpose. He often gives generously to philanthropic endeavors."

"Sarah has prepared luncheon for us. Why not ponder the matter while we eat?"

Justine laid the sleeping baby on his cot and covered him with the thin blanket. "I could cut one of my blankets into four pieces large enough to cover each of these babies," she said. "And we have fresh fruit at home."

Émile drew her from the room. In the dark hallway, he paused. "It is unwise for one small woman to promise everything, especially when your father has not yet approved your plans."

She drooped. "You are right, as always. But I shall pray for opportunity to help." Before he could move away she caught his sleeve. "Émile, did Papa forbid you to see me again?"

"Oui."

"But he promised my mother—"

"I was a child then. I no longer need your father's protection, and I already have other employment. You needn't worry about me."

She gripped his hard forearm. "But Émile, what about me? What shall I do without you?"

He patted her hand. "You must learn to stand on your own faith instead of leaning on mine. God will never fail you. Put your trust in Him, not in me. Now come. I promise I will not leave Paris without contacting you in some way. I am your brother in Christ; your father cannot destroy that connection."

Justine let him lead her along the shadowed passage. "But we are not truly family, Émile. If you marry, your wife will not accept me as a sister."

He chuckled. "Do not borrow trouble, enfant. Today has enough trouble of its own."

After luncheon, Justine thanked Martin and Sarah for their hospitality. They thanked her for helping with the children and invited her to return. This invitation sparked a train of thought that distracted her from her grief during the long walk home.

Émile touched her arm, and she realized they had stopped before her house. "Adieu, Justine."

"How long it has been since you called me by name, Émile! Thank you for today. I am sorry I trouble you with my worries and fears. Perhaps God has allowed this trial to push me into maturity. I promise to pray and learn to trust Him. Of course, you must come see me soon."

Without thinking, she stood on tiptoe and kissed his cheek. As soon as her lips touched his warm skin, she knew her mistake. "Oh!"

Émile looked stricken. His mouth opened then closed. He hitched his pack on his shoulder, turned on his heel, and walked away, disappearing into the crowds.

That evening Justine told her father about her outing with Émile to visit the orphans. Although her father wrote at his desk while she talked, he proved his attentiveness by asking an occasional question. "You say this couple has picked these children from the streets?"

"Oui, Papa. The little ones would have died if not for Frére Martin and Sarah, who are brother and sister. I fear many of them will die yet if they must remain in that dark ruin. Might we purchase a small farm for them, perhaps near la Maison d'Arbre de Cerise? Then when we return home, I could visit the children and help with their care."

Her father peered over his spectacles. "When did you develop this concern for orphaned children? They are not kittens or puppies to be nursed at your convenience. I fear the enterprise would quickly bore you."

Although she wanted to pout, Justine knew he was justified in suspecting her dedication to the cause. Her history of taking on projects and tiring of them before completion argued against her. "Even if I fail, Martin and Sarah will not. And you know Émile's faithfulness."

Papa set his pen in its holder on the desk and folded his hands into a steeple. "We needn't purchase a farm. Due to smallpox, several suitable dwellings already stand vacant on our property. These currently produce no income. The financial loss will be minimal if I donate one to charity."

"Oh, Papa!" Justine leaped up to hug him, but he shrugged her aside.

"These philanthropists require papers in order to leave the city. How many passes will be needed?"

She estimated the number of children. "I should say at least twenty, including two for adults."

He pulled out a stack of official-looking papers, dipped his quill, and started writing. "The children needn't be named, being orphans. This Martin, do you know his surname?"

"Marron. His sister is Sarah Marron. Papa, please tell me why passes are needed. Would I need a pass in order to leave Paris? I'd thought of accompanying the orphans to the farm, where I might be useful in acquainting them with the community."

"Barriers have been raised at the gates to keep undesirables from entering or leaving the city. Any honest citizen must have good reason to travel at this time. You have no reason to leave at present."

"Undesirables?"

"Traitors. Enemies of the people. Tell me, will Émile Girardeau accompany the orphans into Normandy, or does he remain in Paris to worship at your shrine? The inconvenience and cost of donating a farm are as nothing could I but assure myself of his permanent departure. I shall provide a pass for him and fervently hope he chooses to use it."

Justine studied her father's expression. "You speak in jest, *je suis certain*."

"You may be certain that I speak in grave earnest. Once you no longer see that lout, I trust you will come to your senses and accept the suit of a worthier mate." He thrust the papers at her. "I can do no more. If he will not leave the city and continues to force his presence upon you, I shall report him to military recruiters."

Chapter 5

Friday evening, Justine and her father attended the concert performance of an acclaimed soprano. Several other assembly deputies and their families occupied their theater box. Henri Boniface hung over Justine's shoulder, shared her opera glasses, and breathed heavily near her ear until she thought she might go mad.

"Cherie," said Madame Mortimer, an assembly delegate's wife, during intermission after Henri left to obtain refreshments for Justine. "You are the luckiest of women. Monsieur Boniface is every woman's dream. So fine in his tailcoat, and his linens always the whitest! They say his sardonic smile drives women insane with desire, and I believe it must be true. But then, he has set his sights on the fairest flower in all Paris—you."

Justine thanked her for the compliment and studied Henri when he returned. She could see why women found him fascinating, and she suspected he was not a man to frustrate any susceptible woman's desires.

Feeling her father's gaze, she fluttered her program his way. He nodded toward Henri and raised his brows. Justine pretended ignorance of his meaning.

Henri insisted upon escorting her home.

"There is no good reason for you to go out of your way and tire your horses," Justine said. "Papa will hire a carriage." She allowed him to assist her with her silk shawl.

He let his hands linger upon her shoulders. "There is every reason. I've scarcely seen you these two days, and it seems a lifetime. Soon I shall bring your masquerade costume. You will be dazzled, *mon doux*."

"It is ready?" His warm breath on her ear made her shiver. When he called her "my sweet," she felt like a bonbon about to be devoured.

"The *couturière* started working on it months ago when Madame Perotine first told me of her plans for a Grand Masquerade Ball."

He lowered his head as if to kiss her shoulder, but she stepped forward to intercept her father, linking her arm through his. "Papa, you must speak to Monsieur Boniface for he will not listen to me."

Papa patted her hand. "He will not listen? A sorry beginning is this!" He beamed approval. "You must practice persuading the man to your will, which is a woman's proper role."

"Indeed, but she would persuade me not to escort her home. This unworthy objective deserves no such effort." Henri spoke lightly, yet a chill trickled through Justine's nerves. Papa clucked and disengaged his arm, handing her off to Henri. "We are delighted to accept your offer, Boniface. In return, you must dine with us tomorrow evening. You two lovebirds go on ahead while I visit an old friend."

Justine felt her future slip from her grasp as Henri took her arm. "Shall we?" A hint of triumph colored his voice.

The following evening, Cook produced a dinner that drew raves from both men, but Justine tasted ashes. The new maid dropped utensils and spilled soup on the table, listened openly to private conversations, and spoke to Justine with disdain. But these faults paled when compared to the fact that she had taken Émile's place in the dining room.

Not a word from Émile in two days. Between the sweet and the cheese courses, Justine made the decision to find her own way back to the orphanage, deliver the exit passes to Frére Martin, and request information about Émile.

"Justine, I imagine you are eager to see your costume for the masquerade. Henri brought it tonight." Papa's tone urged her to stop sulking.

"Oui, I am eager."

Displeasure at her flat response twisted Henri's fine lips. "Your dressmaker created it to your exact measurements and to my specifications. I am certain its magnificence will be unsurpassed."

Justine tried to smile. "I am certain you are right."

Leaving the men to enjoy their wine, she slipped into the parlor and studied the parcel. A spark of interest flared to life. What might Henri have chosen? She did not know him well enough to hazard a guess.

"Open it."

She started with a gasp. "How do you walk so quietly in this house?"

"The boards dare not squeak when I tread on them,"

Henri said with a smile. "I wish to watch your face when you open your gift."

She untied the strings and removed the wrappings. For the moment, admiration overcame her misgivings. "Monsieur, it is too beautiful!" Slowly she lifted a creamy satin brocade gown shimmering with gold threading in the flounced skirt. White silk covered a mask edged with feathers and pearls. Justine peered at Henri through its eye holes. "Thank you."

He breathed out a long sigh. "My desired reward is to see you wearing it, Justine. You will be an angel here on earth. My angel of flesh to have and to hold."

Justine gaped, then her mouth shut with a snap. "Monsieur, such talk is unfit for a maiden's ears. You must never again speak to me so!"

He smiled, but his gaze still burned. "You know I intend to marry you, Justine. Let us speak to one another as adults and forsake pretense. Although I am a man of strong passions, I shall be to you a faithful consort. Your incomparable beauty cannot help but satisfy my desperate yearning. Only your tender devotion can slake my soul's thirst for meaning."

Her face and body heated in response. To have such a man at her feet, begging her favor! To be the one woman whose love might save him from his lower self and bring him to heights of glory!

He stepped closer, his face glowing with anticipation. "I must have you, my beautiful one. I shall kill any man who stands in my way. You must be mine alone."

He reached for her hand, but Justine evaded his grasp. *Kill any man. . .*

Her mind flashed a picture of Émile falling dead, and the romantic spell dissolved. Horror at her own weakness filled her heart. Silently she prayed for wisdom. "You speak of passion, not love, monsieur. Only God can slake your soul's thirst; only His beauty can satisfy your heart's desperate yearning. Such beauty as I have is mortal and will fade. Even if I did love you, my flawed love could never bring you true contentment. Soon you would search for another woman to provide the perfect love you crave, leaving me alone, consumed and destroyed by your passion."

"Never! I would be content with you, Justine, I swear!"

She put down the mask and stepped back. "I cannot pretend to know your mind, monsieur, but I am certain of my own. I do not intend to marry you. Please take back this costume and put such thoughts from your mind."

Cold anger chased the surprise and hurt from his eyes. "We will see, woman, whose intentions are fulfilled." He waved a dismissing hand at the gown. "Keep the costume. You will need it."

Without another word he slammed from the house.

Chapter 6

After weighing her options carefully, Justine decided to hire a sedan chair to carry her to the orphanage the following morning. Although she did not know the way, she had filed cross-street names away in her memory. The carriers let her off at the corner; from there she ran down the narrow street and pounded on the ancient door.

Frére Martin stared blankly at her before recognition dawned. "Mademoiselle Didier, what brings you here this Sunday morning?"

She pressed a sheaf of paper into his hands. "I bring your exit papers and the deed to a farm for the orphans. I seek Émile. Is he here?"

He studied the papers in evident surprise and increasing delight. "Your father did this? May our merciful Lord bless the man for his generosity." He reached one hand to her. "But enter and rest yourself. You seem distressed."

"I am deeply distressed, Frére Martin. Where is Émile?"

He barred the door. "I do not know, but we shall send for him. If you will tell me your troubles, I may be able to help, and I can certainly pray."

❦

Émile glanced around as he passed beneath the stone arch. "She is here? She is well?"

"Calm yourself and enter my study." Frére Martin closed and barred the great door. "She is with the children. She brought the deed to a farm and exit passes for twenty children and three adults, including you. God has answered our prayers beyond all dreams." He shook his head.

In the study, Émile accepted a chair. "The deed to a farm. . . exit papers. . .and for me? I have prayed, but never did I imagine that Monsieur Didier. . ." He paused as understanding dawned and his mood darkened. "He wishes to be rid of me, no doubt. When do we leave? Paris grows more dangerous by the hour."

"Our projected departure date is Sunday, two weeks from today. Vigilance at the barriers is lowest on Sundays, or so I am told." Frére Martin sat at his desk and shuffled papers. "Now that our means of leaving the city and our destination have been miraculously provided, we must obtain supplies and at least two wagons. All is being arranged." He reached across the desk. "Here is the deed made out to Martin Marron and a map. I pray the farm will provide safe haven for all."

Émile scanned the map and nodded. "I know this farm. Monsieur Didier is generous indeed."

"With hard work and thrift, Sarah and I should be able to eke out a living."

Émile handed back the papers, shaking his head. "It will be more difficult than you think."

"Although we must do our part in preparing for any exigency, at some point it is inevitable that we leave the future in God's hands. As the writer of Hebrews advises: 'Let us hold fast the profession of our faith without wavering; for he is faithful that promised.' "

Émile rubbed his forehead. "I confess I have wrestled against God these many days, striving to place my will above His." He regarded Frére Martin frankly. "But two days of reflection and prayer have cleared my mind, and repentance has cleared my soul. If I place my will above God's, I am no better than the rabble in the assembly who plot to gain power for themselves by inciting the people to violence and murder. A man might gain his heart's desire yet lose all that truly matters."

"Amen, and praise be to God," said Frére Martin. "This is a welcome answer to our many prayers on your behalf, my son. Sarah and I suffered anxiety lest your passion for a woman take precedence over your desire to please God."

Émile felt his face grow warm. "It nearly did. I cannot say that the battle is won, but I am determined to daily, hourly give her back into the Lord's keeping. We believers must continue to encourage each other to do God's will and to leave the results in His hands. Today I must say a final farewell."

The older man's brow creased. "Yet the Lord has promised to give to a man who delights in Him his heart's desire."

Émile leaped to his feet as sudden anger blazed. "First you encourage me to surrender my desires; then you tell me God may grant them. Which is truth?"

Realizing he had lost control, he clenched his fists and stared at the floor. After several deep breaths, he spoke in a quiet yet rigid tone. "Christians often take such promises out of context and assume too much. I love Mademoiselle Didier, but even should her father suddenly approve me as her suitor—an unlikely prospect—God would not force her to return my love just to fulfill my heart's desire."

"I have observed a marked affection between you. Why are you so certain she doesn't care?"

Émile grimaced, turned his back, then whirled around to reply. "*Oui,* she does love me with a child's love for an older brother. I can endure it no longer. I must make a clean break and learn to live without her."

"But is your noble resignation best for her?" Irony sharpened Frére Martin's words. "She deserves as much consideration as any of our abandoned children. You may be God's chosen instrument in procuring her safety, Émile."

Emile's eyes narrowed. "How is she endangered?"

"Henri Boniface desires her as his wife. Her refusal of his marriage proposal has enraged him."

"She has refused? I always believed she would. The man is contemptible." Émile willed his heart to slow its pounding pace. "Still, I fail to see her peril. Monsieur Didier adores his daughter and would not force her to wed against her will."

"Boniface threatened revenge. We both know he has the power to follow through with action." Frére Martin's deep voice held a warning. "I suspect him of darker designs than forced matrimony."

Émile prowled about the room like a caged beast. "Unless he has changed since his childhood, Boniface is a man motivated entirely by self-interest. What do you suggest I do?"

Frére Martin frowned in deep thought. "Talk with her;

watch and listen. If her safety requires action on our part, the Lord will provide a way."

❦

"Justine."

She stirred and smiled at the sound of that beloved voice. Rough and reedy, lacking in refinement yet rich in emotion. "Émile," she whispered before awareness returned.

Her eyes fluttered open. She lay on a cot. Luc snoozed upon her belly with his head pillowed on her fichu. Émile leaned over her, his eyes dark and tender.

"I feared I would never see you again," she confessed. "Where have you been?"

"Nearby."

Cautiously she sat up. Luc gave a little wail but settled back to sleep as soon as she laid him down. "So sweet." She smoothed his flyaway hair.

Émile held out his hand. "Come."

Chapter 7

Do you hear that screaming sound, Émile?" Justine felt blisters forming on her heels as she trotted to keep up. Cobblestones bruised her soles. "What can it be? Where are we going in such a hurry? You are behaving strangely."

He slowed his pace and gave her a troubled look. "The clamor sounds like an uprising. I prefer to remove you as far from it as possible."

"Another uprising? But the king is already held prisoner, and his guards are dead." She felt choked, remembering Henri's descriptions of the mob violence just weeks before. She cast anxious glances around. Henri must have exaggerated for dramatic effect. Surely no human beings could commit such atrocities against their fellow man, certainly not in Paris.

Émile pulled her aside to make way for a party of men and women, some brandishing pikes. They rushed along the street, shouting obscene threats.

Justine stared after them in horror.

Émile turned her around and urged her forward. "Conceal

your disgust or you may be taken for a traitor. Hurry."

"What can be happening, Émile? I thought all would be well once we had a constitution and the new assembly took charge. I do not understand what has gone wrong."

The clamor had faded into the distance before he spoke again. "Let us sit here on this bench and talk. To be overheard could be dangerous, but a public place is perhaps safer than privacy for such discussion."

Justine joined him on the bench beneath a tree and watched sparrows hopping near her skirts. Patrons crowded a nearby café's outdoor tables, laughing and talking. A child skipped along the street, holding her parents' hands. How could life seem so normal yet so surreal?

A breeze rustled leaves overhead. Sunlight caught golden highlights in Émile's wavy hair. He regarded her soberly. Placing his left arm behind her along the bench's back, he tipped his head and leaned so near she thought he might kiss her, but instead he spoke softly.

"Although the king and many nobles and clergymen are imprisoned, radical leaders have been inciting the people to invade the city's prisons and enact their own brand of justice. I cannot be certain, but I fear we are witnessing the result of this wicked plan. The Carmelite Convent, where many priests are held prisoner for refusing to embrace the revolution, is near this place."

Justine watched his lips as he spoke, unwilling to miss a single word. "Surely they would not harm the priests—" She swallowed hard, unable to continue. Despite her heart's denial, she knew her worst imaginings were true.

Émile pulled her to rest her face against his shoulder. Her tears soaked into his jacket. "I've always respected your father's desire to establish a republican form of government in France. Even the Marquis de Lafayette encouraged these reforms and led the struggle to grant justice and liberty to all regardless of birth and station. But while crafting our constitution, the elected representatives failed to take into account one vital truth—mankind's fallen nature."

"My father admires Rousseau and Voltaire," Justine said. "He believes mankind is basically good."

"A government based on the premise of man's basic goodness is doomed to fail. Power has the potential to corrupt the best of men, as shown in the abuse of power by the church and nobility of France. Granting men of the Third Estate this same absolute power solves none of our nation's problems." Sorrow filled his voice. "The current atmosphere of hatred and revenge brings disaster. Anyone can be labeled a traitor for any reason or for no reason at all."

While he spoke, Justine regained control over her emotions. Sitting upright, she wiped her face with a handkerchief. "We must pray for courage and guidance. Yet if the priests are killed, what reason have we to assume divine protection?"

"Whether we live or die, we are in God's hands as were the martyrs of the early church. It would be an honor to die for Christ's name."

Justine felt peace despite her fear. "If we might die together, I could be content."

He looked into her eyes, his expression inscrutable. "We needn't resign ourselves to death as yet. Come." He rose and offered her his hand. "I know a place where we might find refuge today."

Émile led her along back streets until they reached a run-down theater. From the open doorway, music and laughter poured into the street. Justine detected the tempting aroma of roasting meat. Her stomach growled. "Here?"

He smiled and nodded. "Forget your troubles for an hour and enjoy a good meal. This may be our last evening together; let us make it a time to remember with joy."

Despite an eerie sense of unreality about her circumstances, Justine enjoyed the show. Actors portrayed a comedic tableau, then sang and performed folk dances. Another team of players used large puppets to tell a romantic tale.

The meal was also excellent: tender pork, delicate crepes, warm loaves of crusty bread, rich cheeses, and surprisingly fresh vegetables. But the setting was another matter—the room so hot and crowded that men on all sides, including Émile, removed their coats, and women fanned themselves. One man at their table opened his shirt, displaying a vast expanse of shaggy belly upon which he wiped his greasy fingers. The one other woman at their table behaved in a crude and earthy fashion, roaring with laughter at the puppets and leaning heavily upon her male companion.

The stench of unwashed bodies might have sickened Justine had she not concentrated on her meal, the entertainment, and her companion. Émile's shoulders took up more than his share of space at the table. He was obliged to straddle the bench, facing Justine, and eat using only one hand. Each time he leaned forward, his chest pressed against her shoulder.

"Do you recognize the leading lady?" he asked as the curtain fell and rose.

"Should I?" Justine studied the painted woman who bowed and gestured to the crowd. "That is. . . It could not be Adrienne, my maid?"

"It is."

Inner turmoil caught Justine by surprise. Why had Émile brought her here? Recently she had begun to believe, to hope, that he returned her love, that he'd forgotten Adrienne. Had she misread his emotions entirely? Did her obvious infatuation embarrass him? Had he brought her here to remind her that his heart belonged to another woman? Only a year ago, she had giggled with Adrienne about Émile's admiration for the pretty maid, but even then she had suffered inwardly. Sitting bolt upright, she turned to examine his expression. "Do you. . . do you still love her?"

He blinked as if startled then returned his attention to the stage. "In all my life I have loved only one woman."

All her old insecurities and suspicions flooded over her. Drowning in jealousy, Justine struggled to keep from gasping for air. "Is she. . .did Adrienne take you in when Papa threw you out?"

"*Oui,* but it isn't what you think. Her husband, Arnaud, is the clown." Émile smiled. "He is also the swordsmith for whom I now work."

"I see." Justine's brain scrambled to sort out this information. Adrienne, married? The storm of emotion cleared. "Did your heart break when Adrienne married another?"

"If so, I was unaware." He grinned.

"You were?" Confused, she latched on to a subject. "You make swords. Does this work interest you?"

"Oui. These past months I've often worked for Arnaud with your father's approval, when my services were not required at your house."

"Is there anything you cannot do?" His arm rested on the table before her, its rolled-up shirtsleeve revealing a smith's muscles. On an impulse, she smoothed its tangle of golden-brown hair and felt those muscles bunch. He caught her hand and for a breathless moment looked deep into her eyes.

"Émile! Mademoiselle Didier!" A woman's shrill voice called above the clamor.

Chapter 8

"It is Adrienne," Justine said, seeing an arm wave above the throng. "And her husband."

Émile helped her rise from the bench while Adrienne and the tall clown pushed their way through the press of revelers. "I recognized you, Émile, but could not believe my eyes when I saw mademoiselle in the audience." Evidently uncertain how to address her former mistress, Adrienne bobbed a curtsy.

Justine reached for her hand. "You are my maid no longer, Adrienne. We are equals and friends, I hope. Please introduce your husband. Émile tells me he makes swords."

"Mademoi—I mean, Justine, this is my husband, Arnaud Lamorges. Arnaud, cherie, this is Justine Didier. I was her maid from the time she left school at the convent to the time of our arrival in Paris." Adrienne's blue eyes sparkled.

"At which time you met and married me," her husband finished the story. "Pleased to meet you, Mademoiselle Didier; although you lured my assistant away from his work today, for which I find it difficult to forgive you." Arnaud's manners were pleasant. "I need him more than ever now. The assembly has placed orders for swords and pikes that are impossible for me to meet alone. Émile was wise to join me rather than be sent off to war."

"Oui, very wise," Justine said weakly.

"Like you, Arnaud, I prefer making a sword to wielding one," said Émile. "I favor a peacemaker role, but if God calls me into battle, I shall fight with all my strength."

The clown glanced at Justine and gave Émile a sly smile. "Some things are worth fighting for."

Émile seemed startled. "So they are."

Adrienne chuckled. "Are they not an extraordinary pair, Arnaud? This revolution bids fair to bring about the best possible ending to a comedy of errors."

Arnaud waggled his brows, thumped Émile's shoulder, then muttered something into his ear. Émile backed away, his face as red as a tom turkey's.

"I must escort mademoiselle home before dark," he muttered. "If the streets are safe."

"Adrienne," Justine said before Émile could rush her away, "would you consider coming back to style my hair? For the *bal masqué* on the fifteenth."

"Oui, the ball. Arnaud and I will be there also. Certainly I will help you with your hair, *enfant*. And Émile we shall dress up to escort you." Adrienne wrinkled her nose at him. "Why not? In our new France, anything is possible."

Justine opened her mouth but remained silent. Although Henri had provided her costume, she was under no obligation to him. If Émile offered to escort her, she would accept.

But he merely looked uncomfortable and hurried her toward the exit.

Before they stepped outside, Arnaud caught Émile's shoulder. "Take care this night. The people have risen to carry out justice, and the sight may distress sensitive eyes." He glanced at Justine.

"I plan to take a circuitous route," Émile said.

"You might be wiser to bring mademoiselle to our house."

Émile brushed aside Arnaud's concern, and Justine hoped he was being wise.

The sky above Paris gleamed pale blue with gold streaks, though its streets lay in shadow. A cooling breeze off the Seine ruffled Justine's skirts and attempted to lift Émile's cap. When Justine linked her arm through his, he looked down at her with such warmth that joy caught in her throat.

"Adrienne was pleased to see you again." He spoke softly.

"I like her, though I often feel as if she secretly mocks me. I am sure Arnaud is a good man, but I cannot imagine why she would prefer him to you."

"Can you not?" He seemed amused. "He adores her. They are happy together. I would not wish them otherwise."

"Do not tell me you never cared for her, for I know better. She used to ask me to read your love notes aloud. I blush to say we giggled together at your expense." Justine nudged his shoulder.

"I discovered only recently that she cannot read." His smile was crooked.

"Your notes were sweet," Justine said, her cheeks warming. "I don't believe Adrienne fully appreciated their worth or yours."

He appeared to ponder her statement. "I think she did. You see, for a time I considered marriage as a means to distract myself from. . .forbidden fruit. Adrienne, being attractive and amiable, seemed a reasonable choice as wife to a country servant. Using those notes and a few gifts, I attempted to convince her of my affection, but she wasn't so easily fooled."

With an excited flutter, Justine zeroed in on the crux of his confession. "What forbidden fruit did you desire?"

"Inquisitive kittens risk losing their whiskers," he said firmly as they turned a corner. He looked up and stopped cold. Justine observed his stunned expression and turned her head to follow his gaze.

Instantly he caught her shoulders and whirled her around, shoved her back into shadows, and screened her with his body, preventing her from seeing the street. Her face pressed into his shoulder. Justine heard clopping horses' hooves, wheels bumping over cobblestones; then she heard mocking shouts and angry screeches. A hot, acrid stench caught in her throat. She heard Émile's ragged breathing and felt fear in his taut frame. Her own heart pounded in response.

When the last footsteps died away, Justine wriggled loose enough to look up at Émile's face. His eyes were shut, his teeth bared in a grimace. "What was it, Émile? Please tell me."

His shuddering breath sounded like a sob. "Bodies. A wagonload of human bodies, naked, bloody, and limp. Oh, Justine!"

Numb to her bones, she wrapped her arms around him and hid her face in his shirtfront. As one, they quaked and wept and struggled to maintain control. Long minutes passed before Émile spoke again in a rasping croak. "We cannot go up that street toward the prison, yet I do not care to follow the wagon's path."

A lamplighter worked his way along the street, lighting each streetlamp with unusual haste. He scarcely looked at Émile and Justine, his shoulders hunched, his face ghastly. Across the street a well-dressed man scurried past, clutching at his cravat and staring at the ground.

"Maybe we should return to the orphanage for tonight," Justine said, still cowering against Émile. "I hate Paris."

"I must take you home. Your father would worry," he said but continued to hold her close.

Slowly the thought of grisly death receded, and Émile's solid chest, thumping heart, and comforting arms moved to the forefront of Justine's awareness. She sensed a corresponding change in the way he held her, a tiny shift of his arms and catch of his breath. The instant she felt him begin to withdraw, she tightened her grasp around his waist, lifted her face until her nose touched his neck, and murmured, "I want to stay with you."

The sudden tightening of his embrace nearly crushed the breath from her. "You don't know what you're asking," he groaned, his breath warm upon her ear.

"I do!"

His chest rose and fell three times before he gathered strength and pushed her away. "Then you are cruel beyond belief to use me so!"

"*Use* you!" She shook her head. "Émile, I love you!"

"I know you do," he said harshly, turning away and shaking his fists as he spoke. "I am your brother, as you often say."

"Non!" She turned him toward her and stroked his cheek and

the taut sinews of his throat, but he jerked his face away. "You love me as more than a sister, Émile," she said. "You must!"

"I do not deny it." She barely heard the broken whisper.

Joy burst like sparks into her brain. "Then marry me and keep me with you."

She could not interpret his expression by the faint lamplight, but his heaving chest revealed the battle within. Again she reached for him, but he stepped back and folded his arms.

"Listen," he said. "I plan to use the pass your father provided, leave Paris with the orphans, and guide them to the farm." His upraised hand prevented her interruption. "Then I shall take ship for Canada. I need a fresh beginning in a new land."

Justine clapped her hand over her mouth.

"Think and pray seriously," Émile continued. "Consider well before you promise to join yourself to me for the rest of our lives. I would be your husband, not your inferior; head of our home, not a servant. Of my undying devotion, you may be confident." His voice cracked, and he swallowed hard. "If you are willing to leave everything else behind and commit yourself to me permanently on these terms, then I will marry you. You have two weeks in which to decide."

Hearing his marriage proposal expressed in such blunt and practical terms startled her into silence. After a tension-filled moment, he touched her arm. "Come."

In the middle of the street they stepped across a gutter running with dark liquid. The reek of gore and death rose in a cloying mist. "Émile, is that. . . ?"

"Keep moving. We can do nothing to stop the carnage, but perhaps your father can."

Justine forced her rubbery legs to move. To fight against nausea, to keep from thinking, she began to talk. "Papa cannot leave Paris now; he must serve his term in the assembly. He fears the radicals will demand the king's death, which he believes would turn the entire world against the Republic. I do hope the king and queen and dauphin are safe today. Monsieur Boniface talked about Paris being in danger as long as the prisoners lived. He spoke of summary justice. Do you think he meant that this. . .this. . .what you saw just now was necessary?"

"I don't know." Yet Émile's tone said the opposite. Justine agreed with him. Henri Boniface would approve the slaying of anyone opposed to his sacred Republic.

They walked another block before she spoke again. "If I left Papa, he would be entirely alone."

"Justine, please look at me."

Slowly she lifted her gaze to meet his. Behind him the Seine sparkled with stars caught in its depths. A nearby streetlamp cast eerie shadows across Émile's face, darkening his stubbled chin, deepening his frown. "If the choice were mine, I would never leave you. Never."

Bowing his head, he paused to regain control and started walking again before he continued. "But circumstances have changed. I can no longer watch over you as your household servant, and your father will have me arrested if I loiter near your house. The time for decisive action has come. Either you and I must marry, or we must part. I do not ask you to leave your father and choose me; I merely give you the option. I cannot see the future." He broke off each sentence as if afraid of saying too much. "You and I both must trust in God's goodness and mercy and follow His leading."

He stopped. Justine realized that they stood before her house. "Will I see you again?" she asked. "How can I tell you my decision?"

"You asked Adrienne to fix your hair for the masquerade. She will act as messenger between us." Gunfire cracked somewhere nearby. Émile flinched, taking a protective step closer. "Until this unrest subsides, remain inside and take no chances. Pray, Justine. If we never meet again on this earth, you may be confident that we shall meet in heaven."

Silence. Her legs shook as she faced him in the darkness, uncertain. "Émile?"

Then she was in his arms, and his cheek scraped across hers until their lips met in an achingly sweet kiss. She sucked in a sobbing breath and heard him whisper, "You *do* love me!" With a strength of will that ripped her heart up by its roots, he released her and turned away.

Shivering, she watched until darkness swallowed his form and even the echo of his footsteps faded into silence.

Chapter 9

The prison massacres continued day after day. Justine remained cloistered at home, gazing out windows or staring blankly at books. Each evening when her father returned from the assembly, his face was more drawn and gray. She would bring him cognac and a pillow, then kneel on the rug at his feet and listen while he poured out his woes. No longer did he attempt to shield her from the truth; his tales of the atrocities being committed daily in the city turned Justine's blood cold. "Can you do nothing to stop it?" she burst out.

He sighed. "It is terrible, I know, yet justice must be served. The people cannot be as easily controlled as you think. We who would temper their violence are countered by those who encourage it."

"Such as Henri Boniface," she said, giving her father a stern look.

He averted her gaze. "The electorate's mood changes. Ardent revolutionists like your friend Henri rise in power, pushing us conservatives aside."

She set her jaw. "Monsieur Boniface is not my friend."

"He is a dangerous enemy."

Justine regarded him closely. "Has he threatened you, Papa?"

"Not directly." He gave her a quick glance. "You know I would not force you to wed the man, my daughter, but I do ask you to humor him for my sake. Attend the masquerade ball next week. Wear the costume he provided. Smile and be civil. See if you cannot soothe his injured pride."

Justine rested her forehead on her father's knee. "He is all politeness and consideration until he is thwarted. Then his true nature reveals itself."

"His true nature," he said in a thoughtful tone. "Justine, the man was raised in the best of homes and given every opportunity. Why would he choose to be evil?"

"We have discussed the matter before, Papa. The Bible teaches that man's heart is naturally wicked."

He frowned. "Almost I begin to believe this. Yet if this is so, what hope has mankind? Born evil, we practice evil for a lifetime no matter how much we despise it, and then we die."

Excitement built in Justine's heart. She silently prayed for the right words. "In ourselves, we have no hope. Only by God's intervention can we escape this living death and obtain eternal life."

Her father nodded slowly. "What if this God chooses not to intervene?"

"He has already intervened, Papa. He came to earth and lived among us as a sinless man; then He died as the perfect sacrifice to take upon Himself the penalty for our sin."

"You refer to Jesus Christ."

She nodded. "The man whose life changed history. Because of Christ, we can come to God and ask for mercy."

"But will He give mercy? How can we know?"

"Let me read His promises from the Bible." Justine hopped up, ran to the parlor table, and picked up her mother's worn book. Turning pages quickly, she found the passage that had popped into her mind. Holding the book open across his lap, she pointed out the verses. "In 1 John 5, we read: 'And this is the record, that God hath given to us eternal life, and this life is in his Son. He that hath the Son hath life; and he that hath not the Son of God hath not life. These things have I written unto you that believe on the name of the Son of God; that ye may know that ye have eternal life, and that ye may believe on the name of the Son of God.' See Papa? That you may *know*."

He picked up the Bible, frowning, and perused the previous page. "I have never heard this before. Are you certain this is a genuine Bible?"

"It was Maman's Bible."

He cleared his throat. "I prefer to read for myself."

Justine took the hint and excused herself. Tears trickled down her cheeks as she climbed the stairs. "Dear God, please open his eyes!" In her chamber, she fell across the bed and began to pray in earnest. "You do care. You are working in our lives. Forgive my doubts and strengthen my faith! I know You are good, and I know You are all powerful, so I must trust that You will work out Your perfect plan for our future." Sobs choked her words, but in her heart she continued to pray.

Day after day Justine's father attended the assembly, and night after night he sat in the parlor with the Bible open across his lap. She resisted her urge to question him about his reading and continued to pray for the Holy Spirit to give him understanding.

When days passed with no further word from Henri Boniface, Justine began to relax. Events in Paris must be claiming his attention. She hoped this distraction would prove permanent and prayed to that end. But the passing days also reduced her allotted time for prayer and consideration of Émile's marriage proposal, and she found herself no nearer to a decision.

While her heart rejoiced in the certainty of Émile's love, prompting her to give up all for his sake and begin fresh in a new country, love and loyalty for her father forbade such a drastic move. The notion of deserting him seemed traitorous. More than once she resolved to give up Émile and all thought of marriage and family and to devote her life to her father's care and support. But then she remembered Émile's kind eyes, his warm embrace, his beloved voice—and her selfless resolution would again crumble to dust.

Friday afternoon, her father returned home early from the assembly and rushed upstairs to his study. Justine found him seated at his desk, pen poised over a blank paper. His eyes were closed.

"Papa?"

He looked up. Displeasure flashed across his face. "What is it?"

"Is something wrong?"

"Where is Émile Girardeau?"

Justine blinked. "I haven't seen Émile in more than a week.

He works for a swordsmith named Arnaud Lamorges."

Her father stared into space, his fingers twiddling the quill until ink blotched the paper. Exclaiming under his breath, he wadded it up and tossed it aside. "Leave me, but tell Jacques to come to my study within the hour."

"Oui, Papa."

Later, while gazing out the parlor window, Justine saw the young page who ran errands for her father leave the house bearing sealed papers. Curiosity drove her back upstairs to her father's study. His feet resting on a hassock, a robe across his lap, he sat with the open Bible in his hands. His fine features profiled against the window expressed calm resignation.

"Do you need anything, Papa?"

Amusement flickered in his eyes. "Inquisitive as ever." He beckoned. "Sit here beside me. I must speak with you."

Justine obeyed, spreading her skirts and seating herself near his footstool. "What has happened?"

"I've done what I can. The rest is in God's hands. Justine, I have been a poor father to you these past years—"

"Non!"

He held up his hand to stop her protest. "When you returned from school, beautiful and bright, I no longer knew how to behave toward you. I was a proud yet frightened father. Involving myself in politics seemed to me the best way to bring you into good society. I promised myself you would marry well and want for nothing. I am old but not wise, I fear."

"Papa—"

"Hear me out. I am old. My health begins to fail. I would not have my daughter waste her life caring for an old man, though I know she is willing to do so. I want you to leave the city as soon as possible."

Justine brightened. "We are to return home?"

"Wait until you hear all before you begin making plans." His lined features hardened. "Boniface has made his intentions clear. If I fail to give you to him in marriage, he will take you as his mistress by force. I've made quiet inquiries and attempts to gauge his political strength, and I must admit myself powerless to thwart him. According to rumor, he intends to act tomorrow night at the bal masqué."

Numbness crept over Justine.

"Take heart, enfant. God has provided help in our time of need. An acquaintance, a worthy gentleman from England whom I once defended on minor charges, is currently in Paris on business. I've written, asking if he will provide transportation to England for you and Girardeau. He owns a yacht, which is docked at Cherbourg, I believe. If he agrees to aid us, we must abide by his schedule."

"For me and Émile?" Justine whispered.

"While Boniface retains power, you cannot remain safely in France. Girardeau informed me of his intention to immigrate to Canada. I believe I can trust him to escort you there. I sent him a note requesting his assistance in sneaking you out of the city. I shall remain to carry out my duties here for as long as God allows."

Questions spun through Justine's brain. She focused on the most important. "Papa, you speak of God as though you believe."

"I must believe, Justine. Everything I believed in throughout my life has been stripped away, bit by bit, revealing emptiness and darkness. Only when I decided to try believing in the existence of God did I begin to discover purpose and order. Since that discovery began I am overwhelmed by the evidence each day reveals. No longer do I fear death and eternity, for I know that there I can meet Him face to face."

Justine wanted to talk not cry, but tears came anyway. "Do not speak of dying; you must escape to Canada with us."

He wiped her damp cheeks with his thumb. "Trust me, mon enfant, I must remain behind. Deception is our surest weapon against the wiles of Henri Boniface. Until the last moment, he must believe that he has conquered." He bowed his head and tightened his lips, then sighed. "It galls to admit error, but I must acknowledge the superior worth of Émile Girardeau. He will love his wife as Christ loves the church, with eternal fidelity. A father can ask no more for his daughter."

Justine lowered her face to her hands and sobbed aloud.

"This displeases you? I thought you desired to marry him." Distress quivered in her father's voice. "I have again pledged you against your wishes."

She pressed his thin hand to her cheek. "Non, Papa, I weep for joy, not for sorrow. Émile is dear to me. Yet I cannot imagine happiness while I know that your life is endangered here!"

The worry lines in his face smoothed away. "If the Lord wills, I shall live many more years and attempt to rectify many wrongs. But a man cannot add days to his own life, no matter how he tries. My loving daughter will allow me the honor of emulating our Lord Christ in choosing life in death over death in life."

Justine's sobs stilled as she pondered his words. "I honor your choice, Papa. I shall follow your plans as becomes the dutiful child such a father deserves." After a moment's hesitation, she scrambled to her knees and flung herself into his arms.

He rescued the Bible from beneath her, then drew her close and stroked her loose hair. "May God reward your obedience with blessings beyond measure, *ma fille cherie*."

Chapter 10

Émile thrust the partially formed pike into a water tub, rubbed his hands down his leather apron, and reached for the letter in Adrienne's hand. "For me? Are you certain?" Any hope that Justine might have written died when he saw the masculine handwriting.

He looked at Adrienne as he broke the seal. "Merci." She nodded, still waiting. Nosy woman. He glanced over the message, then started again from the beginning, frowning. How could this be true? Yet the signature certainly belonged to Monsieur Didier. Émile's heart picked up its pace despite his doubts. Frustrated, he paced across the smithy and back, then read the letter again.

Adrienne bounced on her toes. "Is it good news? Bad news? Cruel you are, to keep me in suspense!"

Arnaud pulled a sword from the forge, laid it across an anvil, and began to pound it into shape. Between clanging blows, he gave his wife an irritated yet fond glance. "Either way, it isn't your news, woman."

Émile crossed his arms, still clutching the paper in one

hand, still pacing. "It does concern her, and you, too. Our help is requested."

"Who requests our help? Help to do what?" Adrienne asked.

"Monsieur Didier requests our aid in his attempt to spirit Justine out of the city. Monsieur Henri Boniface has evil designs upon mademoiselle's virtue and would force her into his power."

Adrienne and Arnaud exchanged startled looks. "Monsieur Boniface is becoming a powerful man, Émile," Adrienne said. "If he desires mademoiselle, how can she escape? What can we do?"

Émile met Arnaud's frowning gaze, then answered Adrienne. "Monsieur Didier's plan may pose danger, yet I think not. I cannot see how blame could be traced to you, particularly if you disguise yourself."

She lighted up. "An intrigue! How delightful! Arnaud, please say I may help my dear Justine and Émile."

"First tell us the plan. Then we shall see." Arnaud laid aside his work and approached to stand near his wife, arms crossed over his massive chest.

Knowing his friend's sensitive heart, Émile remained confident. "The plan involves tomorrow's grand bal masqué. . . ."

Twice that evening Justine answered a knock at the door and accepted a message for her father. Dutifully she delivered each one, although her heart burned with curiosity. As she handed over the second note, a roll tied with a brown ribbon, her impatience spilled over. "Papa, what does he say? Did Émile agree to your plan?"

Her father merely hemmed and rubbed his forefinger across his upper lip as he read.

Justine stepped back and played with one of her curls. She tried not to stare at her father, yet she knew the instant he lowered the letter. "Please tell me."

"Sir Cuthbert Stuart has agreed to transport you to England, but he insists he must pick you up near Cherbourg ten days from tomorrow, no later. He plans to leave France soon, for the recent carnage has sickened him beyond bearing and he fears for his own safety." Monsieur Didier stared into space for a moment, evidently calculating. "You must leave the city Sunday morning with the orphans, conduct them to the farm, then travel in all haste to the coast."

"Will our presence endanger the orphans?"

Monsieur gave her a considering look then shook his head. "They need Émile to direct them to the farm. Boniface has no knowledge of your association with them, so I believe we can safely avail ourselves of their protection in escaping the city. For now, child, we must pray and prepare for the bal masqué."

❧

Frére Martin listened with sober concentration while Émile outlined the plan; then he rubbed his jaw thoughtfully. "Boniface will put out orders to stop mademoiselle from leaving the city."

"We can disguise her as an orphan. She is small enough to pass for a child. Frére Martin, take thought. Her father provided our exit passes; he can easily revoke them if we thwart his plans. He is a worthy man on the whole, but he will not hesitate to sacrifice the good of many for his daughter's sake."

Émile struggled to control his voice. "The Lord knew beforehand that this crisis would arise. Why not continue to trust in His protection and provision?"

Firelight flickered over Frére Martin's face, hollowing his cheeks. He rose and paced across the room, his fingers laced behind his back. "If your rescue attempt succeeds, you may bring her here. We have sufficient exit passes for one more orphan, and the children love mademoiselle."

"Merci, Frére Martin. My gratitude is greater than I can express." Feeling pressure build in his throat, Émile fell silent. A strong hand gripped his shoulder. He looked up.

"Do you intend to marry her?"

Émile met his friend's gaze squarely. "If she will have me. Her father has withdrawn his opposition."

Frére Martin smiled. "Given the circumstances, I thought he might."

Justine regarded her reflection in the oval glass. "The gown is spectacular, as is my coiffure—thanks to you—yet I do not recognize myself."

Adrienne combed a ringlet around her finger, dropped it into place on Justine's shoulder, then stepped back to survey her handiwork. "You are *exquise*, mademoiselle. I am an *artiste*. Monsieur Boniface will be *enchanté*."

Justine checked the clock on her bedchamber mantel. "If you are to attend the masquerade, you'd better hurry home and prepare."

"There is time in plenty. Never fear; I shall attend tonight's bal masqué. Before I go, I must share my news, for you and I may never speak together again. Soon I shall play the new role of mother. I am carrying Arnaud's child." She glowed with pride.

Justine grasped Adrienne's hands in her own. "A baby! How wonderful! When?"

"Many months yet. But tonight, I play a different part." A naughty gleam entered her eyes. "On behalf of my dear friends. I think in this case God will not mind."

Knowing Adrienne's changeable ways with regard to spiritual matters, Justine wondered what exactly she meant. Adrienne gave her hands a squeeze. "God seems far from Paris these days," she said, "yet He is ever near you and Émile. Arnaud and I think we may decide to believe in Him but not yet. Too much religion is unsafe these days."

"But, Adrienne, how much worse to be without God during these perilous times! Think of your baby."

"We who believe in the revolution suffer no peril. Arnaud and I love you and Émile and would help you escape, for we know as others cannot that you pose no threat to the patrie. The recent killing of prisoners was a dreadful thing yet necessary for the safety of good citizens. Our leaders know best. Your father is a wise man. He would not lead us wrong."

Justine wanted to blurt out her father's opposition to the slaughter of untried prisoners, but caution held her tongue. Better, perhaps, for Adrienne and Arnaud to be ignorant of his altered position.

Adrienne swung their clasped hands back and forth once then let go. "Now I must hurry home and become *irrésistible*. If we never speak again, sweet Justine, be certain that your friend Adrienne loves you." With a little wave she hurried away.

As soon as Justine heard the front door close, she spun to regard her reflection in the glass. How strange she appeared with the mass of shining curls atop her head and flowing down upon her bare shoulders. The creamy gown glittered gold with her every movement. Lifting her skirt, she peeked at a high-heeled golden shoe.

"Justine, are you ready?" her father called.

"Oui, Papa. Is it time already?" She tucked a handkerchief into the pocket concealed within her gown's folds. Hearing his footsteps in the hall, she smoothed her bodice and checked her back view in the mirror. Every ruffle appeared to be in place.

He stopped in the doorway. She heard him suck in a quick breath.

"Is something wrong, Papa?"

"For a moment I thought I saw Marie, your mother." His voice sounded choked. "So beautiful you are, Justine Marie Didier. The gown is exquisite. Whatever his faults, Henri Boniface has excellent taste." He extended a fabric-wrapped bundle. "I shall be honored if you will wear these tonight."

Justine accepted the package while studying her father's face. Feeling hard lumps in the bundle, she unwrapped it. Gold, pearls, and diamonds gleamed amid the folds.

"They were your mother's. I want you to have them as surety in case I cannot come to you. You may sell them at need."

"I will see you again," she said, half questioning.

"I make no promise of that." He lifted a dainty necklace from the bundle and fastened it behind her neck while she held her hair out of the way. Pearl and diamond earbobs, a ring, and a delicate tiara completed the set.

"I look like a princess," Justine said in some concern once the tiara sparkled amid her curls. "What if I am mistaken for royalty?"

"Many bourgeois women possess fine jewels, child. You needn't fear. No true princess would dare attend this bal masqué, even in costume. Every notable personage of the Republic will make an appearance this evening." Her father patted her arm. "I'll watch and make certain your escape proceeds according to plan. Be in constant prayer. Much depends on the loyalty and subtlety of your servant friends."

Arms linked, they descended the stairs. "I believe our carriage awaits," he said, reaching for the door. "Try to appear as if you had not a care in the world."

Justine rose on tiptoe to kiss his cheek. "I love you."

Chapter 11

Enormous chandeliers and countless sconces illuminated the ballroom, their light reflected in sparkling mirrors. Elaborate plaster artwork adorned the recessed ceiling; gilt-framed portraits and landscapes lined the turquoise walls. Violins sang romantic melodies amid the clamor of conversation, the clink of glasses, and the patter of dancing slippers on the hardwood floor. In other circumstances, Justine would have thrilled to the occasion, but tonight she watched the twirling dancers to distract herself from rising fear.

Her father mingled with other political figures across the ballroom, their sober attire in stark contrast to the dancers' brilliant costumes. Nowhere did Justine see Adrienne Lamorges.

Soon after her arrival, she had recognized Henri Boniface amid the milling crowd of masqueraders. A white mask partly concealed his features; a scarlet cape flowed from his shoulders. Numerous women sought his company. In his leisurely way, he had squired woman after woman over the dance floor, but Justine had lost sight of him. Perhaps Papa was wrong, and Henri bore her no lasting ill will. Perhaps—

"Here you are at last," his deep voice purred near her ear.

Justine stiffened and fluttered her fan as she turned. "Monsieur?"

His low chuckle sent quivers through her body. "You forget that I selected your costume. Not that I could mistake you for another woman anywhere. A man can more fully appreciate the perfection of your lips when they are all of your face he can see." Dark eyes seemed to burn holes through his mask. His white teeth gleamed. "Dance with me."

Before she could respond, he dragged her to the floor and fell into step. Dance followed dance, and he gave her no time to rest. Justine began to see him as a cat and herself as a mouse, taunted by his every smile, his every lingering caress. When he led her from the floor into an anteroom partially hidden by a curtain, she followed meekly, her hope fading.

Almost immediately he slipped his arm around her waist. With his other hand he traced a line across her collarbones then clasped her throat. At her slightest struggle, his grip tightened.

"You trusted overmuch in your father's protection, *ma belle fille*. Too late you discover that his career and his life mean more to him than your virtue. I may yet marry you, but first I shall discover whether you are worth the effort. If you please me, a marriage will be forthcoming. If not. . ." He shrugged expressively. "It matters little which you choose. As you informed me recently, even your exquisite beauty will eventually fade. Why should I tie myself to fleeting charms?"

Faint with horror, she felt his lips move across her cheek until his breath warmed her ear. "I believe your father will want you to please me." He pulled back to give her a cruel smile. "For his sake."

Darkness swirled around her. The mask seemed smothering. *"Jésus, m'aider!"* she whispered.

Henri laughed and released her so abruptly that she staggered back two steps. "Cry to your God for help if you will. He cannot hear, for He does not exist. I shall be your god from this time forth; strive to satisfy me, if you can. You cannot leave the city, and should you attempt to, your father will suffer my wrath."

Despite Henri's derision, Justine knew God heard and answered her plea. Peace and renewed confidence flowed into her spirit. Even if everything went awry and she never saw Émile or her father again, God would be with each of them, providing strength and courage to the end.

But to Henri she revealed only her fear.

"Tonight," he said, studying his manicured fingernails, "Mademoiselle Didier forever departs from her father's house. For her I have leased a fine dwelling furnished in gold and white to complement her surpassing beauty. She will soon learn to appreciate her excellent fortune."

With a mocking bow, he pushed aside the curtain and headed toward the tables laden with food and drink. Women touched his arm as he passed, attempting to catch his eye. Justine watched as a shapely woman in a revealing costume stepped into his path and feigned surprise. The creature used every known feminine trick to hold Henri's attention and succeeded, to Justine's mild surprise. Of course, a man like Henri would find such obvious charms appealing. Or perhaps he hoped to rouse Justine's jealousy. Together, the pair moved to the dance floor, his arm around her waist, her hand upon his chest. Justine wrinkled her nose in disgust.

A man's quiet voice spoke behind her. "Do not turn around; it is Arnaud Lamorges. While Adrienne holds Boniface spell-bound, you must exit through the doorway you see on your left, descend the stairs, and leave the building by the large door at the end of the hallway. Once you reach the garden, walk calmly until you pass through the rose trellis arch. Then you must run to the far gate, where Émile awaits you with a carriage. Make haste."

Smiling and plying her fan, Justine moved around a group of seated dowagers and toward the closest doorway. That woman dancing with Henri was Adrienne? And Arnaud allowed it? Once through the door, she descended a dark stair-case and entered a hallway dimly lighted by candle sconces. Probably a servants' hall. Her breath came hot and fast by the time she reached a great wooden door. Lifting the bar, she hauled the door open and felt a rush of cool night air. Stars and torches lighted her way.

The terraced gardens stepped down a gentle slope. Water gushed from the mouth of a dolphin-shaped fountain, flowed over a series of stone steps, and swirled into a stone basin. Marble statues and dark topiaries rose at either hand as she passed along a gravel path, her steps crunching softly. At last she glimpsed an arch ahead, a doorway through a tall hedge.

Émile stroked the horses' necks, but they sensed his tension and stamped impatiently. "Lord God," he prayed, "give Justine's feet wings. Lead her to this gate and calm our fears."

Again he walked to the wrought-iron bars and searched the shadows beyond. Was that a white shape? He blinked and stared again. Something moved in the darkness. His ears caught the rustle of fabric. "Justine," he whispered, then called softly, "Justine."

The figure approached. "Émile? I thought I should never find the gate!"

"Can you lift the latch?"

A metallic clang, and the gate squealed open. Émile closed it, caught Justine's hand, and led her to the waiting carriage. The gate clanged and squealed open again. Panicked, Émile picked up Justine and threw her inside. A blinding flash and a roar slammed Émile into the carriage door. He collapsed backward against the wheel and then slumped to the dirt road, vaguely aware that the horses snorted and whinnied in fear. If they bolted, he thought amid whirling stars, the rear wheel would pass directly over him.

"I thought you might attempt something like this, Justine." Henri Boniface's voice held amusement. "Is this your stupid servant lad again? Your father will proclaim me a hero for rescuing his daughter from her own foolishness."

"Émile!" Justine wailed. "You shot him!"

"Stay where you are. I shall help you climb down to prevent damage to your gown." Footsteps approached. "You know, this Émile desired you as much as I do—perhaps more. Inside every man lurks a tiger waiting to pounce."

Émile opened his eyes. Boniface, spinning round and round against the starry sky, swung Justine down from the carriage in a billow of white fabric. Émile surged upward and plunged his fist into Boniface's belly.

Justine fell away as Boniface doubled over with an animal grunt of pain. Émile didn't wait for the world to stop whirling but punched Boniface's astonished face with his other fist. Pain shot through his hand as his knuckles connected with hard bone and flesh. Boniface's head snapped back. Émile swung blindly and connected again, but the tilting world threw him up toward the sky until the street hit him in the knees. He thrust out his hands and caught air. Solid dirt impacted his cheek. Helpless, he rolled to his back and heard a thud. Down from the spiraling sky fell Boniface.

Justine stared at Émile and Henri on the road at her feet. "Are they dead?"

Arnaud Lamorges knelt beside Émile. "He lives." He patted Émile's cheeks and sat him up.

Monsieur Didier thrust a heavy pistol back into his waistband. "I did not strike Boniface hard enough to kill him. Once you are away, I shall revive him and assure him of my outrage. Climb into the carriage, enfant." His calm voice returned her to her senses. "Your friend Lamorges will drive you to the orphanage." He gently propelled Justine toward the carriage.

"Henri shot Émile." She climbed inside.

"I know," her father said, helping Arnaud boost Émile into the seat beside her. "I should have foreseen that possibility."

"The ball skimmed his head, no more," Arnaud assured her. At least semi-conscious, Émile gripped his wadded-up jacket against his bleeding scalp.

The carriage door closed. Justine heard Monsieur Didier speaking outside. ". . .after you leave them at the orphanage, sell the carriage and horses. Keep the price as token of my gratitude for your assistance. You and your wife are true and brave citizens of France. God will reward you."

"Amen," Émile whispered.

Justine watched as Frére Martin bathed Émile's torn scalp and bruised knuckles. Her mask, gloves, and fan lay discarded on the floor nearby. Her beautiful gown billowed around her chair. Émile lay upon Frére Martin's feather bed in an otherwise Spartan bedchamber. Candlelight turned his hair into gold filigree.

Frére Martin tucked a blanket beneath Émile's chin. "Your head will ache tomorrow, but you should be able to drive a wagon. God blessed you with a hard skull."

Émile smiled but did not open his eyes.

"Do we leave in the morning?" Justine asked. "Arnaud urged us to make haste. Papa cannot keep Monsieur Boniface away from our trail forever."

"We leave in four hours. Sarah and the children sleep tonight in their traveling clothes. She laid aside suitable garments for you," Frére Martin said. "I'll sit up with Émile."

Chapter 12

Sometime in the night Justine awakened to pounding at the great oaken door. With a rustle of satin, she sat up. Fear widened her eyes. This gown would stand out like a beacon to betray her. She struggled to reach its buttons, impeded by her straggling hair.

A quick eternity later, Frére Martin spoke at her chamber door. "Monsieur Didier is here."

"Papa!" Justine refastened the one button she had been able to reach and hurried into the dark passage. Just inside the stone archway, lamplight revealed her father. He opened his arms as she approached. Their embrace communicated a love neither could voice.

He spoke softly. "At present Boniface seeks you on the road to Austria, due to a false lead given by a bribed gate guard. I made inquiry and located the sedan chair carriers who brought you here once before. After learning your location, I bought their forgetfulness." He pressed a leather bag into her hands. "Keep this hidden about your person at all times. Along with funds for your voyage, it contains a letter for Monsieur Stuart when you meet him at Cherbourg. Our estate in Normandy is in your name should you ever desire to return to France."

She nodded, tears rolling down her cheeks.

"I wish to see you marry. Frére Martin has agreed to wed you to Girardeau before your departure."

She looked down at herself. "But I am a mess!"

At the sound of laughter, she turned to see Frére Martin, Sarah, and Émile waiting in the shadows. Émile stepped forward and took her hand. "You are an angel, Justine, if somewhat rumpled. The Lord has provided this moment. Shall we accept it with your father's blessing?"

She looked into his bruised face and could only nod. Émile loved her no matter how she looked.

"I'll help you tidy up," Sarah offered. "No bride could desire a finer gown."

By flickering candlelight, Monsieur Didier gave his daughter as bride to Émile Girardeau, his former servant. Frére Martin conducted the ceremony. Little Luc babbled happily in Sarah's arms while the couple exchanged their vows.

Afterward Sarah helped Justine unbutton the gown and stuff it into a sack for her father to take away. Justine touched the glimmering brocade one last time in farewell. "I married Émile while wearing the gown Monsieur Boniface procured for me. I think he would not be pleased." She and Sarah shared a smile.

Minutes later, Monsieur Didier embraced his new son-in-law, then held his daughter close. "May God bless your union and grant you many years together of service to Him. May you find true liberty in our Lord's faithfulness for all eternity." He cleared his rasping throat, gave Justine's fingers one last squeeze, then disappeared into the dark alley.

Émile comforted his weeping bride while their friends slipped away.

❦

Dawn sent pale streaks into the sky as two wagons—laden with barrels, sacks, three goats, a crate of clucking chickens, and an abundance of children—rumbled into the city streets. Sunday morning traffic was light. Passersby paid scant attention to two farm wagons. Frére Martin drove the lead cart. Despite a raging headache and occasional dizziness, Émile drove the other. Unease gnawed at his belly.

The barriers lay ahead, then miles of travel to Normandy and the coast. Émile dared one glance over his shoulder. His wife sat among the listless children with little Luc asleep in her lap. Justine's head bobbed with the wagon's motion. Émile smiled, comparing this orphan waif with his glorious bride.

The city gate loomed ahead. Émile's horses tossed their heads, sensing his fear. When the guard ordered the wagons to halt, he waited his turn. A guard shuffled through Frére Martin's papers and inspected his passengers. Thanks to Justine's artwork with some theatrical cosmetics donated by Adrienne, the orphans looked sickly and malnourished. "Passes from a deputy, eh? Important orphans, these are."

"Monsieur is a benevolent man," Frére Martin said. "Like all good Republican leaders, he cares even about orphans and widows of the patrie."

After a few more questions and a cursory examination of the wagon's contents, the guard waved them through. Émile drove his wagon forward and stopped at the barrier.

The grimy-faced guard took his papers. "You're with that last crew?"

"Oui."

Another guard hung over the wagon's side to inspect the sleeping children. "Are they alive?" His harsh voice wakened Luc, who began to screech. The guard's eyes narrowed as he watched Justine pat and comfort the baby. "Are you sure this one's a child?" He jerked off Justine's hood. A tangled wig framed her spotted face. She lifted the screaming baby to display the red sores dotting his flushed face.

The guard's mouth fell open, and he jumped away. "Smallpox!"

His superior heard the cry, took one wild-eyed look at Justine and the baby, and thrust the papers back at Émile. "Get them diseased brats out of here!"

Émile slapped the reins on his horses' backs. The grimy city streets gave way to fresh late-summer countryside with touches of autumn color in the trees. Luc continued to cry, although his shrieks calmed to a sobbing wail.

Up ahead waited the lead wagon. Expectant faces peered over its tailgate. Frére Martin and Sarah turned backwards on the seat. "All went smoothly?"

"Thanks to Adrienne," Justine called, pushing the wig away from her mottled face. "She showed me how to make pock sores with cosmetics. This morning I painted my own face and Luc's as an extra precaution."

"The Lord be praised!" Sarah said.

Nearly a week later, the wagons rolled to a stop before a large stone farmhouse amid rolling fields and green hills. As soon as Frére Martin finished leading in a thanksgiving prayer, the children clambered down from the wagons and ran to explore, disregarding the warnings Sarah shouted after them.

The farmhouse door swung open, revealing the plump form of Madame DeFaye, housekeeper at la Maison d'Arbre de Cerise since before Justine's birth. "Welcome all! We cleaned this place for you from top to bottom. Master sent word you were coming, and ever since the family went to Paris, we've little enough to do at the big house. Some of the men are to stay and help run the farm for as long as they're needed. Simone and I hope we can help with cooking and caring for the little ones."

Scarcely pausing for breath, she hugged Justine. "Congratulations to you and Master Émile from all the staff at d'Arbre de Cerise. We never expected Émile to win our *belle enfant*, but we're delighted to see his love rewarded."

Almost speechless with joy and gratitude, Frére Martin and Sarah inspected the house, the tidy grounds, the roomy stables and sheepfolds, pleased to discover grain for feed in the bins and sweet-scented hay in the barn. While Émile and Frére Martin stabled the horses and moved the goats and chickens into their new homes, the menservants unloaded the wagons, and Justine and Sarah prepared the bedchambers for the children. That night after a hearty supper, Justine visited with her old friends, bathed the children, and helped tuck them into bed. Each new proof of her father's generosity and provision for the orphans' future filled her with pride and love.

At last the house was quiet, the children asleep, and Justine and Émile retreated to their small bedchamber. Seated beside a crackling fire, Justine hummed to Luc, rocking him as she stared into the flames. The baby's body relaxed in her arms; he clutched a handful of her *fichu*. Justine's throat tightened. She didn't dare look at Émile for fear she might burst into tears.

"Do you want to bring Luc with us?" His voice was tender.

"I do." Justine nearly sobbed with relief. "I thought my heart would break at leaving my precious baby behind. But can he endure the journey, Émile? He is so small."

"I already spoke with Frére Martin and Sarah. They agree with me that God will make a way." He moved to the settle beside her and gathered his new wife and new son close. Justine leaned against his solid shoulder and soaked in his love. Sucking his thumb, eyes half-closed, Luc sighed with contentment.

Émile kissed her forehead then Luc's. "We are a family."

Early the following morning, the old groom from la Maison d'Arbre de Cerise arrived driving a closed coach pulled by four fine horses. "Master gave orders for us to change horses in Caen. These are for you, Madame Girardeau." He placed several parcels in her hands. "Your mother's things; Master wants you to have them. Don't like to rush you, but that Englishman won't wait if we're late. Word is out in the port cities to watch for you. They say soldiers are coming today to search the big house, but you can count on everyone there to be ignorant." He winked.

Despite the urgency of hot pursuit, Justine and Émile found it difficult to leave their friends and the children. Frére Martin prayed for them then gave Luc an extra blessing and kiss. Many tears and hugs later, the coach set out on back roads for the appointed meeting place on the seacoast.

Waves slapped the ship's sides. Spray dampened Justine's face as she climbed aboard the *Faerie*. Émile, carrying Luc, followed close behind. Shivering, they glanced around the ship's deck and aloft at scurrying sailors and flapping sails. The brisk wind carried snatches of song and shouted orders.

Before them on the deck, feet planted squarely, waited Sir Cuthbert Stuart, a tall, angular man with dark hair and a hawk nose. The slightest lift of his aristocratic brow spoke volumes as he inspected their modest clothing and bulky parcels. His servant stepped forward, welcomed them aboard the yacht in stilted French, and showed them to a cabin in the stern.

"I suspect Sir Cuthbert aids us out of obligation rather than through kindness," Justine said as soon as their last bag was delivered and the door closed.

"We are to be guests in Sir Cuthbert's house until we take ship for Canada. Such generosity shouldn't be despised." Émile slipped a heavy sack from his shoulder and lowered it to the floor.

Feeling chilled, Justine loosened the drawstring of one parcel and tugged out a wool cape. "I hope this crossing doesn't take long. My stomach already grows queasy."

Émile placed Luc on the floor to creep about. "Be thankful we are safely out of France. Another day and we might not have escaped."

"I am sorry I complain. But. . .do you think he is all right, Émile?"

"Your father?" Émile held her troubled gaze and drew her

close. "He is in our Lord's hands, Justine. Sir Cuthbert will try to contact him with news of your safety."

Justine rested her head on her husband's shoulder. "He told me not to mourn but to let him go." She sighed, looked up into Émile's eyes, and gave him a tremulous smile. "Whatever comes, we three are together."

He touched his forehead to hers. "We three and the Lord."

The yacht suddenly tipped to one side, dumping them upon the bunk. Luc let out an excited squeal and slapped his hands on the floor.

"I believe we are underway," Émile observed from amid a curtain of Justine's loosened hair.

She chuckled.

Epilogue

six months later

The carriage arrived to transport Émile and Justine to Portsmouth, where they would take ship for Canada. In the entry hall of Sir Cuthbert's manor house, Justine thanked her host, then hugged his daughters, Melodia and Felice. Little Felice pulled away and ran to her father, but Melodia clung to Justine. "Do not weep, child," Justine said in stilted English, wondering how best to comfort the motherless little girl. Perhaps a parting gift?

She held up one finger and smiled. Blinking back tears, Melodia released her and tried to return the smile. Justine searched through her valise until a fluff of feathers caught her eye. She pulled out her mask and presented it to Melodia. "For you, to remember Justine."

Delight brought a glow to the child's features. "Thank you, madame," she said, taking the mask, then "Merci." She held the mask to her face and peered up at Justine through the eye holes.

"To you I shall write a letter from Canada. You will wish this, no?" Justine asked.

"Yes!" Melodia said. "And Luc?"

Justine took Luc from Émile and let him kiss Melodia's round cheek. He laughed and pulled Melodia's hair, but the little girl hugged him sweetly. "Good-bye, Luc."

"Me! Me!" Felice cried, running to Justine with grabbing baby hands. Justine thought for a moment, then gave the toddler her fan. Felice would probably break the trinket, but for now it pleased her.

Émile shook Sir Cuthbert's hand. The gentleman looked at Justine. For an instant she saw his expression soften. "I am sorry I could not help your father," he said in excellent French. "He was a good man."

Justine ducked her head and fought back quick tears. "I know you did what you could, monsieur. I am forever grateful. May God bless you for your kindness."

Emile took Justine's arm and escorted her down the steps to the waiting carriage. Once they settled inside, the footman closed the door. As the carriage jerked to a start, Justine sat back in the seat, settled Luc on her lap, and smiled wistfully at Émile. "So it ends."

He smiled, pulled her close, and murmured against her ear. "And so it begins."

JILL STENGL

Award-winning author Jill Stengl has written several books and novellas for Barbour Publishing. She currently lives with her husband, Dean, and their family in a log home in the Northwoods of Wisconsin. They have four children and a busy life. Tom is an Air Force Academy cadet, Anne Elisabeth is in college, Jim is in high school, and Peter is Jill's last homeschool student. Jill loves to write about exciting times, historic places, and unusual people. Please visit her Web site at www.jillstengl.com and send an e-mail—she promises to answer.

A Duplicitous Façade

by Tamela Hancock Murray

Dedication

To my talented coauthors, friends, and sisters in Christ:
Pamela, Jill, and Bonnie.

An hypocrite with his mouth destroyeth his neighbour:
but through knowledge shall the just be delivered.
PROVERBS 11:9

Chapter 1

England, 1812

Melodia Stuart stood before her father in his study. She tried not to shiver. Winter's chill hung in the room despite flames burning in the gray stone fireplace. Shivering would indicate weakness, which Father despised. Since he considered the space a man's domain, Sir Cuthbert Stuart seldom summoned her there. Her requested presence bespoke the profound importance of his news.

He studied her, no doubt regarding her slim frame that he had often told her needed to be fleshier to attract a suitor. Yet tonight, he smiled.

"I have news for you, Melodia. Good news." He drummed his fingertips on the armrests of his mahogany chair, in which he had positioned himself in a grand posture more befitting the prince regent than a landed gentleman.

"I am sure if you believe the news to be welcome, I shall share your sentiment."

"Of course you shall." He looked at her with eyes as blue as her own. "I have triumphed, finally. I have made arrangements for you to become betrothed."

"Betrothed?" She took a moment to let the horrific word and its implications sink into her mind. She clutched her hands together in a feeble effort to brace herself before she spoke. "But, Father, I had no idea you were thinking of promising me to anyone."

"Neither did I. While I was visiting London, the occasion presented itself as a surprise even to me," he admitted. "But since the match is such a good opportunity, I could not let it pass."

Visions of their acquaintances paraded through her head. None of them appealed to her. "Who. . .who is the man?"

"Sir Rolf Tims."

"Sir Rolf Tims?" Melodia searched her memory. "I seem to remember that name, but no face comes to mind."

"Ah." A moment of quiet penetrated the brisk air before he continued. "Yes. It was not you but Felice who met him during her stay in Normandy last fall."

"Oh." Melodia recalled how a fever had kept her from vacationing abroad with her sister and father the previous year. "Now that you bring him to mind, I believe Felice mentioned Sir Rolf." A sly idea crossed her mind. "Since she has made his acquaintance, why not betroth her to him instead of me?"

"I have someone else in mind for Felice. Someone more suited to her temperament. A man who is strong enough to rein in her impetuous will."

Melodia remained silent. Despite his admiration for her intellect, Father had always considered her gentle spirit a sign of weakness. If he sought a hard man to control her younger sister, then perhaps his misperception would be to her benefit. She took in a breath and tried not to flinch as she presented another argument.

"I know many fathers match their daughters with men they have never met, but I never thought you would actually do such a terrible thing." Melodia tried not to whine. If she hoped he would grant her a hearing, she had to force herself to take on the calm demeanor of a woman and not display wild emotions of a spoiled little girl. He would indulge Felice in such antics, but not Melodia. "You just cannot!"

His stare caught her attention. "I can, and I will." As he tensed his jaws, graying mutton chops on both cheeks inched forward. "You must understand that my actions are to everyone's benefit."

Since Father prided himself on his logical ability, she sought an appeal to reason. "But surely you would not expect a rational person to agree to a match with an unseen husband."

"Sir Rolf is a reasonable man, yet he has agreed to marry you without a meeting. You should count yourself lucky, at that." Father surveyed her. "Had he seen your stringy hair that cannot hold a ringlet, your lips that are far too red for a lady, and your large feet, he might not have given his assent. I am only thankful I had the foresight to procure a flattering portrait of you from an artist I paid well. And that Sir Rolf did tell me he prefers a woman with dark hair and fair skin—qualities you possess."

Though his description rang true, Melodia's reflection showed that the features God formed to compose her face worked to her advantage. Rather than a bland beauty, her countenance held the benefit of expressiveness. "But how will my betrothed and I converse? We may not have the slightest thing in common."

"Oh, yes, I am glad you bring me to the subject. It is more than evident that Providence granted you a strong mind, but not every man is as appreciative of your intellect as I, your lenient father."

"I would hope any man to whom you would betroth me would be as understanding as you."

"A likely fantasy," he responded. "You are far too high-minded for your own good. If he is a typical man of this age, your husband will not be seeking to engage in intelligent conversation with you when he surely can take advantage of conversing with men. Instead of holding such ideas, you will act as a proper lady—speaking when spoken to, being seen, not heard, and exercising the utmost obedience to your husband."

She flinched.

"I implore you not to resist." He wagged a cross finger. "You know full well that our family name is our first and foremost interest, and your marriage will strengthen our ties to important concerns here and abroad. Through this connection with the Tims family, your offspring will be heirs to one of the most powerful family lines in the empire. You should be grateful for the favor that Providence has bestowed upon you."

"You speak of Providence. Certainly you know I had contemplated giving my life to the Lord rather than becoming a wife and mother."

"I am aware of your childish fantasies, but the time to abandon those has come. If you would read your Bible with more care, you will learn that you can serve the Lord as a wife and mother. Case in point, a young virgin girl named Mary." He tilted his head at her as he made his point.

"I will gladly serve the Lord as a wife and mother, if that is His plan for me."

"Since you and Felice are the only daughters I have to offer, I believe this is indeed His plan for you. And since you are the elder of the two sisters, Sir Rolf has agreed to wed you. You should be thanking God instead of bemoaning your fate."

"I would not be, as you say, 'bemoaning my fate' if you were not marrying me off to the highest bidder."

"Enough!"

"I am sorry, Father. I should not have spoken so boldly." Melodia stared at the edge of his desk rather than letting her gaze touch upon his face.

"Please do not debate me. I only have your best interests—and those of the Stuart name—at heart."

"Yes, Father."

If only her mother were still alive! Perhaps she could have spoken to Father and asked that he not subject Melodia to such an arrangement. She often wondered what her mother had been like. A slip of a woman, like a songbird, she had been told. No wonder Melodia's lanky frame and large feet—despite the fact that both traits had been inherited from Father's side of the family—did not please him. She knew another reason why he found her appearance lacking. Convinced his wife contracted a chill from little Melodia soon after the birth of Felice, he blamed Melodia for such an untimely death.

"Of course you will obey me," Father said, interrupting her

musings. "The wedding is set for the first day of February."

"But that's in less than a week!"

"Precisely. I suggest you begin preparations today."

❧

The moment after Father excused her, Melodia rushed up the front stairs to Felice's bedchamber in the south wing and knocked on the door.

"Come in, Mandy."

Melodia entered to find Felice's maid brushing her hair in front of the vanity mirror. The silver handle of the boar bristle brush glistened underneath the candlelight.

"It is not Mandy. It is I," Melodia said.

"Well, I do wonder where Mandy is with my warm milk. She does dawdle. But welcome, Sister." Despite the fact that the maid continued to brush Felice's hair, she twisted her waist to face Melodia. "Why are you visiting my bedchamber at this late hour?"

"Father has told me the most dreadful news."

Felice set her brush on the table. "What is it?"

"He. . .he has betrothed me to a man I have never met."

Felice didn't seem as surprised as Melodia thought she would be.

Melodia rushed to her sister's side. As the maid stepped back, Melodia took Felice by her woolen-clad shoulders. "Felice, did you know about this? Why did you not tell me?"

"No, I did not. I promise you that. But you know Father. He has always wanted us to marry to his advantage—and to ours."

Melodia let go of her sister. She clutched her hands

together and paced in front of Felice's vanity. "I did not think he would be so cruel."

"Cruel? No, I think he is a generous man who wants the best for our family and our future heirs."

Melodia groaned. "Only you, his favorite daughter, could make such a proclamation."

"But my dear, fathers everywhere betroth their daughters to the best and brightest men available. It is our custom. Surely you are not such a babe in the woods that you are ignorant to our ways."

Melodia stopped pacing long enough to face her sister and to set her lips into a tight line. "I have no taste for your sarcasm."

"And I am sure Father had no taste for the argument you undoubtedly presented to him." Felice leaned her chin against her palm.

"Yes, you do know me too well."

"And knowing Father, he won."

Melodia lifted her forefinger. "He only thinks he was victorious."

"Oh, I suspect he won handily. And I venture you will be married by this time next week. So who is the lucky bridegroom?"

Melodia stopped her useless pacing. "Sir Rolf Tims."

The smile disappeared from Felice's face as she took in a breath. "Father betrothed you to Sir Rolf? The very Sir Rolf I met in Normandy?"

Melodia shrugged. "I do believe Father mentioned that in passing." Suspicion mingled with curiosity. "What do you know about Sir Rolf?"

"Not much. Not much at all." Felice turned back around and motioned for the maid to resume brushing her hair. She stared at her reflection. "But what about your desire to serve the Lord? Does Father not care about your heart?"

"He believes I can serve God as a wife and mother."

"That is what he said?"

The maid set a piece of hair against her palm and smoothed honeyed strands with her brush.

"Not exactly. But I am sure that is what he thinks."

"And you acquiesced."

"I did try to get him to listen to reason, as you guessed. But in the end, how could I not submit? I am his daughter. Even if I were not bound to obey him according to the Ten Commandments, I am duty bound by law to do as he wishes."

"That will be all, Cassie."

Cassie stopped brushing, nodded, and curtsied. "Yes, milady."

As Cassie made a silent exit, Felice folded her arms and pouted, then looked into the mirror and addressed Melodia's reflection. "I am not so sure I would. Perhaps I would run away and find my own destiny."

"Perhaps your high-spirited nature would permit you to take such a course," Melodia speculated. "We shall see when Father announces your fate. Since we are so close in age, I have no doubt that will happen soon after my own nuptials. In fact, if you have a gentleman in mind who has caught your eye, you might implore him to speak to Father now with thoughts of your future. Otherwise, he might saddle you with someone with whom you would not care to share breakfast the remainder of your days."

"I—I am sure Father will consider my feelings." Felice rubbed her hands together.

"Then you might mention Lord Farnsworth. I notice he looks your way wistfully whenever you are near."

"That old pig?" She scrunched her nose.

"That 'old pig,' as you call him, is not so displeasing to look upon, is he?"

"Not if you like a rotund frame and sanguine cheeks."

"Bespeaking of enough food to eat and a jolly disposition—both aspects not to be taken lightly in a marriage," Melodia pointed out. "And he is a church deacon with a significant title and fortune."

"You sound like Father."

"Be prepared, for you will have to face Father regarding your feelings. Only I wish you more success than I encountered."

"Do you really think Sir Rolf is so bad?"

"You know I have never met him. I am hoping since you became acquainted with him in Normandy that you can tell me more."

Felice reached for a bottle of powder scented with the pungent but sweet scent of lily of the valley and dabbed it on what little flesh on her wrists her gown exposed. "Yes. I met him."

"What does he look like?"

"I should think a spiritual person such as yourself would care not a whit what he looks like. Especially since you recommend a match for me with a so-called jolly fellow."

Melodia ignored the snide portion of her sister's observation. "I cannot help but wonder since I will be staring into his countenance for the rest of my days."

Felice shrugged. "I suppose he appears well enough. I do not remember so much about him. A vague image comes to mind of a tall person with fair hair and an indistinguishable face."

"And his ability to converse?"

"As well as the next man, I suppose. He said nothing memorable to me."

"Oh. Well then, you should be grateful that Father did not pursue my suggestion that he betroth you to Sir Rolf instead of me."

"You suggested such?"

"Yes, but he said he has someone else in mind for you."

"I wonder who?"

"I know not. Perhaps I should have made more of an effort to find out for your sake, dear sister, but I confess I was too involved in considering my own fate—and composing arguments opposed to it—to ask."

"Do not let your omission vex you, Melodia. I will learn of his plans soon enough."

"And there is no one you desire for yourself, no one you can bring to Father's mind? I dare not venture another suggestion."

She didn't hesitate. "No. No one. So when are your nuptials?"

"February 1. Father has arranged for us to marry the day after Sir Rolf arrives."

"So soon?"

Melodia winced. "I suppose he is in hopes that Sir Rolf will not have time to change his mind once he sees me."

Felice didn't offer the comforting assurances Melodia sought. Nevertheless, Melodia pressed on with her next request. "Felice, will you be my maid of honor?"

Felice pounced on the offer, which didn't surprise Melodia since Felice loved the idea of romance. "Of course. I shall wear a lovely shade of sapphire, with ivory lace at the neck, cuffs, waist, and hem."

Melodia laughed. "Sapphire blue?"

"Is that not one of your favorite colors?"

"Yes. That and pink."

Felice leaned against the back of her chair. "Well, which should I wear? Blue or pink?"

"I do not think we can afford to be too particular. We need to consult the seamstress to see what fabric is available."

"True." She peeked at her reflection. "Which color do you think flatters me more?"

"You will look beautiful in either."

"Well," Felice responded. "We shall have to decide as soon as we can. With the nuptials upon us, my bridesmaid's dress must be sewn."

❧

The night for her to meet Sir Rolf had arrived. Melodia was packed and ready to leave the only home she had ever known to embark on a journey halfway across England to live out the rest of her days. Why her father wanted to claim lineage to a family living so far away was beyond her, but he had his reasons. He always did. Or at least, so he said.

As her lady's maid, Rachel, styled her hair, Melodia attempted no conversation. She was in no mood for idle chatter. At least Father had agreed to allow Rachel to accompany Melodia to her new home. Becoming acclimated to a new home and husband as well as a staff of servants would prove troublesome enough. She didn't need to be stranded without her well-loved maid.

"Are you pleased with the way I have styled your hair, Miss Melodia?" the young girl asked.

Melodia concentrated on her reflection and noted meticulous rows of curls set around her face. "Yes. This will do."

"Will Miss Melodia be wearing silver or gold earrings tonight?"

"Neither. The pearls. And I want my pearl necklace."

Rachel took the jewels out of the unlocked silver box on Melodia's dresser. Melodia caught a glimpse of silk, a mask decorated with feathers and pearls given to her twenty years before by Madame Justine Girardeau, a beautiful and elegant French woman, when Melodia was but five. With the help of Father, madame and her husband had escaped Paris before the Reign of Terror and now lived far away in Canada.

Justine and Melodia exchanged letters from time to time. She enjoyed the contact even though news was months old by the time a letter arrived from Canada. Melodia had learned that Justine and Émile had been blessed with a large family. The orphan they adopted, Luc, had recently married. Melodia smiled to herself as she recalled holding a scrawny infant whose large voice defied his diminutive size.

Rachel shut the box with a snap, taking Melodia's thoughts away from her friends living across the sea. "An excellent choice, Miss Melodia. These pearls will look well against your fair skin and contrast agreeably with the green dress we have chosen." She handed the earrings to her mistress and then hooked the necklace around Melodia's neck.

"Thank you, Rachel."

"Shall I have tea brought up? And perhaps some biscuits?"

"No. I am not hungry. Thank you."

"I don't blame you for feeling a bit nervous. I'd be, if I were meeting my future husband for the first time."

"I wish you had not reminded me." She tightened her hands together.

"I'm sorry, Miss Melodia."

"No. I am sorry. I did not mean to be irritable." She thought about the little necklace with a gold cross that remained in her jewel box. "I wish I could wear my favorite piece, but Father told me not to wear any religious items. Apparently he doesn't want me to scare off my suitor."

Rachel shrugged. "Your future husband might be well advised to find out about our faith now as later. Surely Sir Cuthbert has not betrothed you to someone who doesn't profess to being a Christian."

"No, I think he would make sure he is a professing Christian." A pang of doubt shot through her chest. She could only hope. "But his faith is not as important to Father as his family name, I am sorry to say. Father's most ardent desire for the evening is for all to go well, and for this marriage to take place. After that, no doubt I am on my own."

Chapter 2

Rolf waited in the drawing room and studied green velvet draperies framing large windows that revealed the wealth of the occupants of the Stuart estate. Larger-than-life oil paintings—one of a man and the other of a woman—graced each side of the fireplace. Rolf surmised the portraits of the couple, dressed in the fussy style of finery his parents wore when they were young, depicted his future bride's parents when they were in the bloom of newly wedded youth.

Aside from the portraits, a large piano crafted from wood polished to a deep hue dominated the room. Rolf judged from such accoutrements that his heirs would be moneyed indeed. Still, he wished for the hundredth time that he hadn't agreed to such folly. Yet Father, battling illness in his London apartment to such extent that he could not travel to witness the nuptials, had spoken to Rolf of honor and duty. Apparently both, considered the highest of virtues, were enough to convince Rolf to promise his father that he would marry a woman he had never met. His sister, Martha, had married and was in her time of confinement as she awaited the arrival of a child. But that was not enough for the elder Tims. By agreeing to the marriage, Rolf was most of all fulfilling the desire to make his dying father happy in the knowledge that through his son, a new generation of heirs would carry forth the family name.

A picture of Melodia playing a tune by Mozart on the piano entered his head unbeckoned. Surely a woman granted such a name was gifted with a talent for music. He would enjoy watching her long fingers move along the ivory keys with deftness and grace. Perhaps he might be moved to join her, strumming his lyre in accompaniment. He took in a breath as the image faded.

Heavenly Father, was I a fool to fall in love with Melodia based on a small portrait?

He contemplated the thought, not for the first time.

Perhaps. But her father assured me his elder daughter prays to Thee with fervor each night, that she blesses each meal, and does not have to be prodded from bed to rise for worship each Sabbath. Otherwise, Thou knowest I never would have acquiesced to such an arrangement. And yet, Father, I pray for Thy strength and guidance, that I am not making a mistake.

Rolf wondered how Melodia could be devout when her sister seemed anything but. He remembered what Felice had been like during her visit to Normandy. According to his memory, she was attractive enough—gathering single men around her with a bat of an eyelash—but too coquettish and flighty for his tastes. When Rolf's own father had first mentioned him being matched to a Stuart, Rolf was afraid that Felice was the one he had in mind. So when Father uttered Melodia's name, Rolf had felt relieved. Yet what if Sir Cuthbert Stuart had exaggerated her love for the Lord? What if she proved to be just as capricious as her sister?

Cuthbert's voice cut into his thoughts. "So sorry for my delay, my boy. It couldn't be helped, I assure you." He extended his hand, and Rolf accepted the gesture.

"Not at all, sir. I have been quite comfortable by the fire."

"Good." Cuthbert eyed the tea table. "I see my servants are also tardy this evening. I had requested that refreshment be brought in to you."

As if on cue, a maid entered carrying a tray filled with biscuits and tea.

"I do not appreciate your tardiness," Cuthbert reprimanded her.

The young girl made haste to set the tray on the low-lying tea table. She turned to them, quaking, and managed a curtsy. "I beg your gracious pardon, milord, but Cook accidentally let the fire go out and we had to restart it."

He harrumphed. "See that does not happen again."

"Yes, milord. May I pour tea, or will you be waiting for Miss Melodia to join you?"

"We shall not wait. Our guest no doubt would welcome a cup of tea to warm his body and spirit after his journey." He motioned for Rolf to sit on a diminutive sofa across from the plush chair he took for himself. Rolf obeyed.

"My elder daughter should be presenting herself momentarily. I trust you are not too nervous, my boy?"

"No." He wasn't sure if he was nervous or not. He hadn't learned enough about Melodia to discern if he should be.

Cuthbert took a sip of his drink. Studying him, Rolf noticed he seemed more like the nervous bridegroom. What was wrong with Melodia? He remembered the portrait and a realization struck him. Melodia had been too ill to go to Normandy with her father and sister. Was she a sickly little thing, unlikely to produce the heir Rolf's father so wanted? Or perhaps she limped. Or was her face pockmarked? Such a detail was guaranteed to be omitted by any artist. Could it be that her ability to speak well had been impaired in some fashion? In a flash, he wondered if he discovered that his future bride bore any of these afflictions, could he get out of his promise?

Just as quickly, shame filled him. How could he be so shallow?

Heavenly Father, I do not ask Thee for the woman with the most stunning outward appearance but for one of healthy body and mind. A woman who loves Thee, a woman who will teach our children to love Thee. I do not ask for happiness. I have been granted too much privilege and too many blessings in this life Thou hast given me to ask for everything. Prepare me to meet with whatever circumstance Thou thinkest fit for me to endure. May I be the meet and right husband for this woman.

"You seem contemplative," Cuthbert said. "I hope you are not thinking of changing your mind." He slathered clear red jelly on a plain scone.

Glad he wasn't prone to blushing, Rolf stirred one lump of sugar into his hot tea with more vigilance than required. The pressure he applied to the handle of the spoon caused the silver filigree pattern to dent his fingertip. "Indeed not. Why would you contemplate such a thing?"

Cuthbert laughed, but his mirth didn't seem sincere.

Melodia entered. When introductions were made, Rolf stopped himself from taking in a breath as he took in her face. The portrait had been accurate. Her eyes were bright, and a thin, pointed nose gave her face a dimension lacking in the countenances of other women he knew. Dark brown ringlets fell against smooth skin. He found her tall, lean frame appealing as well.

"I hope you are not too disappointed." The edge in Cuthbert's voice superseded the playful tone.

"I am not." Rolf found no difficulty in keeping his voice strong and steady since he spoke the truth.

"Good." Was it relief he saw on Cuthbert's face? "Then we may proceed with the nuptials."

Rolf had not even spoken to Melodia, but based on her beauty, he was ready to acquiesce. He swallowed.

Lord, I pray I will not regret this leap I am about to take. May our marriage be in accordance with Your divine will, despite its less than auspicious beginning.

Guilt visited Rolf like a vulture circling a dying beast. He had agreed to the marriage to please his father. The bargain was a desperate attempt to merge the Stuart fortune with the Tims expertise in business affairs. Without the influx of Stuart money to give the business a boost, the Tims family fortunes overseas—in France and Germany in particular—could well become as extinct as a woman wearing a powdered wig on the street.

Melodia gave him a charming curtsey. "I am pleased to meet you, Sir Rolf." Her voice matched her name—melodious.

"And I am enchanted."

Was that a blush he saw on her cheeks? Surely in this ribald day and age, he hadn't happened upon an innocent. But the way she refused to let her gaze meet his, the shy way she held herself, indicated she was no worldly woman. Perhaps she was a prize.

Though he wanted to talk more to her that evening, Melodia's father kept him otherwise occupied. Cuthbert seemed afraid, somehow, that Rolf would back out of his promise. He wondered why.

He had no time to linger on such thoughts when Felice entered.

"You remember my younger daughter from the time we visited the summer home of our mutual friends in Normandy." Cuthbert nodded toward Felice.

"Indeed. A pleasure to see you again, Miss Stuart." Rolf took her hand in his and brushed the back of it with his lips. Felice looked more pleased than she should have. He regretted the gallant gesture. He didn't want to do anything to encourage her. He had seen her look at him in a furtive manner when she thought he wouldn't notice. He prayed the actions were his imagination or her disposition lent itself to flirtation with many men.

❧

"Oh, how lucky you are!" Dressed in her woolen night shift, Felice sat on the edge of Melodia's bed after the happy evening had transpired. "Sir Rolf is even more handsome and witty than I remembered."

"Yes, your enthusiasm for him seems to have grown considerably since I first told you about our betrothal," Melodia observed. "I could see that you enjoyed his company. One might think you were the bride rather than I."

"Silly goose! I will not be seeing him—or you—once you leave here. Is it so wrong for me to be friendly to my future brother-in-law? After all, I may be visiting you soon, and he may have many handsome friends who are looking for a wife."

Melodia shook her head. "That is you, Felice, always looking for an opportunity." Her voice held more of an edge than she intended. Melodia had felt overshadowed by her vivacious sister all evening; her resentment showed.

"Oh, do forgive me, my dear sister," Felice begged. "I only wish I were as lucky as you are. You do like him, do you not?"

"I—I cannot tell. I suppose he is as amiable as I can expect. I really cannot pass judgment yet."

"True. Perhaps Father should have promised him to me since we met in Normandy." Felice laughed.

"Do you really think so?"

"Well, you are the oldest, and he has promised him to you. So now we shall see what Father has planned for me. He still refuses to reveal anything. I confess to not a small bit of fear."

Melodia embraced her sister. "You know you are Father's favorite. Surely he will find a wonderful match for you. You must learn to trust your earthly father as you trust your heavenly Father."

"Perhaps you should listen to your own sermon," Felice suggested. "Then you would not be so vexed about your wedding day."

Melodia knew her sister was right. After Felice left Melodia's bedchamber, dressed in an air of more excitement than Melodia herself felt, she dropped to her knees beside her bed. She rubbed her hand across the quilt, realizing this would be the last night she would sleep in her own bed, the bed she grew up with from her childhood. After the festivities, she would be leaving for her new home, blessed with a new name.

She recalled the last wedding she had attended. She remembered how the couple kissed after they were proclaimed man and wife. A flush of heat warmed her body as she realized the kiss from her groom would be her first. The kiss would take place among people she had known all her life, and Rolf's groomsmen who had journeyed to witness their nuptials. The idea of such an intimate moment occurring in front of everyone left her feeling nervous. She almost wished she had convinced Rolf to walk with her on some excuse—to see the garden statuary, perhaps—so she could practice a kiss in private. But she hadn't, and that was that.

Still, no regret nudged her that Rolf's kiss would be her first. She longed for no other man and had not been curious during her earlier years. The men of her acquaintance were more like brothers to her than suitors. She would be giving Rolf, this man she didn't know, but a man chosen for her, the gift of herself.

Father in heaven, I beseech Thee to take away my fears, and to help me be a good wife in spite of my doubts, since judging by my new situation, Thou hast called me to family life. I thank Thee that Rolf seems to be kind, and that he is not disappointing to look at—handsome, even. I pray that he is a godly man, and that we can make a life together that will be pleasing to Thee.

She rose and climbed into the bed of her maidenhood for the last time.

Chapter 3

Three weeks after they had exchanged vows, Melodia was thoroughly ensconced in her new home on the other side of England and adjusting to an extent that she shocked even herself by how well she took to being a new wife. She had been surprised to discover how well the household was run. Before her arrival, Rolf had lived alone at the estate since his sister, Martha, had long married and moved to Dover, leaving no related woman available to offer him assistance.

Martha had been confined with a delicate condition at the time of the wedding so they had not met, but at the soiree Melodia and Rolf hosted early on to meet the neighbors, she heard nothing but good reports about his sister. She looked forward to the trip Rolf had promised they would take to London after Martha's child was born. Melodia wondered how long the Lord would tarry in granting her a child. A blush of happiness filled her at the thought.

At the moment she sat in the library, rocking in a comfortable chair situated near the fire that warded off early spring's chill. No matter how urgent household duties seemed, she never neglected to indulge in her quiet time each morning. Since her marriage, she had been drawn more than usual to the Song of Solomon. So many of the passages reflected her developing feelings of love for Rolf. She had been warned by more than one experienced matron not to assume love would follow the wedding, but already it had for her, and she could see by Rolf's tenderness that he had developed fondness for her as well. For that, she was grateful.

Most of Melodia's friends had already begun corresponding with her, and Felice's daily missives had kept her up-to-date with news of home. So far, Father hadn't made any announcements about his plans for her. Melodia knew Father felt less insecure about Felice's chances of making a good match than he had felt toward hers. Felice, with her coy wit and appearance of a classic beauty, had many potential suitors. She didn't hesitate to report her current prospects to Melodia, and though any of the men she mentioned would have made a fine husband, Felice always seemed to be waiting for someone better. Melodia prayed Felice would find that elusive man.

Rolf's voice cut into her thoughts. "You appear so peaceful, I am loath to interrupt."

Melodia looked up from her Bible. "Even if you interrupted me a thousand times, I know this passage well enough to recite it by heart, so it matters not. You have something to tell me?"

He drew closer to her. "Yes. I will be spending the next few nights at the Howard estate."

She tried not to pout. "Oh. A hunting party?"

"Yes. I wish you were included, but as you know, Henry is a bachelor and never considers offering diversion for the ladies."

"Then I suspect he shall evermore remain a bachelor."

Rolf chuckled. "And I suspect that prospect is not entirely displeasing to him."

Melodia bit her lip to keep from complaining. If only he were present more. First, business affairs kept him occupied. As for leisure, hunting, fishing, and gatherings with his gentlemen friends seemed to hold more allure than her charms. She supposed Rolf's behavior was normal for a man of his station; after all, how could she expect him to forego the pursuits he enjoyed just because he had placed a wedding ring on her finger?

"You do not mind terribly, do you?" he asked.

What could she say? She felt she had no right to object. "I want what makes you happy, Rolf."

He leaned over and kissed her on the forehead. "You have thus far proven to be the perfect wife."

As he turned to exit, she didn't let him see her wry expression. Perhaps she should consider being less "perfect," as he called her, and more outspoken about her feelings. In the meantime, she resolved not to feel sorry for herself.

But she did.

The next day, a maid interrupted Melodia at the end of her midafternoon toilette and presented her with a calling card the hue of cream and fashioned from thick paper. "Lady Eustacia Cunningham to see you, Miss Melodia."

Standing next to her vanity, Melodia ran her fingers over

the imprinted letters on the card. She had met Eustacia at the soiree, but their time together had been too brief for her to learn much about her. Melodia really was in no mood to receive a visitor, but since she couldn't honestly claim to be indisposed, decorum demanded that she accept Eustacia's call.

She glanced at the mantel clock and saw that teatime had arrived. "Bring tea into the drawing room," Melodia instructed in a voice that, to her surprise, betrayed no anxiety. "I shall meet her there."

"Yes, milady." The maid curtsied.

Melodia glanced at her reflection in the mirror. She hadn't designated that particular day as one when she would be receiving visitors, so she was pleased when she noted that her appearance was presentable enough. Rachel had curled her hair, and though the ringlets weren't as tight as they had been at breakfast, they hung around her face in an attractive manner. The white bandeau she wore in her hair contrasted well with her curls and brought out the natural blush in her cheeks. Her white dress, though an everyday frock, was one of her better and more flattering outfits. She took in a breath and prepared to face her visitor.

As she walked down the large front hallway flanked by oil portraits of Tims ancestors on either side along with occasional tables that displayed ceramic vases, she knew she never need worry herself about the appearance of the Tims estate. She discovered soon after her arrival that the staff was plentiful, efficient, and reliable. The housekeeper and butler who headed the rest of the servants proved competent if not always warm. As long as they held their positions, no dust would be allowed to linger on the furniture.

When he first showed her the estate, Rolf had told her that his sister, Martha, had decorated the home within the past three years during her period of engagement. The fashions and fabrics still looked fresh, and Melodia estimated that they would continue to look well for several more years.

A little smile quickened her lips when she recalled how Rolf asked if the decor was to her taste. She assured him in truth that as long as she felt comfortable and the colors weren't too garish, she could make do in any room. Still, she was glad he had considered her feelings enough to inquire.

Striding over the threshold of the drawing room off to the right of the center hall, she eyed an attractive woman resting on the sofa upholstered in a brocaded fabric the color of clotted cream. Dressed in deep green as she was, with hair a lighter blond than Melodia had ever seen on anyone else over the age of four, the wispy woman cut a striking figure. Had Melodia not been married, no doubt a pang of jealousy would have visited her.

They exchanged greetings. "I was just about to take tea. Will you join me?"

Eustacia tilted her chin toward the tea table and inspected the refreshments, which to Melodia's eyes looked especially delectable that day. "I always have time for tea at the Tims estate. I was great friends with Rolf's sister, Martha, you know."

Melodia took a seat across from her visitor. "Yes, I do believe you mentioned that when we met at the soiree." Which was why Melodia had made a special effort to accept Eustacia's unannounced call and to make sure tea was served. She picked up the teapot and began to pour.

Eustacia inspected her but with kind eyes. "I see you are just as beautiful when caught off guard as you are when ready for an occasion."

Melodia nearly spilled a stream of tea on the table but managed to lift the pot upright in time to avoid a mishap. "Beautiful?" The word escaped her lips unbidden.

Eustacia cocked her head. "Do you mean to say that you are not accustomed to such compliments?"

"Well, no, in fact." She set the pot down for good measure.

"And modest, too. No wonder Rolf likes you."

Melodia considered that Eustacia displayed not a small bit of effrontery to try to catch her unawares and to admit it at that. "Thank you," she managed.

Eustacia took a sip of her beverage and swallowed. "Your cook stocks excellent tea. See to it that she continues."

" 'Therefore I say unto you, Take no thought for your life, what ye shall eat, or what ye shall drink; nor yet for your body, what ye shall put on.' " She hadn't meant to blurt the verse from Matthew. She clapped her mouth shut. Then she saw Eustacia's quizzical look. " 'Is not the life more than meat, and the body than raiment?' "

"Are you quoting scripture to me?"

She stared at her half-filled cup of black tea. "I—I beg your pardon. Force of habit, I suppose."

"Not a very good habit unless you plan to live in the church. Few people enjoy a sermon unless it is from the vicar. And often, not even then."

"I beg your pardon." Melodia stiffened. This was not going well.

Eustacia took a small fruit tart. "So how do you like it out here in the country?"

"I grew up in the country myself, so I am accustomed to it. This estate is pleasant."

"Pleasant? Is that the best word you can find to describe where you live?" Eustacia looked about the room. "That is not how the other nearby women would describe such a grand place."

Jealousy tweaked her heart. What other women had caught Rolf's eye while he was still unattached? She decided not to stray into such territory. "I like it very much."

"Good." She eyed a portrait of Rolf. "No doubt you will be putting your own touches on the decor soon."

"I think I shall keep it as it is."

Eustacia's eyebrows shot up. "Indeed? Well, Martha will be delighted to learn that. She put quite a bit of effort into furnishing this estate in a proper manner."

"Her taste is exquisite, and I am grateful to be the beneficiary of her knowledge of colors and fabrics."

Eustacia smiled as though she meant it. At that moment, Melodia could see that Eustacia had decided they could be friends. She sent up a silent prayer of thanks to the Lord. Melodia had a feeling she would need all the friends she could cultivate.

Chapter 4

A few days later, Rolf hovered by the door of the library and watched his new bride absorb the wisdom of scripture. Since her arrival at his estate, he had been encouraged by her example to increase his own reading of the Word.

Since Melodia didn't lift her head, he knew she hadn't heard his footfalls hitting the thick wool runner on the hall floor. He was glad, since her intense concentration gave him the opportunity to drink in her beauty.

Earlier reservations about his new bride had vanished. She had more than lived up to the exquisite image in her portrait. Her form looked pleasing—neither too wide nor too wispy. Her voice didn't grate on his ears. She stood erect and walked with grace. Had Melodia not debuted only this past season, Rolf imagined she would have been wooed and taken by an attentive suitor long before he met her. He had wondered why Cuthbert had seemed so eager to make a match for her and why he had wanted to rush the wedding after their initial meeting, an arrangement Rolf agreed to only because of Melodia's devout reputation and his father's poor health.

Rolf's first impressions of Melodia did nothing to answer his questions about Cuthbert's odd though unexpressed fears that his daughter was in some way unmarriageable despite her attractiveness and large dowry. Only after Melodia and Rolf had been wed a few weeks did she hint about her father's resentment of her that was nursed by how he blamed her at least in part for her mother's death. Rolf suspected that Cuthbert's contained rage closed his eyes to Melodia's true assets. No wonder she had given more than a passing thought to running away to a secluded life dedicated to God's purpose. Still, as she shared these family secrets, obviously not wanting to show her father disrespect, nothing in Melodia's expression or voice asked for Rolf's pity. If anything, he had a feeling she would rebuff any attempts to make her take on the role of victim.

He admired her strength and was grateful to his father's lucidity in the midst of his own struggle for health that he had suggested a match with Melodia instead of waiting for her younger, coquettish sister. Indeed, Rolf had enjoyed the freedom of bachelorhood, and he had met few women intriguing enough to spur him to more than an idle thought of altering his situation. But as he watched Father grow increasingly ill—his coughing fits growing closer and closer together despite treatment—Rolf felt his obligation as a son weighing too heavily upon his mind to ignore.

During one of his trips to London to see his ailing father, situated in a small apartment where he could be near his doctors and druggists, Rolf broached the subject of marriage. Father's ready response indicated he had contemplated the possibilities. His strong voice demonstrated his joy that Rolf had asked. Melodia Stuart's name fell from his lips, followed by a smile. The answer didn't come as a surprise to Rolf since Father and Cuthbert had been boyhood friends.

Encouraged by Father's response to his query, Rolf took quick action by approaching Cuthbert the following week when they were guests at the same dinner party. After his future father-in-law's acquiescence, Rolf took the news to London. To his delight, Father's face took on a glow for the first time he could remember in months, perhaps even in a year. The look of happiness and, Rolf had to admit, approval told him that the match was well timed and taken in wisdom.

Honour thy father and thy mother: that thy days may be long upon the land which the LORD thy God giveth thee.

Not for a moment did Rolf regret taking this commandment to heart.

Another verse from the second chapter of Genesis came to mind: *Therefore shall a man leave his father and his mother, and shall cleave unto his wife: and they shall be one flesh.*

His wife. Enough of spying on her, however lovingly.

He cupped his hand over his lips and let out a warning cough.

Melodia heard Rolf clear his throat. She stopped reading in midverse.

Her husband was home!

She tried not to look as though she had been waiting for him with eagerness akin to a lover in Song of Solomon. Would he notice that in anticipation of his arrival she wore his favorite dress—or at least one upon which he had commented? She agreed that the yellow frock foretold the advent of Easter, with its meaning of redemption and salvation—the new beginnings promised by spring with its blooming flowers and hospitable weather. Just donning the color made her feel warmer and cheerful.

Despite her attempts to appear indifferent, she knew her enraptured expression upon seeing his fine features must reveal her feelings. As she noticed her heart beating rapidly, she wished he would tell her he loved her. He hadn't yet. But that was too much to expect. The closest he had ventured toward such a declaration was the day he told her she was the perfect wife. She clung to that sentiment for all it was worth.

Though he read scripture each day and conducted himself in a godly manner as far as she could see, Rolf was a man of reserve. Besides, she didn't want him to confess to feelings he hadn't yet developed. She knew he wouldn't in any event. He was too honest for such duplicity.

He smiled, adding to her emotions. "There you are. I thought you would be here."

Melodia closed her book but restrained herself from rising. To her delight, he strode over to her chair, bringing along with him the smell of outdoors—a mixture of new plant life, manure, dust from the road, and sweaty horseflesh. He bent over her for an all-too-brief kiss on the lips, then touched her cheek with manly fingertips before he moved his hand to the back of the chair. She wanted him to linger, wishing he hadn't concluded the contact.

"How was the hunting trip?" she asked.

"Excellent." He stood in front of her straight and proud with remembrance. "I garnered no new mountings for my study, regrettably, but our catch was good enough. We shall be feasting on game for at least a week."

"Good."

"That pleases you."

"Why would it not?"

He chuckled. "Many London women would turn green in the face at the prospect of consuming wild meat even for one dinner, let alone for an extended period of time."

"As you know, I am not a London woman."

"Indeed. And I am glad you are not." He grinned as he took the seat across from her. He settled into the back of the wooden chair and crossed his legs. "No doubt you recall Suffolk?"

The image of a short, stocky man just past his thirtieth birthday came to mind. "Yes."

"He proposed an excellent idea, one I think we should pursue."

"Oh?" She leaned forward.

"After Easter, I should like us to host a masquerade ball."

She gulped. The welcoming soiree had been enough of a crowd for her. She had been relieved when the last guest departed. At the prospect of yet another event, a feeling of shyness overwhelmed her. "Should we be hosting another gathering so soon? Especially an event that promises to require complicated arrangements?" Her brain formed a large list of errands to be accomplished for such an affair—engaging musical entertainment, composing a menu for an exquisite dinner within Cook's capabilities and talent. Or should they hire a caterer? And then the most important—compiling the proper guest list. Her mind whirled.

He chuckled. "Truly you jest. Did you not entertain often at your father's? After all, as the elder daughter, would you not be his hostess by default?"

"Yes, but Father was never one for hosting parties. And I suppose though our standing would have been improved had we been known for lavish affairs, he preferred quiet evenings. I suppose if Mother had been alive. . . ."

"Yes. Forgive me." He leaned over and patted her on the knee. "But you have a new life here, one that promises to be engaging and even exciting if you will allow yourself to enjoy your opportunities to the fullest. I say it is high time that you turned over a new leaf and learned how to be an elegant and popular hostess. And I suggest our first major event should be, as my friend suggested, a masquerade ball."

She tried not to let a frantic look cross her face. "Perhaps as a bachelor, you were not aware of the many preparations that such an event will require."

"Do not worry, my dear. I am confident you are up to the task."

"I—I—"

"Do not tell me you are too shy, because that excuse will not work with me. Especially not since you will be hiding behind a mask. Too bad, since you are such a beautiful woman."

She felt her cheeks blush. Was everyone here in the habit of calling women beautiful? The idea of herself being considered lovely still left her feeling uncomfortable. She had never visualized herself as magnificent, and wondered how others could.

"You have my permission to order an exquisite costume to be sewn for yourself," he continued. "Eustacia's seamstress is sure to take you on as a client. I understand she called upon you while I was away?"

"Yes." A thought occurred to her. "Upon your urging?"

"Not at all. Eustacia never has to be urged to do anything, and if such a thought had crossed my mind and I mentioned it to her, she would have stayed home out of spite."

"Really, now, spitefulness does not seem to be the right word to describe her."

"Perhaps not. High-spirited is more like it. Which is why she has not yet found a husband. For who could tame her?" He winked.

"Despite your levity, you seem to think high-spiritedness is a fine quality."

"In her, yes. But I like my wife demure, as you are, my lovely." His voice softened on the word *lovely*. A warm flush filled her as she recalled their intimate moments, moments that as a maiden she never dreamed she would come to anticipate for their sweetness. She shook thoughts of his hot kisses out of her head. Married though she was, lingering on matters of the flesh could lead to vulgarity.

Such thoughts served to soften her attitude to any idea he might suggest. "I have to say, a masquerade ball might have its advantages. You spoke of a mask. I have one I can wear. It was given to me by a French woman long ago. So it is an heirloom of sorts."

"I am not so lucky. I shall need to have one made."

"I can sew one for you."

"You would do that for me?"

"Of course. You are my husband." The word caused her to look down at her skirt.

"So I have been successful in persuading you to host a ball, then."

"Yes, you have." She gazed into his eyes, knowing he could convince her of almost anything.

Chapter 5

The night of the ball arrived sooner than Melodia could believe. As she watched the partygoers feast on the food, she recalled how for weeks she had immersed herself in preparations, wanting to please Rolf by making a good impression. Over time she had become more comfortable around his friends and neighbors. The soiree they hosted had broken the proverbial ice, and Melodia had formed light bonds with several of the women living nearby. As tradition warranted, Melodia called upon her neighbors, and they returned the favor. She knew the guests on their list would be giving the anticipation of an evening full of lively entertainment priority over criticizing the music, food, drink, and conversation. That fact helped to ease her anxiety.

Still, the ball was only the second event she was hosting as Rolf's wife. The winter soiree had been informal, so this was her first foray into entertaining on a grand scale, and she didn't want anything to go awry. Thankfully the household staff knew how to procure the best ingredients for dishes such as roast beef, stuffed quail, sugary confections, buttery fruit tarts with flavored icing, and other delicacies sure to impress. Melodia was all too aware that a poorly executed party could result in ruin for her reputation as a hostess. The restrictions of the day—the importance of impressions, connections, social rankings, appearances, and style—were some of the reasons why life as a secluded religious had seemed appealing. Until she met Rolf. The temptation to thank her father for making the match crossed her mind.

She stood near the fire that warded off evening's chill. Spring had arrived dressed in her usual array of greens, reds, pinks, yellows, and blues, so the fire's task of keeping the partygoers warm was less arduous than it had been at the soiree only weeks ago during winter's gray pall. A crackle from the fire almost made her jump, reminding her that she wore white silk that would not fare well should it make contact with dark ashes and especially not a stray ember. She moved a step away from the heat and regretted her decision to wear white yet again. Amid vibrant hues of the other ball gowns, she felt colorless. Even worse, would people guess her identity before the unveiling at midnight, perhaps guessing—wrongly—that she had chosen white since she was yet a bride. Instead, she had chosen a color befitting the heat of July because the material went well with her heirloom mask.

True to Rolf's promise, Eustacia had introduced Melodia to her seamstress, who proved more than competent in fashioning a flattering cut for the gown. In matching the mask, she had wisely omitted feathers but had sewn pearls around the neckline and cuffs. The buttons were also fashioned of pearl. Rachel had needed an inordinate amount of time, and no doubt much expenditure of frustration, to dress Melodia in a fashion containing a long row of buttons on the back of the dress and then four on each cuff. Yet the effect had been worth the effort. She touched a dark curl just to be sure it remained in its strategic place peeking out from underneath her pearl-embossed bandeau, the motion leaving her confident she still appeared unruffled.

As she ran an indifferent forefinger over the edge of her saucer, her gaze set itself upon the refreshment table. Several dishes were becoming sparse, a good sign attesting to their popularity but a worry considering she wanted to make sure everyone had enough of the precise offerings they wished to eat. She nodded to a maid and, once she garnered her attention, nodded toward the table to indicate the need for attention. The graying woman bobbed her head and scurried into the kitchen. Melodia had instructed the caterer not to be sparse with the amount of food he prepared for the evening. She was determined not to run out of any delicacies at her affairs—a development that would lead to the most catty gossip the next day and set her reputation as a stingy and disorganized hostess for as long as she remained at the Tims estate.

As she waited for the maid to obey her order, Melodia watched the partygoers flit, chat, and flirt among each other, satisfied that her evening was proving to be a success. She eyed Rolf. Even wearing the black mask she had made him, complete with feathers from a peacock she had retrieved from the grounds, the fine shape of his countenance was unmistakable. Pride in the fact that he was hers and hers alone swelled through her chest even though she didn't beckon such an emotion.

At that moment a tall woman wearing a bold red dress slid through the crowd. Watching her, Melodia admired her mysterious guest's head covering, an elaborate concoction set so closely to her head that Melodia almost wondered if the woman could have been bald. Shaking the ridiculous idea from her mind, she set her admiring gaze on three elaborate feathers that stood from the crest of the headdress. Melodia noted that if she were as tall as the mystery guest, she would have omitted the placement of anything that would add even more height to such a statuesque frame. But since the woman, who even in costume appeared striking, wore red, Melodia could only guess she didn't mind garnering more than her share of attention.

She felt amused until she noticed that the woman drew near to Rolf and reached toward the top layer of a three-tiered sterling silver tray for an egg with creamed filling. Melodia thought the woman's only objective was to acquire the food until she noticed that the woman's skirt touched the thigh of Rolf's velvet pant leg. Before Melodia could react to the close contact the woman's leg made with her husband's, the female turned toward him and laughed in the counterfeit manner of a coquette. Melodia's stomach lurched as she witnessed her whisper in his ear. He chuckled in return. Was he putting on a polite front, or did he find the woman amusing?

Her heart thumped.

Who was the woman in red?

And what had she said to her husband?

She watched for Rolf to move away, hoping he would make a hasty retreat. Just then her view was blocked by a gentleman. Gray curls peeked out from underneath a tricorn hat, and he wore a distinguished costume. She surmised him to be Lord Harrington but resisted calling him by name lest she be wrong—or right.

"I must say, I am having quite the extraordinary time this evening," he observed. "And what of you, my lovely? Are you finding the ball to your liking?"

An instant before, such a compliment—especially given to her by a man who probably didn't realize she was his hostess—would have offered her sufficient pleasure to float for a week. But now, his words seemed inconsequential. Nevertheless, she put on a smile and waved her fan. "Yes, it is. I am having a wonderful time. Have you tried the quail?"

He eyed the table. "Is it good?"

"Splendid."

"As a general rule, quail is not to my liking, but you have convinced me to give it a try." He wagged his finger. "I hope this is not your way of getting rid of me."

She tittered. "Indeed not."

A squat woman wearing a multicolored frock made of silk and decorated with random blue, white, and green oval beads made of glass approached Melodia and shared a few inane but pleasant observations. She guessed her to be Mrs. Snidow, but she couldn't be sure since she wore a blue and green mask with white piping. Melodia tried not to fix her gaze on Rolf, but in her jealousy, keeping her eyes averted from him proved difficult. She did notice that he had moved away from the woman as she had hoped he would and was at that moment conversing with a man wearing a plain black mask and an equally severe black costume. She watched Rolf off and on throughout the evening, but the woman didn't reappear. She felt relief.

Until she realized that perhaps that was their plan. If Rolf were seen talking to the same woman too much—and wearing red made her easy to spot—they might attract suspicion. Melodia wallowed in self-inflicted doubt. The fact that the woman seemed to have vanished left her with little comfort.

Midnight drew near. At that hour, the guests were destined to strip their faces of the masks that concealed their all-important eyes, presenting an unencumbered view of their identities for all to see. Melodia decided to watch for her rival.

"Are you quite ready for the masks to come off?" someone asked.

"I am ready." Her voice reflected the determination she felt. "More than ready."

The grandfather clock bonged the hour. Amid happy music played by the five-piece orchestra that had added much to the atmosphere all evening, the masks were taken off to reveal an array of faces amid gasps of delight, chuckles, and exclamations, Melodia kept her features fixed into a pleasant expression as she scanned the horizon for the unknown woman. Yet no tall woman was to be found. Instead of offering comfort, her absence left Melodia feeling more unsettled.

The brief moments that comprised the rest of the evening seemed inconsequential to Melodia. She remembered people flattering her person and her party, but alarm kept her from basking in well-earned praise. All she cared about was getting Rolf alone so she could question him.

After what seemed like an eternity, the last guest departed, and the butler shut the front door. Amid the last utterances of farewells, whinnying of horses, hooves clomping against gravel, and the occasional squeak of a turning wheel, Melodia watched the Harrisons board their carriage, the vehicle tilting inches to one side and back again as each person encountered the steps and then disappeared inside.

Rolf turned to face Melodia. He let out a triumphant sigh. "The ball was a complete success. I am very, very proud of you, Melodia, my dear." He ventured toward her. Melodia could see from the expression on his face that a kiss occupied his mind. She forced herself to ignore how handsome he appeared and how, at any other time, she would have received the gesture eagerly.

She stepped back. "May I see you in the library, Rolf?"

"The library? After such a successful night, I would think that you might want to enjoy your triumph with me—elsewhere." A mischievous grin played upon his lips.

"No." The word sounded sharp. She decided to soften the blow. "Not until we talk."

"Ah. You want to relive the night by sharing a bit of gossip. Very well. Shall I have tea brought in?"

Her stomach felt so sour with emotion that the thought of eating tempted her not in the least. "None for me."

He shrugged. "Then none for me, either."

As he followed her down the hall, Melodia almost felt guilty that she had allowed him to think he would be enjoying a rundown of the evening's events with her when the conversation instead promised to be unpleasant. Still, she had to know the identity of the scarlet-clad woman. The touch against the thigh, obviously staged by the woman to appear accidental, was not. Melodia knew. She just knew.

Melodia shut the door behind them in the library and held on to the doorknob as though it contained some life-sustaining fluid that would help her keep her balance. She watched Rolf settle into a seat with the ease of a man anticipating an evening with a fine book. She wanted to sit, wanted to appear casual, but no amount of good breeding could keep her from displaying the tip of the poison arrow of jealousy. "Who was that woman, Rolf?"

"Woman?" He clutched the chair's arms. His eyes widened, and his head shook in such a slight manner it almost seemed to jerk. "The question seems absurd when one considers that every woman in the parish was in attendance tonight. With the exception of Mrs. Deal. You were aware that a sudden bout of illness kept her from attending?"

"Yes, and I sent my good wishes for this evening and have every intention of having Peter deliver her a pot of chicken soup tomorrow for luncheon as a sign of our good will."

"An excellent idea. She is sure to appreciate the gesture. She's a lonely old woman, and no doubt she was quite distressed upon missing the ball."

"No doubt." Melodia wished they could remain on the topic of chicken soup all evening, but she had to insist they return to her original question. "Indeed, there were many women here tonight. But one in particular caught my eye when she spoke with you."

"Oh? I had no idea you would care so much now that we are an old married couple." His eyes sparkled with indulgence.

She refused to let him distract her. "The one wearing the red dress."

He chuckled. "There were a lot of red dresses."

"Not like this one."

Obviously sensing that she thought the question to be no laughing matter, he turned more serious. "I beg your indulgence, but you will have to remember that as a man, I have honed little skill in the way of powers of observation regarding women's dresses. I am more interested in you, the woman wearing a perfectly lovely white dress."

She wanted to give in to his flattery, but she couldn't. If she allowed this opportunity to escape, it would be gone forever. "Let me see if I can better enable your powers of recall. The woman was wearing an elaborate head covering with three bright red feathers protruding from the top. Certainly you remember that."

He thought for a moment. "Yes. I do remember that as an unusual hat."

"An unusual hat." She pursed her lips. At least he hadn't insulted her by pretending not to remember such a ridiculous costume.

"And what of this woman?"

"I—I did not care for the way she brushed against you, or the way you seemed amused by her conversation."

"My darling!" He jumped out of his chair, rushed over and, before she could protest, took her by the waist. "Certainly you are not jealous. Are we not still in the throes of newly wedded bliss?"

"I would hope so. But after tonight, I have developed the distinct impression that someone else wishes we were not." She stepped back within his embrace.

"I think not. Everyone wishes you—and us—well. I have never heard the least bit of negative utterance said against you. Please believe me."

"But surely you know who this woman was."

He blanched. "I cannot say with certainty that I do. And that is the absolute truth."

"You know everyone on our guest list. Have known most of them for years. Can you not offer me a clue?"

"I cannot." He took his arms away. Though her speech had been hostile, Melodia regretted the symbolic loss of his fondness. "Do you want to know what I really think?"

"Y–yes." She braced herself for a lecture on how not to be a suspicious shrew.

"I believe the guest crashed our party."

"What? How could something like that happen, especially when the woman was wearing such an outlandish costume?"

"That is just the point. The woman most likely chose a larger than life gown and headdress with the idea that no party crasher would dare appear in such bold attire, and therefore no one would stop her."

Melodia contemplated his idea. "I can see the logic in that." She wanted to believe it. She wanted to believe that the woman attended the ball uninvited, taking full advantage of the fact that all the guests' faces would be concealed by masks. The thought gave her comfort. At least then the woman wouldn't be one of the friends she had recently made. "Yes. I believe you have something there."

"So you see, there is nothing to fear."

"Well then," she ventured against her better judgment, "since you have no idea who the mystery woman might be, can you tell me what she whispered in your ear?"

"I. . .it was hard for me to hear anything amid all the talk and music."

"But you laughed."

"My, but you were watching closely."

She could no longer look into his eyes. "I beg your indulgence. I suppose I am a bit of a shrew, and I have no right to be. You married me even though you knew me only by name and reputation, and you have shown me nothing but kindness since my arrival here. I surmise that not every husband would have been so considerate. Especially since I am so far from my home and family, and no one would ever know if you were cruel."

He took his hands in hers. "I am considerate because I want to be. You are a woman who deserves everything I have to offer as a husband. Now if you will allow me, I would prefer to put aside anything having to do with any mystery woman and concentrate on the lady before me." He caressed her cheek. "I love you, Melodia. And I always will. Remember that."

She gasped. The words she had been waiting to hear! "I love you, too, Rolf."

He took her into his embrace, urgently this time. She didn't resist his kiss.

Chapter 6

"Oh, Melodia, I am so glad you sent for me!" Felice ran into her sister's arms, forgetting all expected restraint in front of the maids witnessing their exchange in the parlor.

Melodia broke the embrace but took her sister's hands in hers. "You must be exhausted after your journey. Come. Let us take tea in the drawing room. The view from the windows is so lovely. You can see the gardens."

"That sounds delightful." Felice inspected her traveling suit sewn from serviceable cotton the color of an afternoon sky just before the first strike of a thunderstorm. "But I am not dressed for tea."

"Indeed not, but teatime is upon us. You can dress in your best for tea tomorrow to make amends for your lack of decorum today, can you not?"

"To keep you from delaying your teatime, I shall. Thank you for overlooking my drab attire."

"Of course," Melodia said. "And while we partake, Peter will carry your trunks to your room just down the east hall.

The Gold Room. I will show you later myself. I assure you, your room is the best guest suite in the house. Not too far from mine."

"That is kind of you, Sister."

"I would never let you stay in any but the best room," she commented as Felice followed her. Moments later, they were sitting together on the sofa. Felice didn't delay in sharing all the news about their friends.

After Felice had exhausted all avenues of tittle-tattle, Melodia posed her own query. "So how is Father?"

"He misses you. But you know how reserved he is. He would never admit to it."

Melodia swallowed. "He must be even more lonely now that you are here. Did you have trouble convincing him to let you visit me?"

She shrugged. "He knows that visiting you would make me happy, so he agreed."

"Are you really so happy to see me, or are you just glad to escape that awful Sir Arnold that Father is determined you are to marry?" Melodia teased.

"Both! Oh, if I can make a good match here, maybe Father will change his mind." Felice looked around the room. Melodia saw that she seemed to notice wallpaper of bucolic scenes and that the windows were framed in damask. Felice's gaze rested upon an original oil painting of a pastoral scene, framed in rich wood. Her observation traveled to the tall pendulum clock, then to the fireplace mantel carved from Italian marble, then to the costly rugs, and around the room to take in the details of each piece of imported furniture. "And I do think I might be able to do well here. Very well."

Melodia chose to ignore Felice's bold observation about her hopes for increased wealth. "And we could live just minutes from each other and visit every day. A splendid prospect, indeed."

She nodded. "So is that why you wanted me to visit? So I would ultimately live here near you?"

"Perhaps."

"Now, dear Melodia, as lovely as such a prospect sounds, I sense that you have some other reason for summoning me here. I hope it is not the result of any unhappiness with your handsome new husband. Is he secretly cruel?"

"No, indeed." She paused. "Although I have reason to believe that at least one of his friends might be."

Felice gasped. "What do you mean?"

"Remember how I told you we were hosting a masquerade ball?"

"Yes. And you also wrote me it was a great success—in the same letter in which you asked me to visit. Surely you did not exaggerate the truth?"

"No. It was a success. Except. . ."

Felice leaned forward. "Except what?"

"A mysterious woman flirted with Rolf."

Felice let out a laugh. "Oh, is that all? Why, women flirt all the time—especially when masks conceal their faces. No doubt many batted their eyelashes at Rolf during the night. You happened to see only one of them."

"I am not sure such a declaration does anything to console me."

"You are much too sheltered from the ways of romance."

Felice touched her fingertips to her curls. "Why, even I have been known to flirt now and again and mean nothing by it. If I did, I would have been wed at least thrice by now."

"Yes, I have witnessed such, and I am sure you could give this particular coquette quite a contest. But there was more to the flirtation than mere frivolity."

"What a ridiculous notion."

"Ridiculous? I think not. A wife can sense these things."

"And you called me here to—to what? Rescue you? How?" Felice stirred her tea.

"I was wondering who she is."

Felice set her silver spoon on her saucer. "And you think I will be able to help you? My dear, I certainly know none of these local people. Why, you would have a much better chance at solving the mystery yourself."

"So the facts would demonstrate, but your mind is sharp, and so are your powers of observation."

"And my common sense as well, apparently. Why did you not make a point of observing this woman at the unmasking?"

"I tried," Melodia said, "but she was gone."

"Oh." Felice stiffened and set her half-empty cup on the table. "Certainly you confronted Rolf?"

"Yes." Melodia set down her own cup. "May I warm your tea?"

"Please do." Felice nodded. "I hope you waited until after the party to ask him about this woman."

"Of course." Melodia's voice betrayed her irritation. "But he offered no clues."

"I am sorry you are so vexed, but I still think I can offer only limited assistance. Someone who knows Rolf's group is much more likely to be of help. I know you have had little time to cultivate friendships here except for perhaps that woman you mentioned." She paused. "Eustacia?"

"Yes."

"Surely she has lived here forever, and I am merely a passerby. Why not ask her?"

"And confide my feelings to her? She has visited me often, and I do consider her a friend, but I still prefer to share my innermost thoughts with my sister."

"Well then. What did this woman look like?"

"She wore a stunning ensemble of red. Her headdress covered her hair, so I have no idea what color it was, or even if it was styled with the curls that are all the rage in Paris. She was tall, about your height." Melodia sent her sister a disgusted shake of her head. "You would have much better sense than to wear large plumage on top of your head to add even more height. Obviously the woman followed poor advice from her seamstress—or someone." She shuddered.

"Indeed." Felice's voice sounded taut. "I suppose then, you should be on the lookout for a woman with a dreadful sense of fashion."

"Or maybe you can advise me to the ways of the world."

"Yes, we are an unusual pair. You, the elder sister, seeking advice from me."

"But you have always wanted to marry. Unlike me. So you have schooled yourself in the ways of romance whereas I paid them little attention all these years."

"True."

"And your visit here will help me be less lonely."

"Lonely?" Felice's brow crinkled. "How can you be lonely?"

"In addition to the woman I told you about, I'm afraid I have other competition for Rolf's attention. Namely, business. And hunting, fishing, and gatherings with his gentleman friends. In fact, he is away on such a trip as we speak. He will not be returning until the night of our next soiree."

Felice's eyebrows rose. "So he enjoys frivolities. He seems not to be home unless a party is planned or in progress."

"I beg your pardon. I did not mean to sound harsh. He is in London visiting his father, who is quite ill."

Felice's lips tightened into the type of tight little smile that showed she wished she hadn't spoken so soon. "I am so sorry. Yes, I did hear he is ill and is not expected to recover. I am so glad you decided not to go and put yourself at risk of contracting his illness."

"Do you not remember what I wrote to you only a fortnight ago?"

"Ah, yes." She nodded. "You did go to see him and found him looking wan and coughing terribly. I suppose I merely skimmed such a depressing portion of your letter. Do forgive me. I much preferred to concentrate on the fine bonnet you wrote of procuring at the milliner's. You must tell me which shop so I can take a peek at her wares the next time Father and I journey there."

"Madame Jullienne's. Yes, her work is exquisite. And I am not surprised that you concentrated on the happy part of my letter, being such a cheerful soul yourself." Melodia took a sip of tea. "I am glad I took advantage of the opportunity to visit with my father-in-law. I had not seen him in years and would not have recognized him had we not been reacquainted."

"I am sorry to hear he seems so ill. I do hope you have not developed a cough since your return." Felice flinched.

"Do not worry yourself. I would never invite you to my home at a time when I thought I could put your own health at risk. I do believe his maladies are caused by old age. I suppose such a condition is contagious for those who live long enough to catch it."

"And the meeting went well?"

"Yes. He was kind to me."

"But Rolf did not see fit to have you accompany him a second time?"

"No. I have seen enough of London to last me for a time. And in any event, Rolf is going to take care of some errands for his father and return home after that. I would only encumber him. Though I do wish I could be with him."

"Ah yes. Loneliness. The plight of many an aristocratic woman. But would you rather be a poor peasant too busy plowing the fields to worry about such trifles as loneliness and jealousy?"

Melodia shuddered. "Indeed not."

"I only hope the woman in red is not from London and that Rolf is not stopping by to see her when he is town to visit his father."

"I am sure the woman in red is not from London." Nevertheless, Melodia wished Felice hadn't brought up the possibility.

"If so, she would have traveled a distance just to brush against your husband and feign it was an accident." Felice chuckled. "But I would not worry about any other woman if I were you."

"Why not?" Melodia hoped Felice would impart some comforting words—perhaps commenting on the couple's devotion to God's commandments or on Melodia's fine character being enough to keep Rolf from straying.

"He would never discard you. As his wife, you are afforded a status that no mistress ever can. You will remain secure, my dear. I am sure of that. But in what state you wish to live the remainder of your days is up to you. You can choose to remain chaste and miserable, or you can choose to carry on great love affairs in a discreet manner and enjoy much frivolity. Once I am safely married, I know I can trust you not to confide in anyone that finding romance on my own is what I plan to do."

"Felice! How can you say that?"

"Easily. You know how much I despise the man Father has chosen for me."

"And you are his favorite daughter," Melodia reminded her.

"That does not seem so, does it? I think Rolf is a much better husband than Arnold can ever hope to be. I know he is much more handsome."

"I would hope that, if you do plan to make a better match while you are here, it will be with the intent of being a good wife and not a faithless one."

"Perhaps with the right man, I can be swayed."

"You are incorrigible!" Melodia tapped her spoon against the rim of her cup. Though her sister enjoyed talking in a daring manner, Melodia knew her well enough to see beyond her boasting. Felice was much like her. She only wanted a happy home and family. Though she flirted now, she was unlikely to live a wanton life as a single woman and certainly not after marriage. Not as she claimed some of the other women did.

As they moved their conversation on to other subjects, Melodia tried to block Felice's warning out of her mind. But the words kept spinning in her head.

I will not give up without a fight. I will be the best wife I can. I shall start by taking Rolf at his word that he will not succumb to another woman's charms.

Still, in the future, she would eye every tall woman who could have been at the ball with the utmost care.

Chapter 7

A week later, Melodia found herself searching the manor house for Rolf. He had been late in making his return from London. Before the soiree in progress that night, she had only been able to discover the most broad details about his father's health—that he was neither better nor worse—and to utter mention of Felice's arrival. At the latter intelligence, she had expected him to react with indifferent pleasantness. She wondered why the news of her sister's stay seemed to annoy him.

Melodia worried. Rolf wasn't in the habit of abandoning his guests in the middle of a night's entertainment. Lord Suffolk had been in the midst of playing a lively tune he had composed himself only the past week. Their audience was the first to hear him perform his work. She couldn't imagine why Rolf wouldn't be present to hear the tune played with immense skill on the piano.

Even worse, her concern about him caused her to forget her manners. She slipped into the dim hallway to search the rooms and gardens for where he might have gone. He was not to be found. The longer she searched, the more alarmed she became. Disgust at having to slip out from their guests, proving herself to be a poor hostess, grew into anger at him for putting her in such a position, then dissolved into fear. Perhaps he had been overtaken by illness. Perhaps even at that moment he was in pain, hoping she would find him so she could administer aid. Or what if something even worse had transpired? She clasped her hand to her throat in horror but nevertheless forced her feet to keep moving. She had to find him!

As she passed a rounded archway leading to the north wing, a woman's voice floated from the turret stairs. ". . .annulled."

The voice sounded familiar, but she couldn't place it. The word made her even more curious. She stopped. "Annulled?"

"I will not have my marriage annulled. And that is final."

Her hand flew from her throat to her side and clenched itself in fear and anger. The man's voice belonged to Rolf. He was defending their marriage to this woman, whoever she was. But why? What could the woman have said that could even give her the boldness to suggest that Rolf's marriage should be annulled?

Curiosity overcoming fear, Melodia peered up the stairs, even though the action risked her getting caught. She had to identify the woman. A hem of gold material told the tale. The woman whispering to Rolf was none other than Eustacia! Her friend!

Why would Eustacia want to spread rumors strong enough to suggest that her new husband annul their marriage?

Unless. . .

Unless she had been the one who was flirting with Rolf at

the ball! But was Eustacia tall enough to fit the description? And hadn't her ball gown been pale blue rather than the striking red gown that the flirt had worn?

Trusting Eustacia was her friend, Melodia never thought before about how tall and regal Eustacia stood. Perhaps she had worn a blue gown, then changed into the red one, then back into the blue one, just to fool Melodia. If Eustacia wanted Rolf for herself, such an effort would be a small concession to make to keep her identity concealed.

Rolf had said Eustacia was high-spirited. Perhaps risk offered excitement she could find no other way. Perhaps Eustacia had deliberately cultivated her as a friend to gain her confidence. A smart move.

But then again, Rolf had told Melodia that he admired her character, not Eustacia's. Was Rolf to be believed?

More thoughts, both logical and preposterous, flooded her head until she thought they might pour out of her ears. She rubbed her palm on the side of her head as though such a motion would help contain them. At the moment, she only knew she felt too confused and befuddled to think about anything. She had to get out of sight before Rolf—and Eustacia—caught her spying on them.

Like the child she suddenly felt she was, Melodia took the only action she knew. She fled to her bedchamber, threw herself on the down-filled mattress, and sobbed.

Moments later, someone entered. She had been missed! Melodia stiffened, shut her eyes, and pretended to be asleep. As the figure drew near, she heard the rustle of a dress. The intruder was female. The strong odor of lily of the valley fragrance revealed her identity. Felice had come to comfort her, but Melodia didn't want to be comforted. She kept her eyes shut.

Melodia felt Felice's soft hand brush her exposed cheek. "Melodia, dear, what is the matter?"

Her eyes remained shut.

"You cannot fool me. I see your eyelashes fluttering. You are not asleep." Melodia felt the mattress sink in one spot as Felice sat on the side of the bed.

Melodia tried to keep her eyes shut but to no avail. Once her sister had determined that she was fooling, there was no turning back. She allowed her eyes to flutter open but remained in a prone position. "I do not wish to speak to anyone, not even you. I am ill. Please give my excuses to the remainder of our guests."

"I will do no such thing. You are to come downstairs with me right this instant. You cannot have it said all over the parish that you abandoned your own party."

"Illness is an acceptable excuse."

"I would not recommend it. And I do not believe you are ill." She inspected her. "You. . .you are crying. Tell me. What is really the matter?" Felice held out a clean handkerchief in a way that reminded Melodia of a carrot being dangled in front of the nose of a horse.

Melodia sat and took the offered item. "I noticed Rolf was missing from the party so I went to look for him. I thought he might be ill. But instead I found him on the turret stairs with. . . with. . ." She sniffled.

"With whom?" Felice rubbed her open palm on Melodia's back.

"You will never believe it."

"Eustacia."

Melodia felt her eyelids widen as far as they would go. "How did you know?"

"I saw him leave the concert and her follow not long after. I had my suspicions that the timing of their departures was no coincidence. And then when I noticed you left in the middle of Lord Suffolk's song, I knew something must be amiss." Felice patted Melodia's back. "So where were they?"

"On the turret stairs."

Felice took in a breath. She opened her mouth to speak but shut it. Clearly, she was afraid to ask what had transpired.

"They were just. . .talking," Melodia assured Felice. "It was what they talked about that concerned me. She said something about annulling our marriage."

Felice gasped. "No!"

"I thought she was my friend." Melodia dabbed the handkerchief against her eyes. "Maybe she still is."

"Indeed?" Doubt dripped from Felice's voice.

"Perhaps Rolf has done something to warrant her suggestion. As I told you, he. . .he is absent a great deal."

"You would think that about Rolf?" Felice paused. "Well, he is a man, after all. But what if he is? Would you really want to leave your marriage?"

"No. No, I do not."

Felice dropped her hands to her lap and looked into Melodia's eyes. "You have come to love him."

Melodia looked into her own lap and nodded.

"Then we must stop Eustacia. She must not be allowed to

play the coquette with your husband any longer."

"I was thinking, and wondering—could she have been the woman behind the red mask that night at the ball?"

"Yes. Yes, I am convinced of that now," Felice said without missing a beat. "I am your sister. You can trust me, and only me, to tell you the truth. Let me prove it to you. Let me help you prove that Eustacia was the masked woman you saw with Rolf that night—a woman hiding behind a duplicitous façade."

"But I asked Rolf—"

"And he lied. He lied to you before, and he will lie to you again."

Melodia swallowed. "No."

"I know such a possibility is heartbreaking to consider, but you must. I regret heartily that I am the one to break your heart, but for your own good, you must face facts," Felice implored.

"I know what we have to do. There is one person we can confront. And we will do so now."

As Rolf listened to Mrs. Snidow play a flute duet with her young daughter, the tune swirled around him but missed his ears and his mind.

Where was Melodia? He looked for his wife, eyeing the door every few moments in hopes that she would reenter. Surely she knew how her absence must appear odd. She had, much to his delight, established herself as an exemplary hostess, yet her reputation wasn't so secure that she should absent herself from the performances.

If only he hadn't allowed Eustacia to pull him away from the gathering! He had been suspicious of her willingness to befriend Melodia but had put aside his reservations in hopes that Eustacia was displaying maturity in spending time with his lonely wife. Rolf wasn't a conceited man, but he knew that not so long ago Eustacia would have welcomed his offer of marriage. And she had many attributes to recommend her—just not attributes that appealed to him. He wanted a woman of spiritual depth, something Eustacia lacked. The longer he stayed married to Melodia, the more convinced he became that their marriage was God's will.

Confident in his union with Melodia, Rolf had believed Eustacia when she said she had something important to share. Like a stunned fly whirring into the spider's web, he had flown onto the turret stairs and heard Eustacia whisper things to him—things he never wanted to hear. Surely they couldn't be true! Surely Melodia didn't harbor some secret love back where she came from and wasn't carrying on with illicit love letters to him at this very moment. Why, she even suggested that the man had been circulating among them at the masquerade ball. That could not have been possible!

The worst confession from Eustacia was that the rumors suggested that Rolf himself was seeking an annulment to their marriage. He was too much in love with Melodia not to forgive her anything.

As Mrs. and Miss Snidow completed their song, he clapped along with the guests and then halfway watched Miss Jane Laurel take her place in front of the audience for a solo. As she struggled to hit notes too high for her natural range, Rolf went over the guest list for the masquerade ball that had been the source of such distress for Melodia, distress he wished she hadn't been forced to endure. He matched a masked guest with each name. He didn't remember seeing any uninvited guests among them—except the woman in red who had flirted with him.

If only he had seen her motive and had fled from the refreshment table the moment she made contact with him! But like a fox cornered by the hounds, he could only stare in disbelief when she whispered in his ear that she loved him. Unwilling to embarrass the woman, he had responded in the only way he knew in public. He chuckled. No matter that he exited as quickly as etiquette allowed. He never should have appeared to enjoy her words. But everyone knew he had recently married. Surely the woman didn't mean what she said. Idle words of flirtation, meant to bolster the emotions of the speaker as much as the receiver.

Heavenly Father, forgive me my slip. I have been wed only a short time, and I still do not know how to act as a husband should. Forgive me! I ask Thee to take away any desire that any other woman except Melodia may still harbor for me, for though I am strong enough to resist their wiles, I wish not to break any hearts. Thou hast seen fit to give me Melodia. Let me be worthy of her.

Chapter 8

Later that evening, as the concert given by their friends and neighbors was still in progress, Melodia and Felice waited for their guest to enter Melodia's private study. She chose the room for the confrontation on purpose, knowing the familiar and intimate setting would make her feel more confident.

Before exiting her bedchamber, Melodia had taken a few moments to compose herself. Rachel had been summoned to touch up her hair, and though the maid's eyes held a curious look, Melodia resisted confiding to her trusted servant. Rachel had brought a few chips of precious ice to help reduce the puffiness of Melodia's tear-stained eyelids, yet despite those efforts the skin around her eyes still looked enlarged from sobbing and her face remained splotched with red. In spite of these disadvantages to her personal appearance, she sat upright in the most thronelike chair available.

"Are you nervous?" Felice asked.

"Yes," Melodia admitted. "But I shall try not to reveal my feelings."

"I am distraught to see you so vexed."

Melodia dabbed her eyes, pleased that the motion was successful in preventing new tears from falling. "I cannot bear the thought of my husband keeping secrets from me—secrets that could affect our marriage. Especially now that. . .now that. . ."

"Now that what?" Felice looked at her with widened eyes.

"Do you promise you will not reveal what I am about to say to anyone?"

"Yes."

Melodia felt herself blush as she peered at her lap. "I think I may be presenting Rolf with an heir this winter."

"Oh, Melodia!" Felice rose from her chair so she could embrace her sister. "How wonderful for you!"

"I—I thought it was wonderful. Now I am not so sure."

"Of course you are sure. A baby is a beautiful blessing." Felice's eyes darkened. "How dare he! How dare he take part in romantic intrigue when he has a wife of whom he should be mindful!"

Melodia didn't have time to answer before Eustacia entered. "You wished to see me?"

"Yes," Melodia answered from her seat, refusing to rise.

Her voice displayed irritation. "I wish you had not summoned me at the peak of the festivities. Lord and Lady Ellingworth were just about to sing a duet when I was summoned here." She stared at Melodia as though thunderstruck. "Are you quite all right?"

"She will be soon, I hope," Felice snapped from her own chair situated near Melodia's.

Eustacia eyed both women. "So you both wished to see me?"

"You might say so," Felice said.

Melodia wanted to elaborate, but suddenly her throat

closed. She took a sip of lemonade, but the cool liquid did nothing to open her vocal chords.

Felice looked over at Melodia, then back to Eustacia. "What my sister wants to know," Felice said, "is why you were lingering on the turret steps with her husband and what vicious rumor you were spreading to him."

Eustacia turned as white as a snowflake. "I beg your pardon?"

"You heard me," Felice prompted.

Eustacia drew herself to her full height and eyed both women. "There must be some mistake. I do not know what you think you heard, but I assure you, I have done nothing improper in relation to your husband, nor do I wish to do so. He has been my acquaintance for many years. Indeed, we were childhood playmates. I would never wish any harm upon him."

"So you do not deny you spoke to Rolf this evening?" Felice asked.

Eustacia crossed her arms. "I know what you imply, and I will not dignify such a question with an answer. And I suggest, Felice, that you not make a pursuit of such prurient pastimes as gossip."

"I beg your pardon," Melodia said, "but despite your protests otherwise, I would guess that you are the one who was engaged in gossip on the turret steps—or worse."

Eustacia's lips tightened.

"I am giving you an opportunity to clear yourself," Melodia said. "If you choose not to accept it, I will be forced to ask you to leave and never expect to return here as my guest again."

"You would say no such thing. I am the only friend you have here."

Melodia clenched her teeth behind closed lips to keep herself from showing emotion. Indeed, at that moment, she had never felt more abandoned. Yet she knew she had gained many companionable acquaintances since her arrival in the country. She felt sure that, given time, she could cultivate many friends.

"And you know full well that Rolf would be sure to object should you try to ostracize me," Eustacia said. "We were once close, you know. And I do not refer to our time together as children."

"No, I did not know he had piqued your interest. But that explains much. Thank you," Melodia said. "You have just confirmed my suspicions about a mystery that has been puzzling me ever since the masquerade ball."

"A mystery? Do tell."

"You." She pointed at Eustacia's nose even though she knew that the gesture was the height of rudeness. "You are the woman in red."

"The woman in red?" Eustacia uncrossed her arms and inched her head toward her. Her mouth slackened into an uneven *O*. "I beg your pardon?"

"Oh, I saw that you were quick to change back into your blue dress in time for the unmasking. But you made quite an impression in your red dress and feathered head covering during the ball."

Eustacia laughed. "Your mind has certainly taken a flight of fancy, Melodia. I am flattered that you think I would devise such an elaborate scheme, but I did no such thing. In fact, I saw the woman you mention. Who would not? She was certainly stunning, and I noticed that all the men seemed enraptured by her presence. In fact, I envy her, whoever she is."

The confession left Melodia shaken. "You. . .you mean that woman really was someone else?"

"Truly. Bring me the Bible you love so much, and I will put my hand on it and swear that I speak the truth."

"No. I do not require such dramatics. I will take you at your word."

"Really? When you have just threatened to banish me from your house forever?"

"I am so sorry, Eustacia. But will you please tell me what you were saying to Rolf while the two of you were on the stairs?"

"Are you saying you have absolutely no idea?"

"No."

Eustacia turned to Felice. "May I speak to your sister alone?"

"I should be privy to anything you have to say to my sister."

"Please." Eustacia sent Melodia a pleading look.

Melodia glanced at Felice, who wore a pout much like the one she would wear as a child when she didn't get her way. Father would always give in to that pout. Melodia decided that since she was in the process of testing an important friendship, she would not be as vulnerable as their father to Felice's wiles. "Felice, I would like to be alone with Eustacia."

"And have my own reputation ruined?"

"What I have to say has nothing to do with you in the least," Eustacia promised.

"I believe her," Melodia assured Felice.

"If I break my word, Melodia is free to tell you," Eustacia added.

Felice let out a dissatisfied sigh but rose from her seat and exited without another word.

"Thank you," Eustacia said.

Melodia motioned to the seat that Felice had vacated.

"I am sorry you saw Rolf and me on the stairs. I never meant for that to happen."

"Obviously."

"I beg your forgiveness for my outburst about my former interest in Rolf. I admit I once wished he would become a suitor. I thought such an arrangement would be a fine thing, especially because of my deep fondness for his sister, Martha."

"I understand." Melodia nodded.

"Good. And now that the two of you are wed, the happiness he wears on his face is something I have never witnessed in him before. I could never have caused him to look like that. Not ever. And because he is a fine man, I am pleased for him. And for you." When Eustacia placed her hand on Melodia's, she decided not to move it. "Please believe me when I say that I am your friend."

"Though moments ago I thought you were not, I believe you now. I can see the sincerity in your face. And you have been a friend to me since my arrival here. I shall never forget your kindness," Melodia assured her. "But you must realize I have not been married to Rolf long, and appearances. . ."

"Yes. We must have looked as though we were in the throes of a love affair. I am sorry that I put Rolf in that position. But I had to speak with him."

"About what?" Melodia kept her voice gentle.

"I wish I did not have to say this, Melodia, but you apparently have enemies here. Someone is spreading rumors that you are in the midst of a passionate correspondence with a secret love you have hidden away—possibly a suitor from home. And of course, since Rolf, as a normal man, is often absent, that only adds fuel to the fire."

Melodia concentrated on Eustacia's declarations, wishing she could laugh and sob simultaneously. "Whoever is saying such nonsense does not know me at all. In fact, do you not remember that I told you myself that I had not even expressed interest in any suitors before my marriage to Rolf?"

"Yes. You had quite a different life planned for yourself. And I believe that. I have seen in your demeanor, the light in your face, the way your love for the Savior shines through you, that you would never deceive Rolf. And that is why I felt I had to tell him what was happening. I wanted to spare you hurt."

"By suggesting an annulment?"

Eustacia gasped. "I suggested no such thing. That is only a tangent running through the rumor mill. You must have heard the end of our conversation when Rolf was expressing to me how preposterous such an idea is. And I agree with him." A tear trickled from Eustacia's right eye. "Melodia, I humbly beg your forgiveness for causing you distress. Please, please find it in your heart to forgive me."

Melodia squeezed Eustacia's hands. "No. Please forgive me for doubting you."

"You have not known me long, and what you thought you overheard was enough to vex any matron. Your readiness to pardon me only proves yet again the depth of your character."

The women embraced, knowing that no rumor would ever come between them again.

Chapter 9

Melodia made her way back to the party, but Felice approached her from the side and grabbed her sleeve before she could return to her seat.

"What happened?"

"Eustacia is not the woman in red, and she was only trying to protect me by speaking to Rolf."

"Is that so?" she hissed. "I am not so sure I would trust her if I were you. So who do you think the woman was?"

"I do not know. I will pray about the situation. Now we must return to the party." She attempted to do so.

"This is an outrage!" Felice whispered. "Rolf is not conducting himself in a proper manner, especially considering your delicate condition. If I were you, I would pack my bags and leave tomorrow. You and I can go back home. You can say you miss Father and want to visit him. Just do not tell Rolf you are never returning."

Melodia thought for a moment. "If I do, then the woman in red may return."

"So what if she does? Rolf does not deserve you."

The night's events had drained Melodia to the point of surrender. "Oh, all right. I will go home for a time with you. Perhaps getting away for a fortnight is just what I need."

Minutes after the soiree ended, Rolf met Melodia in the parlor. Even after the night's events, his touch upon her hand made her feel reluctant to part from him.

"Felice told me you are planning to leave," he said.

"Not for long. Just to visit Father."

"And your sister is returning with you."

"Of course. Why would she stay here?"

"Why, indeed?" He sighed. "Eustacia told me to be sure to see you as soon as the evening ended. Apparently you have something important to share?"

"My, but you have been busy conversing." Her voice sounded sharper than she intended. She jerked her hand from his almost involuntarily.

"You are upset. Please tell me what has happened to vex you so. I will have nothing distress you if it is within my power to stop it."

"I believe you now, but I was not so certain earlier this evening when I spied you and Eustacia on the turret stairs."

He gasped. "What did you hear?"

"Enough. And then I confronted Eustacia, and she explained the full conversation. I know about the rumors. Rolf, I promise you they are not true."

"Of course they are not true. I regret that she told you. Such vile accusations were not meant for your ears."

"Who do you think is saying these awful things about me?

The woman in red, perhaps?" Melodia's stomach lurched.

"I can promise you no one is saying anything negative about you now. I started another rumor, only this one is true. I am making it clear that anyone who tries to sully your name will have to face my wrath."

Love for him surged through her. She took his hands. "But how can you stop them from saying things behind our backs?"

"Perhaps I cannot. But my name and reputation mean something around here. I doubt anyone will want to cross me." He squeezed her hands. "I will defend your honor now and forevermore. And as you are my wife, you will obey me as you agreed in our vows, yes?"

She looked at her toes, clad in kid leather, peeking from underneath her soft green skirt. "Yes."

"Then I want you to obey me now. Stay here. With me."

She looked up. "Do you really want me to?"

"I would not ask if I did not." His eyes took on a sad cast. "Why do you doubt that I would want you to stay?"

"I. . .the rumors."

"No. I never want you to mention such a thing again. Do you understand?"

For the first time, Melodia saw Rolf's eyes narrow and his features tighten in anger. She could see why Rolf had a reputation as a great hunter—and why he was feared by his enemies.

"I cannot bear the thought of your departure under such circumstances." He clutched her waist and pulled her toward him. She surrendered with abandon to his urgent lips.

She forced herself to pull away from him. "I will stay but only on one condition. You must tell me the truth. You say you spoke to the source of the rumors. Who is it?"

At that moment, Felice rushed into the parlor. "No. Do not tell her."

"You were listening to us?" Melodia asked.

"Yes. But it is for your own good." She placed an urgent hand on Rolf's arm. "Do not tell her. She is in no condition to be upset."

"No condition?" Rolf looked at Melodia. A smile of cognizance flooded his face.

She averted her eyes. "Yes, it is as you guessed. If all goes well, I will be presenting you with a gift from God—an heir—this winter."

"Melodia!" He lifted her in his arms and whirled her around.

"Careful!" she jested.

Laughing, he squeezed her in an embrace. "Oh, Melodia, this is one of many moments in our marriage I have been dreaming of! An heir! I hope his eyes are as bright as yours."

"And his form as fine as yours," Melodia said.

"No doubt he will be beautiful," Felice said. "But, Melodia, we must prepare for our departure on the morrow."

"No," Rolf said as he sat Melodia back on her feet. "I do not want her to leave. Especially not now. She is in no condition to travel. Undoubtedly you suggested such folly, Felice?"

"I—I thought visiting Father would do her good."

"You thought nothing of the sort." Rolf's eyes took on an anger Melodia didn't expect. "Felice, it is time your sister knew the truth."

"No." A light of fear visited her eyes, and she clutched her throat.

"I have been protecting you all this time but no longer."

"Protecting her?" Melodia asked. "Rolf, what do you mean?" She looked at Felice. "What is happening here?"

He looked at Felice with a cold sternness. "You should be ashamed of yourself, Felice. If I were you, I would rather die than let my sister know how little I thought of her."

Melodia felt more confused than ever. "The truth, Felice. I want to know."

Felice concentrated her attention on Melodia and looked at her with flashing eyes. "Rolf has never belonged to you, Melodia. He is mine, and you do not deserve him."

She pressed her hands to her heart. "What?"

"You were supposed to live the life dedicated to God, remember?"

"Yes. But Father forbade it."

She regarded the floor. "Yes, I am aware of that. Even though I am his favorite daughter, he would not listen to reason."

"Are you saying that Father knew you wanted Rolf for yourself but insisted that I marry him?" The thought was too much to bear. Only a few months before, Melodia would have been more than happy to throw Rolf straight at Felice and never look back. Now the thought left her throat dry and her heart heavy. She looked at him, a fresh wave of love rushing to her being.

"I am indeed." Felice crossed her arms. "You were more than happy never to marry, yet he was not willing to, as he said, 'waste' an opportunity to marry you to Rolf to bind our family's fortunes. Then that would leave me free to marry Arnold." She grimaced.

Melodia felt shamed. While Rolf was no fool, to have him spoken about as a commodity left her with embarrassment. "Stop it, Felice."

"Do not worry about sparing my feelings," Rolf assured her. "I know the ways of the world."

"Remember Normandy? How we dined and danced?" Felice reminded Rolf. Her voice held a tantalizing tone that left Melodia cold.

"I dined and danced with many lovely ladies. I am sorry that what I thought was polite behavior on my part was interpreted as much more by you, Felice." Rolf's voice held an edge Melodia had never heard.

"But. . .but. . ." Felice stopped herself and sighed.

"That is correct. You cannot think of any promise I made or anything else I said that would have led you to believe I harbored any feelings for you beyond the pleasures of polite conversation. I am sorry, Felice. I have come to love your sister. No matter how many masquerade balls you attend uninvited or how many rumors you spread, you cannot change my mind—or my feelings. And I do not want you to try."

Realization struck Melodia. "Felice, you are the woman in red!"

Felice countered with more rage than Melodia knew her sister possessed. "You!" She shook her finger in Melodia's face. "You ruined everything."

"I? I ruined everything?" Melodia paused to bring down the tension in the room. "Just what do you think you were trying to do to my marriage? I suppose you told Father you were visiting a friend."

"Of course." Her voice held no remorse. "Although Father did insist that I bring three servants."

"And you chose three who fear you too much to reveal your secret," Melodia guessed. "Father always lets you have your way, regrettably."

"I must say, the Goat's Head Inn proved quite a disappointment. I never saw so much riffraff in one place at the same time."

Rolf shuddered. "I never would have allowed my sister-in-law to stay at such an establishment."

She shrugged. "It was only for one night."

"But why, Felice? Why did you go to so much trouble just to come here in secret and whisper to my husband?"

"Do you want the truth?"

"If you are capable of telling it."

Felice flinched. "I suppose I deserve that. I flirted with Rolf because I assumed you were not in love."

"Oh, but we are in love!"

"Yes, I can see that now. And I never should have interfered. Only. . ."

Melodia could see the hurt of lost love in her sister's face. "I am sorry, Felice. I never wanted to be the cause of any unhappiness for you. I love you too much."

"You do?"

"I know she does," Rolf said. "And you should be grateful for such a wonderful sister. I know I am thankful that God gave me a gift in Melodia far greater than I deserve."

Melodia took Felice's hands in hers. "You are my sister, and you shall always have my love. But for now, I think it is best if you return home to Father. I will write him a letter imploring him not to betroth you to Arnold. I cannot promise he will comply, but I can try."

"You would do that for me?"

"Yes."

Obviously overwhelmed by Melodia's forgiveness, Felice kissed her sister on the cheek. "I shall be taking my leave of the estate on the morrow."

Seeing Felice's sincerity, Melodia nodded. Felice exited the room, her demeanor humble.

Melodia turned to Rolf. "I beg your forgiveness for doubting you."

"No, I am the one who should be asking forgiveness. I allowed myself to appear faithless when nothing could be further from my mind—or my heart."

She smiled, knowing they could forgive each other anything for the rest of their lives. "I must ask one favor. Can we dispose of the costumes we wore to the masquerade ball? The memories they evoke—ones of doubt and torment—are too great to bear."

"I agree. I never want to see the dress you wore or that mask or my costume ever again. I promise I will donate both costumes to charity—somewhere in London, where we are unlikely to attend an event where we would find anyone else wearing them."

"And I certainly never want to see a crimson dress again. Never."

"Crimson would not be becoming on an expectant mother in any event." As Melodia giggled, he caressed her curls and took in a happy breath. The kiss they exchanged let Melodia know they truly would enjoy a happy ever after.

TAMELA HANCOCK MURRAY

Tamela Hancock Murray is an award-winning, best-selling author who lives in Northern Virginia. She and her husband of over twenty years are finding the nest is beginning to empty now that their first daughter, an honors student, is a college freshman at Tamela's alma mater. Their second daughter, an outstanding student at Christian school, keeps them busy with her activities.

Writing inspirational stories blesses Tamela's life. She loves to take minivacations with her family, and she also enjoys reading and Bible study. Visit her Web site at www.tamelahancockmurray.com.

Love's Unmasking

by Bonnie Blythe

Dedication

To my husband, who is everything a hero should be.

Acknowledgments

Special thanks to Tamela for recommending me
for this anthology and to Pamela and Jill
for making me feel so welcome. As always,
I am indebted to my critique partners
in the Crits and ACFW#11 and to my main writing buddy
Vickie McDonough for her unwavering encouragement.

Man looketh on the outward appearance,
but the L*ORD* *looketh on the heart.*
1 SAMUEL 16:7

Chapter 1

London, 1814

Oh, dear! Is everyone in London so intimidating?

Amaryllis Sinclair peered up at the face of the butler while standing on the front steps of her aunt's West End London townhouse. Fatigue made her limbs leaden after the long journey from Dorset to London. Lady Agatha's traveling carriage had not been particularly well sprung, and Amaryllis looked forward to a quiet nap after her trip.

"You are expected," the butler said in sepulchral tones. "Step inside."

Amaryllis took trembling steps into the dim hall, noting the black-and-white tiles and a hall table flanked by two heavy Jacobean chairs. A large painting on one wall depicted a stag being savaged by hounds.

"This way, Miss Sinclair," the butler intoned. "My lady is in the Blue Room."

Following the butler's stately tread, she heard the sound of barking somewhere deep inside the house. She nibbled her lip in anticipation of meeting her great-aunt for the first time. In point of fact, she'd never known of Lady Dreggins's existence until a week ago when a crested letter arrived at her home, offering the sponsorship of a season.

At twenty summers and busy with the needs of a small church parish, Amaryllis had begun to lose hope of marrying. The letter had seemed like an answer to prayer. Perhaps in London, she would find a godly man for her husband—a man not swayed by the dictates of fashion or pleasure but with his attention turned toward what was most sober and worthy.

The butler pushed open a door and preceded her into the room. "Miss Sinclair, my lady."

Amaryllis stepped across the threshold. Her gaze fastened on a woman reclining on the arm of a backless sofa, and she put a gloved hand to her mouth.

Here was no diminutive lady with the sparkling eyes and white locks she'd envisioned during the long trip. Instead, a squat woman, powerfully built with freckled arms and a bulldog jaw, stared back at her with small, bearlike eyes. Two tiny pug dogs shuffled forward, barking and wheezing. Amaryllis took a step back, not wishing to be bitten.

"You Sinclair's daughter?"

"Yes, my lady."

"Is he still too busy with botany to spare time for his flock?"

"Er, well—"

"Are you mealymouthed? Speak up!"

She took a deep breath. "My father is very fond of flowers, my lady."

The woman smiled smugly and petted one of the dogs on

the head. The dog seemed to have an asthmatic fit. Amaryllis struggled to compose her expression, not daring to give away the shock that assailed her.

"Not planning to give you a season, was he?"

"No, my lady."

She patted the cushion next to her. "Well, Lady Agatha will take care of that."

Clutching her reticule in her hands, Amaryllis crossed the room and perched on the edge of the sofa. Her smile felt more like a grimace.

"I think you'll do," Lady Agatha said. "Maria Ashbury has a young charge, whey-faced and with red hair. Most unfortunate hair color, red. The Duke of Wellington even went so far as to shave his son's red eyebrows off. What do you think of that, hey?"

"I—"

"Your opinion's not important. The key is to stay quiet and smile prettily. Men hate intelligent women, so if you're unfortunate enough to have much book learning, keep it to yourself. A lady only needs to be able to write her name so she can sign her dressmaker's bills. Beyond that, her sole occupation is to be a pretty ornament to a man and bear him heirs."

Amaryllis glanced at her aunt's puce-colored gown, constructed with many gores, flounces, and bows, and wondered if she had ever married and had children. "It's very kind of you to offer me this opportunity, my lady," she ventured.

Lady Agatha touched her mop of curls tinted an improbable gold color. "That's me, generous to a fault. You may repay me by marrying well."

A frisson of alarm skittered down her spine. "My lady?"

Lady Agatha sat up and fixed her beady gaze on her. "My boon companion, Maria, and I have something of a wager. She insists she can make a superior match with her charge. Because the girl has an ample dowry, she thinks she can puff her off to a duke."

Alarm mushroomed into panic. Amaryllis worried that her rate of breathing might soon match the wheezing of the dogs.

"She won't be able to compete with your looks, however. I had a notion Sinclair's daughter might be a diamond of the first water. Your mama was a reigning belle of London in her day."

"Thank you," Amaryllis said faintly.

"And the icing on the cake will be the tidy dot I'll settle on you if you do as I say. No one will be able to say you don't have a dowry." She peered closely at her face. "You don't, do you? Poor as a church mouse, hey?"

"No dowry, my lady."

She leaned back, seeming satisfied. "Well, we'll put a spoke in Maria's wheel this very night. Colette, my maid, will be able to alter something. I took the liberty of choosing a few gowns for you. That's me, generous to a fault. Now off with you."

A petite woman entered the room, with dark hair, darker eyes, and sallow skin.

"Go with Colette. She's French, so ignore her prattle."

Amaryllis rose from the couch and swallowed. "Am I to understand we are to attend an event this eve, my lady?"

Lady Agatha turned to her, her face an angry purple. "Now didn't I just say that?"

"I had thought to rest after my journey from Dorset—"

"Pah! There's no time to be wasted. You ain't one of those milk-and-water misses, are you?"

"No, my lady," she said with an inward sigh.

"Good. Now show your appreciation by going with Colette. Make haste, girl! There's a wager to be won!"

"A curse on all these newfangled ways to tie a cravat!" Lord Matthew Leighton snarled, tearing the offending garment from his neck and tossing it onto the floor where several others lay piled in a heap.

He heard his friend, the Honorable Peregrine Haddon—Perry to his friends—chuckle from where he sat in the corner of the bedchamber.

"Faith, I've never seen you in such a pother. Surely you don't suffer from a case of the nerves. This is hardly your first ball!"

Matthew peered at his expression in the cheval glass and wondered if his plan to appear as a fop was worth the effort. His dark hair had been teased so high he resembled a Friesland hen. His face still bore marks from the recent scrubbing he'd given it after deciding he couldn't bring himself to wear paint.

Matthew wrinkled his nose at the pungent musky cologne with which he'd liberally doused himself, and the lurid red-and-magenta stripes of his waistcoat made him cringe. His brown-eyed reflection stared back at him as if he'd gone mad.

Maybe I have.

"Tonight's ball," he said evenly, "is my first since the lengthy convalescence from my leg wound at Salamanca. Naturally, I want to look my best."

Perry scoffed good-naturedly. "What I think is now that you hold the title of viscount, you plan revenge on all those debs who ignored you when you had no money."

"Now, Perry," Matthew said with a note of sarcasm in his voice, "you know I would never stoop to such levels. I am rather too bookish, too religious a man, to involve myself in such a Machiavellian scheme."

"Much to the dismay of those pretty *señoritas* who plied for your attention back in Spain. I wish I'd garnered such attention, but I possess neither your figure nor your fortune."

"Spare my blushes, Perry," he said, glancing at his rather chubby friend. Perry had round blue eyes and a mop of black curls. "You're well enough in your own way. And it goes to prove the fickle, petty snobbery of London females. They pass over a heart of gold for some old lecher with moneybags. Or in my case, ignore the fact that I had to bear the loss of my father and brother to get the title, never mind that I'm barely out of mourning. To the fairer sex, I'm nothing more than a means to an end. It's enough to send me back to the fighting."

"It's the way of the world, Leighton. Only you seem not to understand that. Too sensitive for your own good."

Matthew made a final pleat in his cravat. "Then all the more reason to stiffen my backbone and accept my fate as a rich, eligible bachelor. I shall enjoy the hurly-burly spectacle made to secure my newly acquired fortune."

Perry sighed loudly. "By courting the simpering misses, that's what you'll find. Better to look out for a sweet girl, unspoiled by avarice or cynicism."

Matthew placed a ruby stickpin into the snowy folds of his cravat and regarded his friend with a mocking smile.

"It is you who are the romantic, Perry. Such a girl does not exist!"

Chapter 2

Amaryllis trembled on the threshold of a mansion, waiting to experience her first ball—something she never had imagined would happen.

A red carpet had been rolled down the steps. Blazing torches flanked the entrance. Light from hundreds of beeswax candles poured out from the doorway, and the scent of hot-house flowers hung in the air. She followed her aunt into the ballroom.

"Lady Agatha Dreggins and Miss Amaryllis Sinclair," the butler announced. After curtsying to Lord and Lady Taylor, the purveyors of the ball, she followed Lady Agatha to the rows of rout chairs lining the dance floor.

Amaryllis gazed about with wide eyes. As Lady Agatha settled onto one of the chairs, her avid gaze ranged the room. "Hmmm, Maria has not made an appearance. Mayhap she realizes the futility of trying to compete with such as I!"

Amaryllis perched on the edge of the chair, trying not to allow her benefactress's words to alarm her further. The idea that this whole undertaking was based on a wager!

She glanced across the crowd. Dancers swayed to and fro in a cotillion. Ladies dressed in every color of the rainbow flashed and twirled around men dressed mostly in black evening garb. Amaryllis glanced down at her celestial blue gown worked with silver embroidery, and a portion of her dread eased. Perhaps she would meet a worthy man here, someone who would be kind and cheerful. Someone who shared her faith in God.

Suddenly, Amaryllis became aware of a huffing and puffing beside her. She looked over to see Lady Agatha breathing hard and fastening a gimlet eye on a bony, long-faced woman who was leading a wispy-haired girl toward the chairs.

As the two older women glared at each other, Amaryllis chanced a smile at the young lady. The girl, who had gray eyes and light red hair, smiled back. Warmth flooded Amaryllis at the response. Surely this girl was as sweet-natured as she appeared, and Amaryllis very much desired a friend.

"Maria," Lady Agatha said gravely as they came to a stand before them. "Meet my charge, Miss Amaryllis Sinclair."

"And meet mine, Miss Fanny Elwood."

Curtsies were traded all around. Fanny sat down on the chair on the other side of Amaryllis. "Are you as nervous as me?" she whispered behind her fan.

Amaryllis felt instantly comfortable at the girl's merry expression. "I'm terrified," she confided.

"Well, don't worry too much. You'll undoubtedly win the wager."

"You know about that? I don't mean to disparage my hostess, but it seems a rather odd way to go about things."

"It's dreadful! But when you've got pots of money and no husband to keep you in check, I guess there's a risk of becoming totty-headed!"

"Shh!" she whispered, horrified Lady Agatha might hear.

Fanny gave her a conspiratorial wink. "I may be a trifle blunt, but it's the truth. Anyway, there's no contest. With your looks, you'll be engaged within a week!"

Amaryllis felt her cheeks warm. "Don't talk fustian! Even I know blonds are unfashionable." She waved her fan in the direction of the dance floor. "That woman there is in the current mode of beauty." A dancer with dark brown hair, liquid brown eyes, and a tiny, pouting mouth, swished past them in the arms of her gallant.

Fanny shrugged. "I suppose." She leaned close. "What do you say about having our own wager? *We* could see who gets engaged first!"

Amaryllis fanned herself. "No, thank you." She shuddered at the notion of making a game of finding a life partner.

Fanny grinned. "You must be the only one who doesn't gamble in this town. Just the other day, I overheard two men bet on which fly would climb a wall faster. Ludicrous!"

"Indeed!"

A party of men strolled past. Amaryllis gazed at them with interest. Most were soberly dressed in black coats, white waistcoats, and clocked stockings. One, however, stood out like a peacock among crows. He wore a pink satin coat over a garish waistcoat set about with an absurd assortment of fobs and seals. Purple silk breeches, striped stockings, and red-heeled shoes completed the unbelievable ensemble.

She had read about such excesses in the newspapers but assumed they'd been exaggerated. Here before her stood what she could only describe as a dandy. His voluminous cravat nearly covered the lower part of his face. A quizzing glass swung idly from his slender fingers. She hid a smile behind her gloved hand.

"Leighton," she heard Lady Agatha boom. "Meet my charge, Miss Amaryllis Sinclair."

Amaryllis looked up with expectation, wondering which man her aunt addressed. The colorful fop put up the quizzing glass and stared at her with a horribly magnified eye.

"La! She's a beauty, but I can't be bothered," he said in a mincing voice. "Your servant, Lady Dreggins."

When he started to walk away, Amaryllis sucked in a little breath. The man had cut her! The rude, uncouth—

"Ah, I must insist. The girl needs a bit of town bronze, and one dance with you will establish her in society."

Amaryllis was even more shocked by Lady Agatha's coercion. *What a dreadful moment!*

The man called Leighton stopped and gave Lady Agatha a haughty stare.

"Your mother would've wished it," she pressed, dabbing a lace handkerchief to her eye. "We were great friends, as you know."

The man dropped the quizzing glass and turned back to Amaryllis. She cringed under his scrutiny, glancing at Fanny for support. Fanny gave another wink and whispered, "He's rich as Croesus."

Amaryllis hoped the floor would open beneath her and swallow her up. A look at the man, and the frown marring his features, told her he'd heard Fanny's comment.

He made an elaborate bow, flicking a delicate handkerchief, his nose almost touching his knee. "Would you do the honor of dancing with me, Miss Sinclair?" he drawled.

There was nothing for Amaryllis to do but accept. She rose and put her fingertips on his proffered arm. She avoided looking back at Lady Agatha or Fanny, knowing they were somehow delighted with the turn of events.

On the dance floor, they took up positions for a Scottish reel. Amaryllis hoped she could remember the steps. She and the housekeeper at the vicarage had practiced to while away winter afternoons. As they waited for the music to commence, she studied the man before her. His heavy-lidded expression and mocking smile didn't seem to match the absurdity of his clothes.

"Is this your first season, Miss Sinclair?"

"Yes, my lord."

"And you are on a hunt for a rich husband?"

Amaryllis gasped. Before she could respond, the music began, and she was forced to follow his lead. The dance lasted half an hour, and the figures kept them separated for the most part. She took a measure of relief from each reprieve, but whenever they met, his glinting gaze seemed to find her wanting. Amaryllis experienced a savage urge to cry.

By the time the dance came to an end, she felt tears well up in her eyes. Exhaustion from her travels made her want to collapse, and her head ached from trying to remember all the steps. As Lord Leighton promenaded her around the room, the dancers blurred into a dizzying swirl, and she stumbled.

"Are you unwell, Miss Sinclair?" he asked in a deep voice at odds with his earlier falsetto. His surprisingly strong arm encircled her waist.

Amaryllis pressed a hand to her forehead as the floor seemed to heave beneath her. "I feel faint."

She was vaguely aware of being hustled from the dance floor. A rush of cool, musty air hit her face, and she realized the viscount must've taken her into an unused room.

"The crush in the ballroom was such that I could not return you to Lady Agatha quickly enough," said Lord Leighton, depositing her onto a sofa. He took a branch of candles and lit them from a smoky sea-coal fire in the grate.

Amaryllis lowered her head in her hands and concentrated on taking deep breaths. After a moment, she glanced at the door and was relieved to find it open to the hall.

"Now that you've established the conventions are being observed, you may forget your plan to compromise me."

She stared up at the viscount in wonder. He stood with his arm along the mantel of the Adams fireplace, glaring at her.

"My lord?"

"Don't play the country innocent with me," he snapped. "I heard your friend mention the state of my finances. Well, I can tell you, you shan't get your hands on it!"

Amaryllis shot up from the sofa. "That's absurd!" The room lurched crazily. She staggered. As if from the wrong end of a telescope, she saw Lord Leighton lunge for her—and saw his leg buckle from beneath him when he tripped on the edge of the sofa. He fell forward, knocked her backwards onto the sofa, and landed on top of her. The air whooshed out of her lungs.

In her supine position, blood rushed back to Amaryllis's head. She blinked owlishly at Lord Leighton's face only inches from her own. He scrambled to his feet, glowering down at her, his handsome face flushed a dark red. He brushed his sleeves in a finicky manner as if to remove all traces of their encounter from his person. *It wasn't my fault!* Amaryllis bit her lip.

"Well, Miss Sinclair. Was that one of your little tricks?"

Before she could answer, Lady Dreggins stumped into the room. She waved her fan at Lord Leighton in a menacing manner.

"I saw the whole thing, Leighton! You compromised my charge, and now I demand satisfaction. You will marry Amaryllis to save her reputation!"

Chapter 3

Amaryllis sucked in an icy breath. She put her gloved hands to her cheeks, unable to believe her aunt's accusation.

Lord Leighton's words dripped with venom. "You are mistaken, madam. I have no intention of allying my name with that of your charge or anyone else at this time."

Lady Dreggins peered up at his tall form, apparently unmoved by his stature. "On the contrary, you placed Miss Sinclair in a delicate position and were caught." She thumped her cane on the floor. "That sort of behavior will have to wait until after the honeymoon."

Amaryllis let out a low groan. She longed for the poky little Tudor pile she had called home her entire life, despite the threadbare furniture and damp patches on the walls. Her father, a timid, bespectacled man who cared for nothing but flowers, transformed in her mind from an emotionally absent parent to a loving one with his arms outstretched. Surely, any place was a haven compared to the likes of London and its inhabitants!

She peeked up at Lord Leighton. As if aware of her attention, he turned and fastened his gaze upon her. Amaryllis shrank back against the cushions of the sofa.

"What do you have to say for yourself, you scheming little minx?"

His dark eyes glittered in the pallor of his face. His lips were thinned in a white line. He appeared to be in pain, as well as justifiably angry. She remembered the way his leg had collapsed from under him. She clasped her hands together.

"Are you hurt, my lord?"

Matthew scowled. Was he that obvious? The vixen peered up at him with wide blue eyes, looking admittedly fetching with her flushed cheeks and blond hair in disarray from their tumble. He fought the sudden temptation to believe her concern was genuine. Her air of innocence was an act, of that he was certain. Despite his inclination to believe the worst, he found his senses quickening at the girl's loveliness.

"La, my Amaryllis is all solicitation," Lady Dreggins said, waggling her fingers. "She'll make a fine viscountess."

Matthew opened his mouth to deliver her a stinging set-down. He heard a disturbance in the hall. His cousin Bertie Snell ambled into the room, gazing about with obvious interest. A brunette floated alongside him, her limpid gaze taking in every detail. Matthew remembered her as Lady Olivia Thorpe, a dazzler with whom his cousin had made him promise to dance.

"What's to do, Leighton? Lady Thorpe is simply pining for you. Remember, you are engaged with her for the supper dance."

Matthew looked with disfavor upon Bertie. His oily behavior and darting dark eyes gave him the manner of a horse trader.

Bertie raised his quizzing glass at Miss Sinclair and sent her a haughty stare. Although Matthew had done the same only a short time before, Bertie's action irritated him. Miss Sinclair's color was high, but she held herself with quiet dignity.

"Well, Leighton," Lady Dreggins thundered. "What are you going to do about my charge, hey?"

"What's this?" Bertie squawked. He gave the older woman an outraged glare, flicking his handkerchief as if to shoo her away.

Matthew's bad leg throbbed and burned from his stumble. The room seemed to close in on him. Lady Thorpe glided up to him and slid her hand around his arm. Her liquid brown gaze threatened to swallow him up. He glanced at Lady Dreggins, whose humorless smile and hard eye boded a scandal if he refused to come to heel.

Miss Sinclair kept her gaze averted to her clasped, gloved hands. Only the quick rise and fall of her chest indicated her high state of emotion. The bugle beads of the cap in her lap winked in the low light of the room.

Matthew breathed a silent prayer for forgiveness for what he'd done—for what he was about to do. *My vanity has brought me to this point. Now I must suffer for it.*

The pressure of Lady Thorpe's hand on his arm increased. Lady Dreggins's wheezing breaths quickened in tempo. Bertie flicked the lid of his snuffbox and took a generous pinch.

Matthew made a decision. He must choose the lesser of

two evils. And perhaps he might find a way out of his conundrum before he found himself wedded to a stranger.

Straightening, he looked at the older woman and cleared his throat. "Lady Dreggins, permit me to pay my addresses to Miss Sinclair for her hand in marriage."

Lady Dreggins thumped her cane on the floor, swelling up until she looked about to burst from the confines of her corset.

"Done!" she boomed. "My charge accepts!"

That was when Miss Amaryllis Sinclair fainted dead away.

Returning from an early morning ride in Rotten Row before his staff had arisen, Matthew strode into the hall of his London townhouse and stripped off his gloves. His butler, Steves, took his gloves and hat, and inclined his head.

"I hear congratulations are in order, my lord."

Matthew started. "Congratulations?"

"On your forthcoming nuptials."

He thinned his lips. "News travels fast in this town."

"Actually, I ascertained the information from the morning newspapers."

Matthew ground his teeth as a fresh wave of fury washed over him. "No doubt that Lady Dreggins inserted it *seconds* after she trapped me into marriage with her equally conniving niece!"

"My lord, this is not joyful news?"

"No, it is not," he snapped. "I find myself affianced to some country bumpkin who set a neat trap for me." He tried to make Amaryllis Sinclair's image into a cunning, shrewd female. Instead all he could remember was the way her blue eyes filled with alarm when she woke up in his arms after her faint. He also remembered the purity of her skin, the light fragrance of her perfume. . . .

He grimaced. Surely such an innocent countenance was just a ruse. He'd seen it before when his male friends had been enslaved by belles of the ball only to find themselves married to empty-headed harridans.

"The Honorable Peregrine awaits you in the breakfast room, my lord."

Matthew's frown eased a bit. He entered the breakfast room to find Perry filling a plate with kippers and a rasher of bacon from the chafing dishes. He looked up with his usual cherubic smile.

Before he could speak, Matthew put up his hand. "Do not congratulate me, whatever you do, Perry."

Perry grinned and brought his plate to the table. "Still huffy, eh? Thought you might've settled down by now."

Matthew grabbed a plate and began filling it with eggs and toast. "Your wits have gone wandering, my good friend. I'm still quite livid and will make every effort to escape this debacle."

Perry grunted. "Don't see what all the fuss is about. Miss Sinclair is a pocket Venus. A real shiner. Make a fellow proud to have a girl like her on his arm."

Matthew raised a brow as they sat down at the table. "Looks can be deceiving. I'll grant that Miss Sinclair is, as you so delicately put it, a 'real shiner,' but I also know she's sly, scheming, underhanded, tricky—"

"Are you sure about that?" Perry interrupted with his mouth full. He stabbed the air with his fork. "Maybe she's as sweet as she looks. Maybe it's that dragon aunt of hers who's behind any scheming. Give the girl a chance."

"Give the girl a. . ." Matthew pursed his lips and shook his head, deciding he'd had enough talk of Miss Sinclair. "By the way, is there a reason you stopped by this morning? Although I'm always happy to receive you."

"Breakfast," Perry mumbled around his food. "I'd starve on what my cook prepares."

Matthew sent him an amused smile. "Fire her. Hire another."

"Can't. She terrifies me. Easier to come here."

He laughed. "You're welcome anytime, Perry."

His friend drained his teacup. " 'Sides, thought you might want to know what Snell said in his cups after you left last night. Mumbling something about seeing you dead before he'd see you wed."

Matthew leaned back in his chair, drumming his fingers on the tabletop. "That cousin of mine bears watching. He's been acting awfully strange lately."

"He was certainly surprised when you returned to London a fortnight ago from Spain. Like he'd seen a ghost." Perry blotted his mouth with the edge of the tablecloth. At Matthew's raised brow, he belatedly noticed the folded napkin next to his plate.

"Can't get used to these newfangled French inventions."

Matthew chuckled.

"Enough of your creeping cousin. This is a beautiful day and as such deserves a visit to a beautiful girl."

"Forming a *tendre* for someone, eh, Perry? Who's the lucky lass?"

He turned red. "No such thing, Leighton. I'm talking about us paying a call on your fiancée."

Chapter 4

Amaryllis winced as pale light flooded the room when the chambermaid pulled the curtains open. She struggled to a sitting position, her brain fogged by something dark and ominous lurking just outside her memory. Her throat ached, whether from crying or a cold, she didn't know.

"What time is it?"

The maid bobbed a curtsey. "Just past one, miss."

"One in the *afternoon*?"

"My lady and miss didn't return home until after four this morning."

Amaryllis slumped back against the pillows as the shadow hovering over her burst into unhappy brilliance—she was being forced into marriage to someone who didn't want her. And her aunt had insisted they stay for the duration of the ball to make sure *everyone* had heard the news.

She put her hands over her face and began to cry.

"Your chocolate, miss."

Amaryllis looked up to see the placid face of the maid through a blur of tears. She accepted the cup and saucer with trembling hands, struggling to compose herself.

"My lord the viscount is accounted a good catch, miss."

She stared in surprise. "You know about it?"

The maid lowered her gaze. "The announcement was in the papers this morning. Mr. Biggs, the butler, told the staff."

I doubt Viscount Leighton sent that announcement to the papers. It had to be Lady Dreggins! She sniffed mournfully, wondering how to cope with such a cascade of humiliations.

The maid fluffed her pillows behind her. "And they say he do be a brave man."

Amaryllis looked up after venturing a sip of the chocolate. "The butler?"

The maid's lips firmed. "No, miss, the viscount."

She thought back to the foppish dress and mocking gaze of her supposed fiancé, wondering if they were speaking about the same person. "Brave? How?"

"In the campaigns. The battle in Salamanca was written about in the papers, and my lord was mentioned especially." The maid bobbed another curtsey and left the room.

He was a soldier? She tried to imagine the fribble she danced with last night leading troops into battle. A hysterical giggle escaped her lips.

The momentary merriment faded away. *How can I ally myself to such a man? Dear Lord, surely this is not Thy will for my life. Surely Thou wouldst not have me yoked together with an unbeliever!*

Colette swept into the room and began laying out an ensemble. "Time for miss to arise. Lady Dreggins wishes you to be ready for callers."

"Callers?" she said faintly. "Does anyone in this town ever rest?"

"No, miss. They are here for one purpose and one purpose only—to marry well."

Amaryllis sensed an underlying mockery in the tone of the lady's maid. She swallowed a shaky sigh and got out of bed.

Lady Agatha Dreggins visibly preened over her apparent coup as they sat in the drawing room, awaiting callers. "Maria was fuming, Amaryllis. I tell you, it was my finest hour."

Amaryllis bit her lip. "Aunt, I'm not sure it is wise to take glory in gambling."

"Stuff. It's the way of the world."

The way of the world meaning the city of London. Amaryllis eyed the wheezing pug dogs in her aunt's lap, wishing with all her heart she was back home in Dorset. Her gaze fell on the skirt of her morning gown of green crepe edged with blond lace. On the other hand, she could never have afforded such a wardrobe back in the parish, and she was feminine enough to enjoy a pretty frock.

Worries about her supposed fiancé suddenly eclipsed the beauty of her dress. She leaned forward. "Aunt, I beg of you, do not hold me to this engagement. What happened was purely an accident."

Her aunt's expression became mulish. "Doesn't matter. Besides, Leighton needs to marry and set up his nursery, not prance around throwing away his fortune on himself."

"I'm sure that is for the gentleman to decide."

"Have no fear, Leighton will do what's expected of him."

Amaryllis experienced a pang of pity for the viscount in the face of her formidable aunt.

"And it's important that his cousin does not inherit. Leighton *must* have sons."

Lady Dreggins stared at her as if Amaryllis could present sons by sheer force of her will.

"Cousin? That man who came into the room when. . . ?" Her voice trailed away as renewed mortification rushed to the fore.

"Bertie Snell is a wastrel," her aunt said, "and would run the Leighton estates to rack and ruin. He almost got his hands on them when your fiancé nearly died. Leighton is the last of his family." One of the pugs lumbered onto her lap. "He does have an older married sister whose daughter, Regina, is due to make her come out next season, and a good thing, too. The girl is beautiful, but positively wild. She needs to be matched with someone with a strong hand to keep her from doing something scandalous. When you and Leighton marry, perhaps you can befriend her."

"Of course," Amaryllis murmured. "But what's this about my fiancé almost dying?"

"Took a ball in the leg during a campaign. Was invalided home, and a fever almost finished him off. It's amazing he's alive." She patted the asthmatic dog on its head. "Might not last much longer though if his dandyism extends to lead paint. But t'wouldn't be a bad thing if he departed for foreign shores after you've produced a couple of heirs."

"Travel to America?"

"I'm talking about death, child."

"Aunt!"

"Tish. My Leon had the good sense to pop off six months after we were married. I have done a much better job with the estates than he would have."

Amaryllis wondered if her dreams of love, marriage, and children were just that—a dream in this world of unions as business contracts and heirs merely a guarantee that fortunes remain in the family. She began to feel sorry for the viscount.

The butler entered the room. "Lord Leighton and the Honorable Peregrine Haddon, my lady." He stepped aside to allow the two gentlemen in.

She caught her breath when her gaze met her fiancé's eyes. He wore a blue morning coat of Bath superfine stretched across his broad shoulders, nankeen breeches, and glossy Hessian boots. His dark hair was styled in the windswept, and his conservatively pleated cravat exposed the clean lines of his jaw. There was no sign of the fop in the imposing figure that stood before her.

Amaryllis almost wished for his return.

His friend Mr. Haddon peeked around from behind and smiled beatifically. "Good morning, ladies. The weather is fine, is it not?"

Lady Dreggins waved them to the couch opposite. "Do sit down, gentlemen. Biggs, tea and cakes, if you please."

"Yes, my lady."

As the butler quit the room, Amaryllis peeked at Lord Leighton. He sat ramrod straight, resting his hands on the knob of a silver-topped cane. His dark eyes surveyed her with an air of disinterest. She felt her cheeks growing hotter by the minute.

He turned to her aunt. "Lady Dreggins, I must say you

were most prompt in sending the betrothal announcement to the papers."

Aunt Agatha wiggled her fingers at him, a toothy smile stretching across her face. "Tol rol, you fellows are so forgetful when it comes to such things. No need to thank me."

Mr. Haddon cleared his throat. "How did you find your first ball, Miss Sinclair?"

Amaryllis's gaze flew to the viscount's friend. *Is he mocking me?* She glanced at Lord Leighton. He returned it with a limpid gaze of his own.

She took a deep breath. "I found it most singular, sir."

Matthew regarded his apparent fiancée with something approaching appreciation. *That's an understatement, if I ever heard one.* And though her beauty captured his attention, he hardened his heart when he remembered the way she had trapped him. How to get out of it? He'd chosen not to appear as a fop today because of the disastrous result on the previous evening, though he might revisit the ploy at some future date.

His gaze dropped to her lips. *Perhaps I should take some premarital license.* His conscience panged him, but the injustice done to him burgeoned in his mind.

She sent him a seemingly shy smile. "How is your leg, my lord?"

Matthew jerked in surprise. Lady Dreggins harrumphed. He notched up his brow. "My, what free and easy manners must thrive in the country. My, er, *leg*, as you so delicately put it, is much improved. I thank you for your concern."

His temporary fiancée bit her lip, her blue eyes wide. She

looked down as a blush mantled her cheeks.

"Lady Dreggins, might I have a few moments alone with my betrothed?"

Miss Sinclair looked up, her lips parted.

"No, Leighton, you may not."

Mr. Haddon cleared his throat, eyeing his friend. "I say—"

"Alas," Matthew said coolly, "I must insist."

Lady Dreggins thumped her cane and rose to her feet, decanting the dog onto the floor. "Ten minutes and not a moment more."

When Mr. Haddon, who darted nervous, meaningful looks in his direction, and Lady Dreggins left, he regarded the young lady where she sat with her gaze fastened squarely on her clasped hands.

"That is a vastly fetching hair ribbon, Miss Sinclair."

She snapped her head up. "I beg your pardon?"

"I meant that I was only able to view the top of your head. I prefer this aspect much better."

Her cheeks turned fire red. *Quite the little actress,* he thought cynically. "Do take a turn of the room with me."

She stood and slowly took his arm, careful not to touch him any more than she had to. It struck him as odd behavior if it was true that she'd planned to trap him into marriage. Perhaps she *had* been forced into it by her aunt, as Perry had suggested. A plan to repulse her materialized in his mind as he thought once more of her lips. "Miss Sinclair."

"Yes?" She looked up at him, her eyes the color of a warm summer sky.

He felt his own face heat at what he was about to do, but

he stiffened his spine, rationalizing that it would be unwise to succumb to a sham of a marriage with a stranger—even if she was pretty. "May I kiss you?"

She pressed her hand to her chest and took a step back. Her frozen expression matched the ceramic gaze of the shepherdess on the mantle. "I barely know you!"

Matthew was unable to keep the irony from his voice. "And yet we *are* engaged to be married."

He moved closer, effectively blocking her into a corner between the fireplace and an escritoire. She backed up until she bumped into the wall.

"Are. . .are you really going to kiss me?" she squeaked.

He placed a hand on the wall next to her and lowered his head, wondering if becoming unengaged might be more pleasant than he thought. "Perhaps."

Miss Sinclair gulped. "Are you healthy, my lord? I fear I woke up with a bit of a sore throat."

He raised his brows.

"Because," she rushed on, "Aunt Agatha said you were once quite ill and might even pop off right after we're married."

Matthew raised his head and narrowed his eyes, regarding his oh-so-innocent fiancé. Was this part of her game? To cast herself as an unwilling victim, to make him somehow sympathetic to her plight and allow the engagement to stand?

Well, I won't be a pawn in some matchmaking busybody's scheme. Despite the delicious temptation Miss Sinclair presented, he decided he wouldn't attempt to kiss her. It could actually cement their betrothal in *her* mind. Better to stick to playing the part of the fop.

He pulled out a handkerchief and held it up to his nose. "La! Stand back, Miss Sinclair. I do not wish to be a victim of your contagion." He flicked the handkerchief at her. "Get thee hence!"

Amaryllis glared at him in surprise and marched over to the sofa. She sat down, her back stiff with outrage.

The drawing room doors opened. Lady Dreggins lumbered in. "Well, Leighton, not up to anything havey-cavey, I trust."

"Here now," Perry sputtered as he walked in behind her. "Leighton doesn't resort to such goings-on."

"In fact," Matthew said in a falsetto voice, "this Miss Sinclair is quite a forward girl. She got close enough to kiss me, then informed me of her contagious status. Really, Lady Dreggins, you should chose charges only from the healthiest stock if you plan to loose them into society."

The older woman puffed up with anger, her gaze darting from him to Amaryllis. "What's this all about? Are you bamming me, Leighton?"

"I had it from her own lips." He let out a shriek of laughter at his pun and glanced at Amaryllis for her reaction.

Distaste had curdled her gentle features, which gave weight to the notion that Miss Sinclair had no more interest in this marriage than he. A reluctant admiration for her sprang up within him. Still, he needed to disaffect her to the point of begging her aunt for a release from the engagement.

Even if it meant playing the fool.

Once Lady Dreggins had delivered herself of the stern dressing-down on the impropriety of mentioning the word *leg* in polite society—*nether limbs* being the appropriate term—Amaryllis was given leave to go to her room.

At the window of her bedchamber, she pressed her forehead against the cool panes and looked out at the jumble of rooftops and birds wheeling against the cloudy sky. *This is not at all what I expected, Lord. Is there still hope that I can find a husband this season? It will be dreadful if I don't marry, and Aunt has to endure the expense of the season for nothing.*

But to marry some coxcomb who minced and pranced in that disgusting way? She closed her eyes. It was either him or some man in his dotage back in the parish.

Amaryllis released a weary sigh and wandered over to the fireplace, where a cheerful applewood fire crackled against the chill of the day. She sank down onto an upholstered ottoman and thought of her surprise when Lord Leighton had arrived in somber morning dress. The tall, masculine man had been far and away divergent from the fop she'd become engaged to—until it served his purpose to play the fool again.

So which was the real Lord Leighton? The dandy or the dashing man of fashion?

A plop of rain fell down the chimney, landing on a fire castle with a hiss and crumbling it into a pile of embers. Was that happening to her dreams? Because dandy or dashing, what remained of import was finding a godly man to take as husband.

Chapter 5

Amaryllis was allowed to rest the following day before a busy schedule of evening events, and she was thankful for the reprieve. She spent the time in her bedchamber reading a Minerva Press novel. While she enjoyed the distraction of the gothic romance, Amaryllis felt the heroine was rather trying, always swooning and fainting about the place.

Remembering her own swoon in that musty room with many avid spectators made her cheeks grow warm. But that reaction had been real. Surely a mere apparition was no match for the discovery of being betrothed to a ridiculous stranger.

She thought once again of seeing Lord Leighton without the popinjay veneer. She had actually found herself attracted to him—actually had wondered if she would like it if he kissed her.

Amaryllis set the book down and jumped up from the chair. *This is not the proper direction for my thoughts. Marrying the viscount will surely never come to pass—somehow the Lord will spare me from such a poor match.*

But what if He doesn't?

Amaryllis groaned. Somehow she had to stop this farce of a

betrothal. Besides, the viscount didn't want her any more than she wanted him. And to help him along, perhaps she might even dabble in a little masquerade of her own. Something to give him a disgust of her.

Her restless gaze landed on the cover of the novel, reminding her of the cloying, clingy heroine who was prone to faint at every little noise. She blinked. Of course! The perfect way to repulse someone who didn't want her was to cling and pine and wheedle—and to press her unwelcome attentions on the skittish object of her pretend passions.

She giggled at her own melodramatic thoughts, but images of clutching the viscount's arm, of gazing into his eyes—of risking a kiss—assailed her untried senses. It would be a dangerous game—a deep game where she might be burned instead of spurned.

But do I really have a choice? Imagine a lifetime joined to a posturing fop. Think of the consequences!

Amaryllis firmed her lips and raised her chin, her heart pounding in her ears. *I'll do it!*

Butterflies took flight within Amaryllis's stomach as the carriage stopped in front of a large mansion later that evening. Flaming torches lit the entrance, and once again, she felt the frightening thrill of venturing into the unknown. What would be the result tonight?

She took a measure of comfort in the fact that she was in looks—at least that's what the cheval glass had told her. Colette's choice of a round train-dress of rose Moravian muslin and silk roses nestled among her curls made her feel like a princess—and a little wistful that she had yet to meet her special someone.

"You know, we neglected to set the amount of a wager because I surely owe you some money!"

Amaryllis turned to see Fanny Elwood approaching with Maria Ashbury. She impulsively reached out to give the young woman a hug.

Fanny regarded her with a mischievous twinkle in her eyes. "I knew you'd get engaged soon, but this surprised even me. Congratulations!"

Amaryllis bit her lip, hesitant to divulge the details of her bizarre betrothal to her new friend. "Thank you."

As they sat down and arranged their skirts, Fanny leaned over. "I want all the details, you know. It must be romantic to receive an offer on one's first evening in town!"

Fiddling with the lace of her reticule, Amaryllis wondered how to answer in such a way as not to be dishonest. "Um, well—"

"I spy the fair charmer now," someone shrieked. "Make way!"

Amaryllis looked up in the direction of the disturbance to see Lord Leighton tittupping toward her on high boot heels. He made an elaborate bow with many flourishes of a lacy handkerchief in front of her and straightened, regarding her with a mocking smile.

"I am come," he said in that absurd voice, "to claim your hand for the waltz."

The viscount had outdone himself tonight. His coat of a virulent purple was worn over a waistcoat embroidered with a pair of showy peacocks. His cravat foamed up over his chin, and the points of his collar nearly touched his nose.

Out of the corner of her eyes, Amaryllis saw Fanny holding up her fan to hide most of her face, but sensed her friend was laughing at the outrageous spectacle of this Pink of the Ton. The grand plan to shame her fiancé into breaking the engagement suddenly seemed imperative.

Lord Leighton held out his arm. Closing her eyes briefly to summon strength, Amaryllis stood and accepted his escort. He led her to one side of the room, sweeping her into the crowd as the strains of the waltz began.

She spent most of the time adjusting her steps to the crush of dancers, while trying *not* to notice the pressure of the viscount's hand at the small of her back. Despite the fact that the Prince Regent had given his blessing to the once-forbidden dance, it still seemed disgraceful to be so closely entwined with a member of the opposite sex. Finally, the dance came to an end. Amaryllis remembered her plan to cling to her fiancé. *It's now or never.*

As he promenaded with her around the room, she hung on his arm and gazed up into his eyes. "I just dote on the waltz, don't you, Lord Leighton? It is a rather scandalous dance, I suppose, but don't you think it was *made* for us?" She batted her eyelashes for good measure.

The viscount blinked rapidly. "Er, yes, Miss Sinclair."

She pressed up against his side and lowered her voice. "I cannot wait to see your home, my lord. Pray tell me, does it have a large ballroom? I simply dote on dancing and will want to have many balls and parties. I look forward to redecorating your—our—home."

She stopped and faced him, peering up at him with her most appealing expression. "*Do* say you'll get a special license so we may marry as soon as possible. I simply dote on quick weddings. Not the pomp and circumstance of a Hanover Square wedding for me. On the contrary, a small, intimate wedding of modest proportions will suffice. What say you, my lord?"

Lord Leighton tugged at the top of his collar, his face flushed a dark shade. "Really, Miss Sinclair, I wouldn't dream of marrying you in such a hole-in-wall way. You deserve the grandest of weddings. Take a year or two to plan, you know, no rush and all that."

Amaryllis rapped his knuckles with her fan. "Silly boy! You act as if you are getting cold feet, which is surely far from the truth. Admit it, you long for immediate nuptials as much as I."

"Ah, here is your aunt, Miss Sinclair. Deary me, I see Mr. Haddon frantically waving me over. Must be some kind of emergency. Your servant."

He bowed quickly and scuttled off into the crowd.

Amaryllis released a pent-up breath and leaned back against the chair, wondering if she'd laid it on too thick.

Matthew strode outside to the balcony facing the back of the property. He nearly bumped into Perry, who followed him out.

"I say, where's the fire, Leighton?"

Matthew ground his teeth then forced himself to inhale a deep draught of cool night air. He took out his handkerchief and mopped his brow.

"Is anything the matter? You look affright."

Tucking away the handkerchief, Matthew gripped the iron railing. "Perry, I'm in trouble. Apparently Miss Sinclair wants me to obtain a special license and marry right away."

Perry slapped him on the back. "That's capital news. Just capital."

Matthew gave him a haughty stare. "Are you mad?"

"Miss Sinclair is all that is suitable. She'll make a beautiful bride."

"Perry, may I remind you my sole intent this season was to avoid matrimony, not find myself deep in the middle of it!"

His garrulous friend shrugged. "Got to get married sometime, you know. Set up a nursery, carry on the family name, eh what?"

"You're missing the point!"

"Here now, no need to get huffy."

Matthew raised an eyebrow and straightened his shoulders. "I never 'get huffy,' Perry. Please do see reason."

"What I see is a perfectly charming young lady who you, mind you, proposed to. Look around at the debs. Won't find one like Miss Sinclair. Sad crop of debs this year, sad crop."

Matthew shook his head, realizing he was getting nowhere. He replayed Amaryllis's little performance in his mind, wondering what her angle was. "She's already talking of redecorating Leighton Hall, the grasping female."

"Place could use a bit of sprucing up. Last time I was there, it smelled of dust and damp dog."

"Perry, are you on my side or what?"

"Think about it, Leighton. If you don't snap her up, someone else will."

"Tcha!" Matthew spun on his heel and stomped from the room, regretting the pain shooting up his thigh—which did little to improve his mood.

As he headed back into the ballroom, someone passing by clipped his shoulder.

"Hey, coz, we were just looking for you."

Matthew turned and saw Bertie and Olivia Thorpe on the fringes of the crowd. Desiring to avoid conversation with his annoying relative, he bowed to Lady Thorpe.

"I believe I still owe you a dance from the other night, my lady."

She smiled and took his proffered arm. As they began the steps of the cotillion, he studied the woman with whom Bertie seemed to want him to become better acquainted.

Her deep brown eyes matched his in color, and her pomaded hair shone in the candlelight. He wondered what she saw in Bertie.

"How do you find the season, Lady Thorpe?"

"Very well, I thank you."

The measures of the dance separated them for a time. When they met again, she smiled. "And how do you find the prospect of marriage, my lord?"

He remembered Amaryllis's words. "Singular, my lady."

His dancing partner emitted a silvery laugh and sent him an understanding smile. "These misses out of the schoolroom can be a trifle *farouche*. . .and rather forward, if you ask me. Even to the point of trickery."

Matthew frowned at the tone in her voice. She had been witness to the disastrous proposal and surely knew he'd been backed into a corner. But for some reason, he was offended by her judgment of his fictional fiancée. Something prompted him to tease her a bit.

"I admit the matter presented itself most awkwardly, but now that it's accomplished, I confess, I look forward to love in a cottage, surrounded by doting children."

Lady Thorpe cast him a sly look. "Ah, you are funning. Love in a cottage, indeed."

The dance came to an end. He smiled stiffly and returned her to his cousin, who was leaning against a pillar at the edge of the ballroom, watching them.

As Matthew walked away, Lady Thorpe's words plagued him, echoing the throbbing wound in his leg that refused to completely heal.

Love in a cottage. For some reason, the notion echoed something in his heart, something unidentifiable at the moment, while Amaryllis Sinclair's face rose to mind.

Chapter 6

"At least here, Perry, we may find refuge from the trials of women." Lord Leighton ushered his friend ahead, and they filed up the aisle of the rapidly filling church to the private box. He looked forward to focusing on God and forgetting his troubles over a country miss.

As he settled himself in his private box, he gazed across the way to see others who were in attendance. When he saw the owner of a smart chip straw bonnet adorned with cornflowers, all his expectation of a peaceful service fled.

"What is *she* doing here?" he grated.

"Who?" Perry asked in a disinterested voice.

"That woman!"

Perry leaned over the box to view the one below. " 'Pon rep, that's Miss Sinclair."

"I am aware of the identity of the person, Perry," he said in freezing accents. "She is here to torment me, to rob me of my last refuge, to—"

"Why are you in such a taking, Leighton? Perhaps she's here to commune with the Lord as you are."

"Pah!"

Several people turned around at the noise, including his fiancée. When she caught sight of him, her eyes widened, and her lips thinned. She sent him an irritated glare before turning back around.

"Well!" said Matthew, offended despite himself. "She acts if she's the one who is put out, when I have the prior claim."

"Oh, do hush," admonished Perry. "The service is about to begin."

Matthew failed to bring his rioting thoughts under control—anger and attraction warred within him. Regardless of her pretty face and well-turned ankle, he would not succumb to entrapment. He would *not*.

"Well, that was a fine service, just fine. Might I repair to your place for luncheon?"

"Of course," Matthew said distractedly. He was ashamed to admit that his fixation with Miss Sinclair and the troubles she presented had blinded him to the entire service.

"Going to greet your fiancée?" Perry asked cheerfully.

"No, I am not. Why give her the satisfaction since she followed me here to torture me?"

As if he didn't hear, Perry waved to Miss Sinclair and Lady Dreggins and hurried to meet them out on the steps of the church.

Matthew followed, seething with a fresh wave of anger—then belatedly felt a sense of shame for his unrighteous attitude. *Dear Lord, I pray for Thy forgiveness for the darkness of my heart in Thy house.*

After greeting several parishioners, trading bows for curtsies, and exchanging innocuous remarks about the weather, Matthew finally made it out onto the steps where he could hear Perry talking with Miss Sinclair about her friend, Fanny Elwood. Schooling his expression into one of blandness, he headed toward them.

Amaryllis sensed Lord Leighton before she saw him. Then, from the corner of her eye, she spied him approaching their group. Despite her angst at seeing him this morning, she couldn't help but notice his fine appearance.

She flushed when she remembered the verse the vicar had used for his sermon. Still, the short frock coat with brass buttons worn over a tan waistcoat with matching breeches made her wonder how she ever thought him a fop. His shiny top boots, beaver hat tilted at a rakish angle, and walking stick completed the picture.

Amaryllis released a breath, sternly reminding herself the truth from God's Word: "Man looketh on the outward appearance, but the Lord looketh on the heart."

"What was that, Miss Sinclair?" Lord Leighton asked, raising her gloved hand to his lips in a perfunctory greeting.

She felt herself blush as she realized she'd spoken the verse out loud. Lifting her chin, she cleared her throat. "I was referring, my lord, to the scripture text used in this morning's sermon from the first book of Samuel."

His lean cheeks seemed to darken as he raised a brow. "And you are, er, familiar with the books of Samuel?"

"Indeed, my lord. I especially enjoy reading the exploits of David."

"What are you prosing on about, Leighton?" her aunt demanded. "Of course Amaryllis is familiar with the Bible. Her father is a vicar!"

"But I also enjoy perusing God's Word, Aunt Agatha."

Lady Dreggins bridled. "What's this? You ain't turned Methody, have you, hey?"

Amaryllis refrained from rolling her eyes. Before she could answer, Lord Leighton leaned forward.

"And what, pray tell, is your favorite book of the Bible?"

She regarded him, determined not to let his proximity affect her senses. . .much. "I take great comfort in the Psalms, naturally, but I hold the Gospels dearest to my heart."

The viscount straightened, his gaze considering. Amaryllis wondered what he was thinking, wondered how he could make her feel hot and cold by turns.

"And the scripture today was?"

Returning his steady gaze, she said in a low voice, " 'Man looketh on the outward appearance, but the Lord looketh on the heart.' "

"Apt, Miss Sinclair. Very apt." He sketched a brief bow and walked away.

Amaryllis watched him go, having no idea what he'd meant with his cryptic statement.

"Wonder what's up with Leighton," her aunt groused. "Must be a disordered spleen. Remind me to have my footman take round some rhubarb pills."

The following day, Lady Dreggins took Amaryllis to tea at Maria Ashbury's home in Berkley Square. Regardless of who'd won the wager, Mrs. Ashbury maintained the better address and accordingly lorded that fact over her friend.

"Lady Dreggins! So good of you to come all the way from Green Street," she said archly. "I trust you passed a pleasant journey?"

Lady Dreggins removed her cloak and handed it to the butler. "Indeed, I take much comfort in Amaryllis's betrothal to such an eligible *parti*. How goes the hunt for Miss Elwood?"

Mrs. Ashbury's heavily rouged cheeks turned a deeper red. "My drawing room has been filled with many callers—"

"Ah, how many offers has she received?"

Mrs. Ashbury affected not to hear and led the way to the drawing room. Amaryllis suppressed a sigh at the behavior of her elders.

In the drawing room, decorated with a great quantity of Egyptian furnishings after the current mode, she saw Fanny and several other ladies.

"Lady Dreggins and Miss Sinclair, allow me to introduce to you some here whom you may not have met. Mrs. Barton and her daughters, the Misses Tabitha and Jane."

An elegant older woman sat next to two dimpled daughters with butter blond ringlets and china blue eyes. They bobbed curtsies at the introduction.

"And Lady Olivia Thorpe. Unfortunately her mama is unwell today and could not be with us."

The pleasure at seeing Fanny faded somewhat when Amaryllis saw the woman who'd witnessed the sordid proposal scene at her first ball. The young woman, with her brown eyes, straight nose, and perfect rosebud lips, nodded from where she sat regally on a backless striped sofa.

"Pray be seated ladies, and I shall ring for tea."

Fanny patted the cushion next to hers, and Amaryllis thankfully crossed the room and sat down next to her.

"I'm so glad you're here," Fanny whispered. "Perhaps we shall be able to have a real visit. You're always too busy dancing at the balls for us to have a comfortable coze."

Amaryllis blushed and regarded her friend, who wore a pretty apple green morning gown with a fringed shawl, which brought some color to her pale eyes. "You are funning me, Fanny. Now, tell me all about your prospects. Is there a gentleman you favor above all others?"

Fanny covered her mouth with her hand and giggled. "Indeed, and you shall be shocked to hear his identity." She glanced around the room as if afraid of being overheard. "Your fiancé's friend Mr. Haddon."

Amaryllis smiled. "I am not shocked but rather pleased. Mr. Haddon is all that is amiable. Unlike—" She bit her lip against the unkind words about the viscount. Clearing her throat, she continued. "Does Mrs. Ashbury attend church? Mr. Haddon attends with Lord Leighton at St. George's."

"Oh!" Fanny bounced on the cushion. "I must get her to take me next Sunday."

The tea service arrived, and cups were passed all around. Amaryllis's aunt and Mrs. Ashbury talked exclusively with one another. The two Barton girls lisped and giggled their way through several cups of tea and plates of cakes.

Suddenly, Lady Thorpe approached Amaryllis. "Miss Sinclair, I have long wanted to make your acquaintance.

Do take a turn about the room with me."

Fanny sent her a rueful smile. Amaryllis stood and followed the woman to the perimeter of the room, her heart pounding at the certain direction of conversation. Lady Thorpe linked arms with her and smiled as if they were boon companions.

"As you know," she said in a low voice, "I was witness to what happened with Lord Leighton. And I want you to know you have my gravest sympathies."

"Um, well, that is very kind of you—"

"Of course, there's no doubting that the viscount is accounted rich and is fiendishly handsome, but sometimes that is not enough to make up for other things."

The ominous tone of her voice made Amaryllis stop. "Other things? What do you mean?"

Lady Thorpe increased her grip on her arm, tugging her forward. "Far be it from me to gossip, but rumors have been circulating for some time. . . ."

Amaryllis's respiration increased, mixed with a growing sense of annoyance. "Rumors," she said flatly.

Olivia peered around to confirm their privacy. "A string of mistresses," she whispered. "And 'tis said his heart is as hard as stone, and society shudders at the poor victim he will take as wife."

"What I've seen of society," Amaryllis said tartly, "is that many are hard-hearted, yet that stops no one from marrying."

"But I've heard he beats his servants, his horses, and I fear he will beat you, too!"

Lord Leighton might be a slave to fashion, but she could not imagine him beating anyone. "Fustian!"

Olivia Thorpe's smile faded. "My apologies for trying to warn you, Miss Sinclair. Beatings you may endure, but you will wish you had heeded my words when you learn he has left you for the arms of his mistress after your marriage. That will surely be beyond bearing, even for you!"

Lady Thorpe abruptly dropped her arm and walked away. *Managing female,* Amaryllis thought crossly. Yet as she returned to Fanny's side, the image of Lord Leighton in the arms of another woman seared itself into her brain. She balled her hands into fists as an unexpected emotion slithered into her heart.

Jealousy.

Chapter 7

"Do you really think Amaryllis Sinclair has any intimacy with the Holy Scriptures?"

Perry leaned on the pommel of his saddle, gazing out to the foggy green distance as they wended their way through Hyde Park. "Stands to reason. Vicar's daughter and all that."

Matthew grimaced, patting the neck of his roan. "Perhaps she learned of my interest in that direction and is using the knowledge to further her hold on me."

"Perhaps if you took the scriptures to heart you'd stop mincing around like a coxcomb and simply ask Miss Sinclair outright."

Matthew felt as if he'd been struck, made doubly painful by the truth in the words. "I'll thank you to keep such observations to yourself," he said in a chilly tone.

Perry let out an apologetic grunt. "Think on it, Leighton. You haven't been yourself this last week."

His conscience panged him. He *had* been behaving badly lately. "Perhaps you are right, but I don't always find myself forced into an engagement!"

"Then break it if you are so set against it."

He sighed. "You know very well I cannot break the engagement. If I did, doubtless that Dreggins woman would have me in court. That is why I must give Miss Sinclair a disgust of myself so *she* will initiate the break."

"It's a lot of nonsense if you ask me."

Matthew shook his head as if to clear it. "My apologies, friend, for snarling at you. Let us endeavor to forget such 'nonsense' for a time, eh? We've been trotting sedately along long enough. What say you to a bit of a race?"

Perry grinned. "You're on!"

He pointed with his whip. "To that tree yonder."

Nodding, Perry yelled, "Heeyah!"

Matthew spurred his mount, and together they flew across the greensward. The wind in his face was exhilarating, freeing him from the confines of his troubles.

Suddenly his horse jolted to a stop—and he went sailing through the air—sky, clouds, and grass, spinning before his eyes.

Matthew landed on his back with a dull thud, the air evacuating his lungs. The thundering hoofs of another horse approached. Dazed, he closed his eyes, willing himself to draw in air.

"Leighton! Are you all right?" Perry skidded to a stop and knelt at his prostrate form.

Matthew held up a hand as little by little air seeped into his lungs. He took a gasping breath and struggled to a sitting position. After a moment, he clambered to his feet, holding onto Perry's outstretched hand.

"How's the leg?"

Matthew gingerly twisted his previously injured leg, noting

no new pain. "I'm all right," he croaked. After a few more minutes, he walked to where his horse stood, its eyes rolled back and muscles quivering.

"Easy, boy." Matthew gripped hold of the reins and ran his hand along the horse's neck, speaking in soothing tones. Something wasn't right. As he examined the animal's legs for any sign of injury, he noticed a wetness on its flank. When he touched the substance, his fingers came away sticky with blood. "Perry, look at this!"

Matthew checked under the saddle and blankets and found a large thorn embedded in the horse's flesh. Perry calmed the horse while Matthew pulled it out. The animal whinnied, then stilled when the object had been completely removed.

"What do you make of it? This is bigger than anything I've ever seen. And how did it get under the blankets?"

Perry took the thorn. "Wicked looking thing, I'll warrant that. Show it to your groom and see what he makes of it."

After a long, hot bath to ease his aching muscles, Matthew felt more the thing. Not only had his body taken a beating, but his conscience, as well. Perry was only speaking the truth that he'd been treating Miss Sinclair shamefully. Fiancée or no, she deserved better.

Later, as his valet brushed his evening coat, Matthew determined to behave with impeccable manners tonight at the rout where he would surely see her. Regardless of whether he'd been tricked or not, he must treat her with delicacy and kindness, especially as she was an apparent sister in the Lord.

After presenting his invitation to the long-faced butler at

the mansion and entering the evening's festivities, Matthew mentally prepared himself for the crush of fighting his way up the stairway among the other rout goers to greet the host and hostess at the top, then fight his way back down the other side of the stairs, all without the added benefit of refreshment or entertainment.

He craned his neck, looking for a diminutive blond among the pushing and shoving guests. *Now where is she?* His groom had heard from the Dreggins's groom that they'd planned to attend tonight. Matthew made it all the way up the stairs, greeted the hosts, and was almost all the way back down before he spotted her.

❧

This is madness. Amaryllis struggled to breathe amid the mass of perfumed, unwashed bodies of the ton. A wizened old man with a pink scalp to match his satin pink evening coat leered up at her from his smaller stature. She pressed herself backward, hoping to eel through the crush without damaging her new gown embroidered with gold thread.

Her formidable aunt seemed to be in her element, conversing with practiced ease in the press. Amaryllis fought down a rising feeling of panic. *Lord, please help me get down these stairs!*

"Miss Sinclair!"

A familiar voice drew her attention downward. *Lord Leighton!* Remembering Olivia Thorpe's words that had festered overnight, Amaryllis turned her shoulder and refused to face him. Her heart pounded, and she felt dizzy—whether from the crowd or from pique, she didn't know. Regardless, she wanted to be well away from that philanderer.

"Miss Sinclair, take my hand and allow me to lead you out of the fray."

She peeked back at him only to see one old dowager rap him on the head with the sticks of her fan for getting too close. Amaryllis winced on his behalf but edged upward away from him. The ancient man who had given her a fright moments before leaned closer and clicked his false teeth at her in a terrible leer.

Oh, for pity's sake! Desperation made her turn toward Matthew and grasp his outstretched hand. His grip was warm and strong as he gently threaded her through the crowd, down the steps, and out to the hall. Breathing a sigh of relief, she sent a sideways look up at her benefactor.

Once more he had forgone the foppish attire and was resplendent in a black double-breasted wool coat with tails worn with gray trousers. A diamond winked from the sculpted folds of his cravat. She hardened her resolve, remembering to look beyond the appearance and to the heart.

"Forgive me, Miss Sinclair. I have not yet bid you a good evening."

Amaryllis flicked open her fan and shielded the lower half of her face in an attempt to gather her wits. His open expression and seemingly genuine smile made her feel more out of kilter than when she'd been on the staircase.

She averted her gaze. "Good evening to you, Lord Leighton. Are you alone tonight or did you bring a friend?"

"Unfortunately Mr. Haddon is feeling a trifle under the weather and elected to remain home."

"I'm sorry to hear that, but I wasn't referring to Mr. Haddon."

Amaryllis almost choked on a fresh wave of jealousy.

He raised his brows. "Whom are you referring to, I pray?"

"A lady friend, perhaps?"

"A lady friend." His brow arched upward

"Of cracked reputation?"

Blood rushed to the viscount's face, and his expression was like thunder. "I beg your pardon!"

That's torn it. Amaryllis too late realized one of her aunt's rules of decorum: never, ever mention a man's mistress to his face.

Lord Leighton took hold of her upper arm and marched her to a less populated area. His voice sounded like a hiss. "What on earth could compel you to allow such filth to pour from your mouth?"

"Are you going to beat me next?"

White to the lips, he stared down at her with eyes that smoldered like coals. "Would you mind explaining to me how you came to believe such a farrago of lies?"

She bit her lip, realizing she was in deep trouble. *If Aunt Agatha catches wind of this, I'll be packed off to the country quicker than a wink.* But the poison of Lady Thorpe's words had infected her heart and mind. Amaryllis's eyes filled with tears of mortification.

"Did someone tell you this?"

She nodded, unable to speak.

"What utter rot! I demand to know who."

"Is it true?" she asked just above a whisper.

He pulled her close, his face only inches from hers. "Miss Sinclair, I am a man of faith, and as such I do not fraternize with ladies of certain reputations, neither do I beat anyone! Now, I want to know who is spreading such lies about me."

"You're a Christian?"

His features softened somewhat. "Yes, Miss Sinclair."

"Oh. I didn't know there were any in London."

A smile tugged the corners of his lips. "Yes, even in London." He gave her a gentle shake. "Now will you tell me who gave you such wicked information?"

Amaryllis gazed up at him, taking in the details his proximity afforded. He had long, thick lashes and a small scar over one eyebrow. He smelled of soap and cologne, and even better, he was a believer. "How did you get that scar?"

"Miss Sinclair," he growled. "The name, if you please."

There's no going back now. "Olivia Thorpe told me you had a string of mistresses and that you beat them as well as animals and servants."

His expression grew grim. She wondered how she ever thought him effeminate. He tucked her arm through his and drew her from the shadows to where Lady Dreggins stood waiting for the carriage.

"There you are, you naughty child. I have been looking for you this age. Leighton, be so good as to call for our carriage."

He bowed and, as he straightened, sent Amaryllis a look she was unable to decipher. "As you wish, madame."

After he left, her knees felt decidedly weak. She took a deep breath to calm her nerves and grabbed hold of the revelation that Lord Leighton's heart was in the right place after all.

Chapter 8

"I tell you, Perry, I felt as if she'd slapped me." Matthew paced in front of a window in the library of his townhouse. He looked up to see his friend taking his ease in a large, leather, winged chair and regarding him with twinkling eyes.

"Was it that she mentioned it to your face or that she imagined you to have a mistress in keeping?"

Matthew stopped and took a breath. "Both. To hear such language from her lips." He slapped his gloves against his thigh. "Dash it all, it's her look of innocence that gulls me. I keep forgetting she's not what she seems."

Perry grunted. "To Miss Sinclair, neither are you. What would the young miss think if her foppish fiancé had once considered the curacy?"

"I told her I was a Christian."

"Fan me ye winds! What did she say to that?"

Matthew slumped onto the facing chair. "Said she didn't know there were any in London."

Perry chuckled. "Can't say that I blame her for such a supposition. And when she finally meets one, he's a far cry from anything she's seen in her parish." He leaned forward. "Do you know what I think?"

Matthew leaned against the back of the chair. "You will tell me regardless," he said dryly.

"I think that the Lord orchestrated this meeting with Miss Sinclair."

"What!"

Perry put up his hand. "She's apparently a believer, and you did not think they existed. Well, here's one right under your nose. Couldn't be more perfect."

"You've got windmills in your cockloft, Perry. I doubt very much that Amaryllis Sinclair is a believer. Don't forget she tricked me into a betrothal." When his friend raised a supercilious brow, Matthew cleared his throat. "Besides, why would she tell me Olivia Thorpe said such lies about me? Lady Thorpe would have no reason to act that way. Another strike against Miss Sinclair!"

"Fiddle," Perry said pleasantly. "Olivia Thorpe is an intimate of your obsequious cousin, who can't be trusted under the best of circumstances."

"It's probably just a coincidence."

Perry stood and went over to the bellpull, giving it a tug. "Not like you to be so stubborn, Leighton. You act as if you're in love with Miss Sinclair."

"Love!" Matthew expostulated, jumping to his feet.

"You rang, sir?"

"Ah, Steves," said Perry rubbing his hands together. "Got any of that seed cake about?"

"I shall ascertain if the cook has any in the larder, sir."

When the butler left, Perry grinned. "All this argufying makes me hungry, and your cook's seed cake is sublime." He sat back down.

Matthew shook his head, half-amused, half-exasperated at his friend's behavior. "Love, indeed. When I marry, if I marry, it will be to a sweet-natured girl from a good family far away from London, I can tell you that."

"You've described your fiancée to the letter."

Matthew put up his hand. "Enough! We are getting nowhere. And still the question remains, why would Lady Thorpe say such things about me, if Miss Sinclair can be believed."

The butler appeared with a tray of cakes and two dessert plates along with tea. Matthew watched as his friend piled several cakes on his plate and bit into one with a look of exaltation on his face. "Stands to reason she's doing it on behalf of Snell," he mumbled around a mouthful. "If you don't marry and produce a son, he inherits."

Matthew sank down onto the edge of the chair, unwilling to allow such a thought to flourish. "I cannot believe such a gothic scheme, Perry. Been reading Mrs. Radcliff's novels, have you?"

Perry set down his teacup after taking a noisy drink. "Don't need to. Watching you and Miss Sinclair is more novel than anything I could read."

"Droll, my friend. Very droll."

"Well, what if it's true? Snell doesn't want you to marry. Say he tells the Thorpe female to drip poison in your fiancée's ear so she'll break off the engagement."

Matthew eased back against the chair, surveying his friend

from under heavy lids. "And how do you come up with such a Banbury tale?"

"Just popped into my head. After your groom told me that the thorn must've been placed under the blanket of the horse deliberate-like, well, it just adds up."

"My groom said that?" he asked faintly.

"You were still wobbly from being thrown. Must not have heard."

Matthew closed his eyes, unwilling to acknowledge such madness. *Dear Lord, it cannot be true! Please help me find out the truth.*

"Yes," Perry said after demolishing the last of the cake, "looks like your cousin has murder on his mind!"

Amaryllis gazed out the window down to the street below, watching the carriages fly over the cobblestones. Would Lord Leighton call today? She longed to look in his eyes again and ascertain if he spoke the truth.

Could the viscount truly be a Christian? And if he was, was he the man God intended for her? She blew out a breath and smoothed the folds of her morning gown trimmed with Valenciennes lace.

"You are not attending, child!"

Amaryllis jumped at the gruff sound of her aunt's voice. The dog wheezed in agreement. "Yes, my lady?"

"You must help me address these invitations."

She moved across the room to where her aunt sat at the escritoire. "Invitations to what? Are you to have a rout?"

"Don't be silly. These are for your wedding."

"My wedding," she said in a colorless voice. "Has a date been set?"

Lady Dreggins harrumphed. "Not yet, but I'll pin Leighton down next time I see him. Regardless, there is much to be done. No one will say Agatha Dreggins does not do right by her charges!"

Amaryllis wondered at the anxiety mixed with longing that filled her. *Will I really marry Lord Leighton?* A delicious shiver went over her until she remembered his strange behavior.

She glanced at her aunt. "What is the viscount's Christian name?"

Lady Dreggins peered at her with her small eyes. "His Christian name? Why, it's Matthew, I believe." She looked up as the butler entered the room with a letter on a salver.

"Yes, Biggs?"

"The post has arrived, my lady."

Amaryllis retrieved it for her aunt and watched as she broke the seal and read the contents.

"Make haste, Amaryllis. Leighton is to call at five. You are to join him for a carriage ride at the fashionable hour."

A dizzying assortment of feelings swirled within Amaryllis—excitement, fear, and a suffocating longing for the unknown. As she hurried up to her bedchamber to change into riding dress, she thought of the viscount's Christian name.

Matthew. His name is Matthew.

Matthew helped Miss Sinclair up onto his curricle. He'd forgotten what a fetching creature she was. She wore a scarlet velvet spencer over a fine muslin gown, and a dashing shako hat was perched atop her golden curls. The cool afternoon air lent color to her cheeks.

With an effort, he forced himself to remember she might not be all she seemed. As he climbed up next to her, he sent her what he hoped was a charming smile. He planned to test her, to test Perry's assumption that the girl was religious.

Matthew nodded to the boy who held the horses' reins. "Stand away, Jimmy!" He snapped his whip above the team of matched bays, and the curricle lurched forward as Jimmy hopped onto the back.

They headed for the ring, where many of the nobility drove at this hour, and he wondered how to broach the subject and discern a genuine response from his fiancée.

"The day is very fine," he ventured. "Even here in London, one can see the beauty of God's creation."

She gazed up at him, her searching look seeming to divine the secrets of his soul. "Yes, my lord."

Matthew cleared his throat, determined not to become befuddled by a mere slip of a girl. *He* was the one doing the investigating.

They entered the gate to the ring and joined the queue of carriages making the circuit around the loop. Quizzing glasses were raised, and people craned their necks to see who was with whom. Matthew nodded to a few acquaintances before turning his attention to Miss Sinclair.

"I've been thinking about our conversation. The one where we discussed Lady Thorpe telling you some untruths about me."

She glanced at him and blushed.

"Do you have any idea why she would do such a thing?"

Miss Sinclair furrowed her brows for a moment. "If she did lie, then it must be that she wants to thwart our marriage." Her face turned an even deeper shade of red. She looked away.

Matthew considered her words, which echoed Perry's. If they were true, then just about everyone was attempting to thwart his marriage to Amaryllis—including himself.

"Hmm. An interesting perspective. Here's something else to consider. The other day I was thrown from my horse."

"My lord!" Miss Sinclair put her gloved hand on his arm, her eyes wide. "Were you harmed? Was the war wound in your, um, nether limb, aggravated?"

Matthew bit the inside of his cheek to keep from laughing as his defensiveness eased. Surely he wasn't misreading the concern in her eyes. If she was acting, she'd be fit for Drury Lane.

"I was unharmed, Miss Sinclair. But a large thorn was found under the saddle blanket, giving rise to the notion that it was no accident."

She gasped. "Who could do such a thing and why?"

"That's what I'm trying to discern."

Matthew guided the horses to a nearby park and stopped under a stand of oak trees. "As a matter of fact, I thought we could work together to solve the mystery, and I hoped we could begin by beseeching the Almighty for His aid."

Amaryllis stared at the viscount, wondering wildly if he was mocking her. She gazed into his eyes, longing to discern the truth in their dark depths.

Deciding that prayer was the best option regardless, she swallowed and nodded her head. When he took her hand in his and smiled, her heart fluttered like a trapped bird. Suddenly his lashes swept downward, and it took a moment for her to realize he'd begun to pray.

Amaryllis caught her breath and closed her eyes, striving to focus on the Lord instead of the viscount's deep voice.

". . .We ask for Thy favor to discover any plot intended to harm me or Miss Sinclair. And help my cousin and Lady Thorpe to seek Thee in all their ways. Amen."

"Amen," breathed Amaryllis. She looked up at Lord Leighton, astonished that a simple moment of prayer could establish a sweet intimacy with a man she longed to trust but still feared. Would she ever learn the whole truth about him?

Chapter 9

Amaryllis was no nearer to the truth a week later. Lord Leighton, back to his mode of a dandy, sat at the long dining table crowded with guests, wearing a black- and yellow-striped coat and yellow silk breeches that made him look absurdly like a wasp. His dark hair was teased to a ridiculous height, and he spoke in that high, mincing voice that so grated on her nerves.

What had happened to the seemingly godly man who sought the Lord on her behalf?

She frowned at him from where she sat down at the lower end of the table, away from the higher ranks that included Lord Leighton's cousin and Lady Thorpe. He caught her glance and his cheeks darkened as if he'd been caught doing something unseemly.

Amaryllis looked away and scowled down at her turtle soup, wishing something made sense about this season. Had she really been silly enough to indulge in dreams of romance and marriage to a good man? At this rate, she worried she was well on her way to becoming just another cynic who filled the salons and ballrooms of London.

She glanced at the footmen who stood at attention along the back of the room. One of them, a tall and broad-shouldered Adonis, placed a second bowl of turtle soup in front of Lord Leighton, who continued sipping spoonfuls and talking a great rate, interspersed with dreadful shrieks and giggles.

Just above her, Mr. Haddon also frowned at his friend. Was he thinking the same thing? Next to her sat Fanny, who was attempting to get Mr. Haddon's attention with the vigorous application of her fan. Amaryllis sighed. It seemed everyone's hopes this eve were destined to be thwarted.

Two hours later, the dinner came to an end. The hostess stood and nodded her head for the ladies to retire to the drawing room and await the gentleman.

Lord Leighton jumped up. "Let us dispense with ceremony and join the ladies, shall we?" He waved his fan in Amaryllis's direction. "I positively pine to be with my ravishing fiancée."

Amaryllis flushed. His tone made the words sound like an insult.

The other gentlemen looked resigned. Since the viscount was of the highest rank, they couldn't refuse and appeared to acquiesce with bad nature.

Once they were all settled into a large drawing room painted a pale green with frescoes on the ceiling, Amaryllis found a quiet corner out of the glare of the flaming branches of candles. She played with the sticks of her fan, wishing the evening were at an end so she could lie down in her bedchamber with a cool handkerchief on her forehead.

"My cousin and Lady Thorpe acquit themselves well, wouldn't you say?"

She looked up into the glittering, dark eyes of her fiancé. "My lord! I didn't hear you approach."

Lord Leighton flicked up the tails of his coat and settled beside her on the sofa. "No doubt you were lost in dreams of planning our wedding?"

Amaryllis clenched her fists, longing to box his ears. Despite his occasional attractive manners, how could she for even a moment consider opening her heart to such a hardened fribble—especially one who played fast and loose with his faith? She shook her head, too angry to speak.

He waggled his fingers at her. "Tol rol. Mayhap you should, since I have reconsidered a long engagement. A love like ours must not be made to wait, so I shall acquire a special license from the bishop that we may marry with haste."

"You shall do no such thing," Amaryllis said in a quavering voice. She swallowed, finally realizing what she must do. A glance at her aunt, who would go into histrionics at the broken betrothal, made her shudder. But she could not, would not marry such a man!

"My lord, I fear I must inform you of a sudden change of circumstances." She glanced up at him to see if he ascertained the direction of her words.

The viscount blinked several times and pulled at his neck cloth. "Faith, 'tis hot in here."

Amaryllis bit her lip as her courage ebbed. She took a deep breath and stiffened her posture, resolved to follow through on what was right. "I'm sure you would agree with me that we would not suit—"

The viscount stared at her, his eyes taking on an odd, glazed aspect. Suddenly, he subsided to one side of the sofa and slid onto the floor.

"Lord Leighton!" Amaryllis fell to her knees next to him and chafed his wrists, half-furious that he might be playing a prank to shame her, half-terrified he was truly ill.

Her shout had roused the other guests, who rushed to her side as she cradled his head in her lap. One of the ladies waved a vinaigrette under his nose. The viscount blinked once, turned sheet white, and passed into unconsciousness. Mr. Haddon lightly slapped his friend's face to no avail, then yelled for a doctor.

Some of the men laid bets as to when he'd recover, several ladies fainted, and still the viscount lay unnaturally still in her lap. Amaryllis began to pray.

"My lord is resting now."

Amaryllis twisted around when she heard the doctor's words. She jumped up and hurried to where Mr. Haddon stood next to the small man who wore a bag wig, an old-fashioned frock coat, and buckled shoes.

"I have given him a purge," he said in a low voice, "and in time the fever will most likely abate."

"Fever?" she asked, clasping her hands together, not caring if she appeared rude to the guests still assembled in the drawing room an hour later.

The doctor peered at her through his spectacles. Mr. Haddon intervened. "This here is the viscount's betrothed."

The doctor nodded. "Ah, yes, you must not worry, young lady. Men home from the battlefield are often beset by fevers."

"Who is with my lord now?"

"A chambermaid of the house, I presume."

Amaryllis stood trembling, engulfed by a fear she could not identify. Without waiting to speak to her aunt, she rushed from the room and ran out to the hall.

"The viscount!" she said to the butler. "Where is he?"

The butler raised his brows and swept her with a disapproving look. "Is there something I can help you with?"

She stamped her slippered foot. "I am his fiancée, and I demand to see him!"

"Very well," he said frostily. "Follow me."

Amaryllis followed him, longing to scream in frustration at the slow pace as they traversed long corridors toward the guest wing.

A movement to her left caught her eye. She turned to see what it was. Down a short hall, ending in a shadowed alcove, she saw Bertie Snell drop several guineas into the hand of the footman who'd served the viscount's turtle soup.

What are they doing in this part of the house?

The butler gave a discreet cough. "We have arrived, miss."

Amaryllis glanced at the butler, dismissed both him and the consequences of her actions from her mind, and entered the bedchamber. She found a chambermaid sprinkling rose water in the room, who stopped at her entrance.

"Would you please bring me several strips of cloth and a basin of water? I shall now sit with my lord."

The chambermaid bobbed a curtsy and quit the room.

Amaryllis looked at her surroundings. A branch of candles on a toilet table flickered in the gloom, casting eerie shadows. The red bed curtains were closed. Stepping quietly to the bedside, she pulled them back.

She put her hand to her mouth. Lord Leighton looked so pale, she feared for his life. The frilly nightshirt he wore lay open revealing the strong column of his throat, but the white color of the garment heightened his waxy pallor. All her angst fled before a rush of unexpected affection.

She dragged a chair over to the bed and sat, taking his icy hand in her own in an attempt to warm it.

"Heavenly Father," she whispered, "I beseech Thee to make my lord well. Bring him comfort and healing."

The maid returned with the requested items. Amaryllis released the viscount's hand and turned to the toilet table. From her reticule, she produced a small flask of cologne, which she emptied into the basin of water. She placed the strips of cloth into the water and, when they were soaked, took one, gently wrung it out, and bathed the viscount's forehead.

Matthew opened his eyes, and he took her hand in a weak grip. His sleepy gaze held hers for a long moment. "You look like an angel, Amaryllis, with the candlelight glowing on your hair."

A blush heated her cheeks at the compliment combined with the use of her Christian name, making her wonder if she had a fever herself. *And yet his skin is not warm but cool.* She forced her features into a smile. "Flirting even from your sick bed, I see."

He gave a little tug to her hand. "Not flirting, but proud to be affianced to one as beautiful as you."

She swallowed, longing to believe his loverlike words were genuine but fearing he was playing with her emotions despite his illness.

Voices echoed up the hall. Amaryllis eased her hand from his and went out into the hall, closing the door behind her. Mr. Haddon, with Fanny on his arm, and Lady Thorpe accompanied by Bertie Snell approached the chamber. Lady Dreggins brought up the rear.

"How's the fellow?" Bertie drawled. "Turtle soup is too rich for some, eh what?"

"The doctor said he had a fever," Amaryllis said quietly. "But his hands are like ice."

"Tut tut, Miss Sinclair," Lady Thorpe said. "The fact is you should not be in a man's bedchamber at all. Leave the viscount to the servants, and he shall do very well."

Amaryllis regarded Lady Thorpe, knowing she was right, then directed her gaze to Bertie, who fidgeted with his snuffbox. The memory of him paying the servant lent a suspicious air to his actions. She remembered what Lord Leighton had said about the thorn hurting his horse and about Lady Thorpe's lies. What if there had been something put into the viscount's soup? She suppressed a stab of alarm.

Fanny sent a small smile, and Mr. Haddon's expression revealed worry for his friend. Lady Agatha harrumphed that it was all a rum do.

Amaryllis firmed her lips. "Nevertheless," she said clearly. "I will sit with my fiancé until he is quite recovered."

Matthew slowly opened his eyes and for the longest time didn't have any idea where he was. Candlelight wavered on red bed curtains, but otherwise the room was shrouded in darkness.

Images flickered through his mind—images of Amaryllis glaring at him, then seeing her mouth go slack with distress. He remembered many voices and a lot of fuss, and now he was here—but here wasn't his home.

Matthew turned his head slightly toward the candlelight and was rewarded with a breathtaking pounding in his skull. He closed his eyes, waited for the pain to subside, then risked moving his head a little more. After a sensation of dizziness faded, he saw someone else in the room.

He blinked to bring the vision into focus and realized Miss Sinclair was in the bedchamber. She sat in a chair next to the bed, her head pillowed on the mattress by her folded arm, asleep. Her other arm was stretched across the counterpane, her fingers wrapped around his own.

Well, now that her reputation has been compromised, I will have to marry her after all.

The notion did not depress him in the slightest. Instead, he came to the unexpected realization that he'd fallen in love with her.

From her contempt at his dandyisms, to her knowledge of the scriptures, and now her compassion at his bedside, Miss Amaryllis Sinclair had clearly demonstrated she was no gold digger determined to trap him into marriage—and he was ashamed he'd ever entertained such thoughts.

He tried to squeeze her fingers, but his grip faltered. He blew out a sigh and closed his eyes, praying for a speedy recovery. What had landed him in this bed anyway? He could only remember his stomach suddenly roiling combined with a feeling of overwhelming confusion.

A little gasp drew his gaze back to where Amaryllis sat. She had awakened, and her eyes were filled with tears.

"Lord Leighton," she whispered. "You're awake!"

Chapter 10

A knock sounded at the door. Amaryllis tore her gaze from the viscount's and brushed the tears from her eyes with the back of her hand.

Mr. Haddon popped his head in the door. "Lady Dreggins is demanding your presence in the drawing room, Miss Sinclair."

"Please give my compliments to my aunt, Mr. Haddon, but I cannot leave until I am assured of the viscount's health."

"Go ahead, Amaryllis," the viscount said in a low voice. "I believe I am much improved."

She turned and gazed at him, noting that a touch of color had returned to his face. "Are you quite certain, my lord?" The nightmare she'd woken from moments ago in which he had died clung to her with frightening intensity.

Lord Leighton inclined his head ever so slightly and offered a feeble smile. "Perry will apprise you if there is any change in my recovery."

Amaryllis released his hand, suddenly embarrassed to be caught holding it. She dropped her gaze and rose on unsteady legs. Smoothing down the folds of her dress, she sent a shy smile toward her fiancé and turned to leave.

Mr. Haddon stood outside the door. "How long have I been here?" she asked him.

He pulled a watch from a pocket in his waistcoat. "About five hours, I should think."

"And did my aunt leave and return for me?"

"No, she has been here this age along with all the other guests. They have been playing cards as was planned."

"What!" Amaryllis stared at him in shock. "Entertaining themselves while my lord was at death's door?"

"Well, er, yes, Miss Sinclair. In fact, they didn't seem to believe Leighton was all that ill."

She grabbed hold of his arm. "Yes, he was, Mr. Haddon, and I think he may have been poisoned."

Perry's eyes bulged. "Steady on! How can you be sure?"

"The footman who served my lord his soup was later seen by me receiving money from Mr. Snell. I know it's circumstantial, but can it be a coincidence? No one else got sick, and Lord Leighton did not have a fever."

"I say, Leighton was right. Gothic goings-on and all that." He patted her hand. "Tell you what, you put in a good word for me regarding Miss Elwood, and I'll send round notes to you keeping you apprised of Leighton's condition. Have we a bargain?"

Amaryllis smiled. "Yes. Thank you."

He sketched a bow and disappeared inside the bedchamber. She sagged against the wall next to the door, exhaustion assailing her. Surely she'd only nodded off moments before Lord Leighton had awakened. She remembered long hours keeping watch, fervently praying for his recovery.

Amaryllis heard a muffled shout through the door. Realizing it had not been latched, she eased it open a few inches. She squelched a stab of guilt at eavesdropping and inclined her ear to the conversation inside.

"And based upon Miss Sinclair's suspicions," Mr. Haddon was saying, "tonight's events may not be a coincidence."

"I believe you have the right of it," Lord Leighton said in an angry voice. "And the time has come to confront this once and for all!"

"Isn't it exciting? I confess I'm in high alt and don't know how I shall be able to wait a whole week!"

Amaryllis smiled at Fanny's enthusiasm. Everyone was talking of the masquerade ball at Lord and Lady Ackers's Berkley Square mansion. At first Lady Dreggins and Maria Ashbury had pooh-poohed the notion of their charges attending, as masquerades were known to encourage loose morals, but Mrs. Ashbury had been overheard admitting high hopes that Mr. Haddon was *epris* in Fanny's direction and might use the occasion of the ball to propose.

All that remained was the choosing of fripperies to complement their costumes. Amaryllis decided to stop worrying about Lord Leighton's health and enjoy the sunshine of their outing to Exeter Exchange. Mr. Haddon had been faithful with his missives, but she wondered if he were too quick to assure her. If he could be believed completely, Lord Leighton had improved immeasurably and was planning to attend the masquerade.

Gazing about the shops from the windows of the carriage, Amaryllis couldn't suppress her own hopes of dancing with the viscount to test her tender new feelings when she wasn't terrified for his health. The carriage came to a stop, and a footman opened the door and let down the steps.

Exeter Exchange on the Strand quivered with the noise and bustle of shoppers and stalls filled with every imaginable ware, including scarves, cheap jewelry, toys, and fans.

"Amaryllis, do come here!" Fanny cried. "I found the perfect mask for my costume!" She held up a satin sequined affair with rainbow feathers.

"I agree, Fanny. It's perfect!"

"And a mask for you, miss?" the vendor asked. He had swarthy skin and a bushy black mustache and sideburns.

Amaryllis looked over the selection, trying to decide which would be the best match for her white gown. She had decided against the usual shepherdess, gypsy, or Turk costumes that were so popular and planned to wear a pretty mask with regular fancy dress.

"May I be so bold as to ask what will you be wearing, Miss?"

She told the vendor, whose fingers flew over the selection. He picked one up and showed it to her with theatrical flair. "For a night of mystery, this will be the best. This is not just any masquerade mask but one worn during a ball as the wearer fled the Terror in France. And later, by a lady who thought her lover false. Be not alarmed, their paths led to true love."

"And just how did you come by all this information?" Amaryllis asked, biting the inside of her cheek.

He closed his eyes. "The mask, it speaks to me, I sense this intrigue and romance in the glint of the pearls and—"

"The gossipy servant what gave it to him told him all about its owners, that's what," said a ruddy-faced woman who was apparently the man's wife. "Blimey, Jem, you an' yer stories."

Amaryllis laughed as his face turned red. Covered in white silk with seed pearls and white feathers, the mask was pretty and would be just the thing to match her gown. She paid the price of five shillings and couldn't help wondering what might be in store for her when she wore the mask.

After another hour spent choosing ribbons and gazing at everything offered, they headed home. When Amaryllis arrived back at her aunt's townhouse, Biggs held out the salver. On it was a note folded like a cocked hat.

Her heart beat a little harder. Mr. Haddon only sent plain letters sealed with wax. Amaryllis took the note to her bedchamber and opened it with trembling fingers.

Miss Sinclair,

Mr. Haddon and I launched upon an investigation, and after searching for the servant you saw receive money from my cousin, we discovered him in his cups as he apparently has a weakness for drink. We found out that he had been paid to put arsenic in my soup and had also been paid earlier to put the thorn under my saddle, all 'for a lark.' I decided to speak to the groom at Leighton Hall about the carriage accident that took the lives of my father and brother. He believed there was evidence that the ridge poles had been sawn through, but I had earlier dismissed such a notion as he was known to be rather touched in the upper works.

Amaryllis put her hand to her mouth. *Murder?*

All together, this is simply too much to ignore. Apparently, Bertie thought I had died when I was wounded in the war and so assumed he was heir to the title. When I appeared in London, he had to find a way to get rid of me, and in part thanks to you, he has not succeeded.

I do not have direct evidence except for the ramblings of a drunk man and the mutterings of an old groom, so I cannot involve the local magistrates at this time. I have however, decided to embark on a plan which I will carry out at the masquerade ball Thursday next.

I tell you this so you will not worry if events seem odd that night. I covet your prayers for the endeavor to be successful and for my cousin to be brought to justice. Please destroy this letter after you have read it.

I remain humbly yours,
Leighton

Amaryllis bit back an exclamation. Worry that the viscount was embarking on a foolhardy scheme conflicted with disappointment that his words contained not a trace of affection.

Shoving the letter through the grate into the fire, she watched as the paper curled and turned into ash. She hoped her dreams would not follow suit.

As if confirming the theme of the masquerade, a thick yellow fog crept through the city streets, masking the night of the ball. Amaryllis shivered and pulled her cloak more closely around her frame to protect her gown of white spider gauze over a white silver embroidered satin slip with paste diamond clasps.

Her heart beat erratically at the eve to come, not from debutante nerves but from worry over Lord Leighton's plan—a plan to which she was not privy. She glanced at her aunt, who dozed as the carriage clip-clopped over the cobblestones to the mansion in Kensington.

Dear Lord, please protect Lord Leighton—Matthew—from any harm tonight. The prayer seemed somehow incomplete but worry fragmented her thoughts. Amaryllis glanced out the window and saw the flambeaux outside the mansion. They had arrived.

She looked down at the satin mask winking in the gloom, wondering what the night might reveal. Taking a deep breath, she quickly tied on her mask. The carriage door opened, and the footman let the steps down. Lady Dreggins awoke with a snort. Amaryllis alighted and marshaled her reserves for whatever lay ahead.

Matthew leaned against a pillar and watched the dancers in their glittering, feathered masks and colorful costumes. He wore a simple black domino over his evening clothes and a plain black silk mask.

I hope my plan works. If it doesn't, I will be made the fool. He had the idea put about that he was considering wearing the costume of a Renaissance gentleman before making it known he would be unable to attend. Matthew regretted using deception to achieve his aims, but this had become a matter of life and death.

He stiffened. A man clad in a doublet, hose, and plumed hat strolled past.

"La," the costumed figure said in a high falsetto. "I just pine to waltz with my fiancée Amaryllis Sinclair. Have she and that dragon aunt arrived yet?"

Bertie! He took the bait! His cousin was of a similar height and physique and spoke in that ridiculous voice, making it easy for someone to take the imposter as the viscount. He cringed as Bertie continued to make a complete cake of himself. *Poor Amaryllis! Did I disgust her as much as my cousin disgusts me? Faugh, what a coxcomb!*

He continued to watch his cousin prance and simper. *Now, if only Bertie will take this charade all the way.*

"Matthew!"

The soft utterance made him twist around. He saw Amaryllis, a vision in shimmering white and silver satin, looking past him to the Renaissance imposter she obviously thought was her real fiancé. Despite her mask, he saw her rigid stance and the high color of her cheeks.

Bertie approached her, flickering a lacy handkerchief in her face. "Remember my rank and title when you address me, my pert country miss."

Amaryllis's lips firmed, and she sank into a low curtsy. "My lord viscount."

Matthew glared at his cousin for his impertinence, only to realize Snell was just mimicking what he'd seen.

Bertie held out his arm. "Your manner pleases me, therefore I shall deign to dance with you for the cotillion. No, I shall accept no words of gratitude. It is enough to know you will cherish this for years to come."

Matthew seethed, breathing through his teeth as they whirled away in the figures of the dance. *Posturing popinjay!*

Amaryllis bit her lip, fighting against a wave of tears. Her fiancé was behaving like the veriest fool! Surely he didn't need to act so when they were together. To think she'd allowed her feelings for him to grow warmer.

How can he be party to any plot while he's leering at me like any half-pay captain? She lowered her gaze. *But Matthew never leers. He plays the part of the fop, but he has never taken such license.*

Amaryllis studied her cavalier when they met in the figures of the dance. Dark eyes glinted from his heavily sequined mask. Despite the similarity of color, something wasn't right. Could it be someone else? Could this be part of Matthew's plan?

Deciding to do a little investigation of her own, she smiled at her partner. "Such a comfort to join you in prayer the other day, my lord."

"Prayer!" he scoffed. "Waste of time, Miss Sinclair. Religion is naught but for women and fools."

A wave of relief washed over Amaryllis. Even in jest, Matthew wouldn't speak so. Heart pounding, she confined her comments to harmless prattle for the remainder of the dance.

At last it came to an end. Before she could scan the ballroom for a glimpse of her true fiancé, a man in a black domino approached her and bowed over her hand. Suppressing a surge of disappointment, she bobbed a curtsy and joined him in the waltz.

Chapter 11

Looking for someone, miss?" Matthew asked in a purposefully husky voice, watching as Amaryllis's masked gaze swung back to him.

Coloring up, she shook her head and stared at his cravat as they whirled about the room. Silk flowers with jeweled centers winked in her hair, and the stuff of her gown floated around her body. He thought of the sweetness of her spirit, and the quiet dignity with which she comported herself.

The newness of his feelings, discovered when he was at his weakest, had been shaken in the cold light of day by the incessant worry that she was marrying him for his money. If only he could be sure.

"Your fiancé, perhaps?" he pressed. "You are fortunate in securing such a prize. 'Tis said he's rich and you naught but a poor parson's daughter."

"Sir," she said through clenched teeth, "your manner is most unbecoming."

A savage desire for the truth urged him on. "It's more becoming than that of a scheming adventuress."

Amaryllis stopped and stared at him with a fiery gaze and clenched fists. "You go too far, sirrah! I would marry Viscount Leighton if he didn't have a farthing!" She spun on her heel and pushed her way through the dancers.

Matthew watched her go until she disappeared from view, the meaning of her words heaped like burning coals on his head. He cursed his hard heart—and his lack of trust—and feared his harsh words might have cost him the woman he loved.

"Aunt Agatha," Amaryllis said breathlessly when she reached that lady's side, "have you seen Lord Leighton?"

Her aunt stared at her. "Are you blind?" She pointed with her fan. "There he is, heading for the card room."

Amaryllis saw the man with whom she'd danced the cotillion. How could she voice her doubts that he was her real fiancé?

Lady Dreggins turned to a dowager, with whom she'd been conversing. "Imagine, a girl not even recognizing her own betrothed!"

Amaryllis loosened the strings of her mask and removed it, intending to find the ladies repairing room where she could sort through her jumbled thoughts. Had she really just declared herself to a complete stranger?

Had she really fallen in love with her own fiancé?

The motion of the crowds heaved like waves of the sea, making her dizzy. She wanted nothing more than to find Lord Leighton and—

And what? Tell him you love him? Tell him you want to marry him? Tears burned her eyes. *He's made it plain he doesn't want you!*

Amaryllis put her hand to her head, taking deep breaths to

clear her mind. *If I tell him, his reaction will be that of the man in the domino—cynicism and suspicion.* She glanced up to see Fanny being led by Mr. Haddon in the figures of a Scottish reel. She envied their simple courtship. They had no secrets between them.

Suddenly she knew she must tell Matthew the truth, regardless of his reaction.

More than anything, Matthew longed to find Amaryllis and reveal himself, but at that moment, his cousin sauntered by, heading in the direction of the card room. Matthew threaded his way through the crowd at the edge of the dancing, barely able to keep sight of the florid hat bobbing ahead of him. Bertie disappeared into the card room.

Matthew tried to go faster but was impeded by the ball guests gathering to watch the leaps of the more talented dancers. One dancer jumped up only to lose his balance and careen to one side.

A wave of people was pushed back from the impact. Costumed guests stumbled in his direction. A man, obviously drunk, reeled against Matthew, knocking his mask askew, crashing him to the floor, and landing on his bad leg.

Ladies shrieked and went into faints while others chanted the showy dancers to greater heights. Ripping off his mask in fury and pain, Matthew pushed the sodden man off his leg and struggled to get up.

A gasp right above him caught his attention. He looked up.

Amaryllis!

"Matthew," she whispered, hardly able to believe her eyes. His dark gaze and flushed face seemed to mirror her own thoughts. Beyond them, a kaleidoscope of humanity twirled past, oblivious to the quiet tableau in their midst.

She stretched out her hand, attempting to help him up. He took it and slowly rose. Leaning against her, he staggered out into the hall, where he collapsed onto a bench and struggled to catch his breath.

"I fear this wound will not heal completely," he said in a low voice. "I feel like a doddering old man!"

"I'm sure you just need more time, my lord, and. . .and I shall offer my prayers on your behalf." Amaryllis twisted her hands together, knowing her face was scarlet. The real issue was not Matthew's leg but what he must think of her after her declaration. His steady gaze gave her no answers.

"Who was that man I danced with earlier?" she ventured as he remained silent. "He said he was you."

Matthew looked away and shook his head. "It's too late," he said in a choked voice. "I can barely walk right now."

She stared at him, frowning. "What's too late? Why would that man say he was you? I don't understand."

"Make haste, man!" Perry Haddon appeared, as out of breath as his friend. "I just heard that Snell insulted Lord McAlister in the card room."

Suddenly, the fog cleared in her brain. Bertie! The plot! Amaryllis turned and dashed toward the card room, ignoring the oaths that followed her as she rudely shoved past the bodies congregating around the card tables.

The man in Renaissance garb struck a man in a red silk domino, Lord McAlister. "Name your seconds!"

Amaryllis felt faint as she understood Bertie's intention of masquerading as Matthew in order to get him killed in a duel. McAlister would expect Matthew, not Bertie, to meet him on the field of honor—and when Matthew didn't show up, the man would be even more incensed and challenge him personally. Even if Matthew survived, his reputation would forever be in ruins. She struggled to formulate a plan, knowing she had to do something.

"Stop!"

Her clear voice rang out. Everyone turned toward her. Several men eyed her and made lewd comments about her appearance in a man's domain. Amaryllis suddenly wished for the anonymity of the mask but didn't have time to put it back on.

"It is a trick!" she continued, struggling to get air into her starved lungs amid the cloud of tobacco. "That is not Lord Leighton whom you have challenged, but his cousin Bertie Snell!"

The man in the red domino bridled like a horse. "What's this, Leighton, some kind of schoolboy prank? Remove your mask!"

Bertie impaled Amaryllis with a hate-filled gaze before spinning and bursting through the crowd surrounding him.

"Get him!" someone yelled.

Suddenly all the languid, drawling London bucks acted as one man and went after the escaping imposter. Shouts of *Halloa Halloa!* rent the air, as though it were a fox hunt.

Amaryllis gripped hold of a drape as they rushed past, needing something to keep her anchored. She closed her eyes, striving to regain her composure. *Please, Lord, let Bertie be discovered and Matthew kept safe!*

Finally, when all was quiet in the card room, she opened her eyes and walked out to the hall on trembling legs. The noise inside the ballroom took on a fevered pitch when Bertie was caught. She heard her name, along with the viscount's and his cousin's, among the babble of excited voices.

It worked! Thank You, Lord.

Amaryllis turned and saw Matthew where he sat on the bench in the deserted hall, his head in his hands. He looked up at her approach, his eyes dark and unreadable. She paused, unable to think beyond the thundering of her heart. A tenuous thread of emotion seemed to hover between them.

Matthew put out his hand. Amaryllis quickly closed the space between them and took it. He pulled her down next to him.

Her mouth dry, she took a deep breath. "I think Bertie has been exposed."

Matthew gripped her hand. "Miss Sinclair. . .Amaryllis," he said in a low voice, "what you said, was that true?"

She knew he wasn't referring to his cousin or the foiled plot. She gazed down at their clasped hands, her heart swelling with a suffocating longing for him to return her feelings—and with fear that he might be readying to make a mockery of her.

Deciding to unmask the burgeoning truth of her heart regardless of the consequences, she looked up at him and nodded. "It is true that I have fallen in love with you, my lord—"

"What's this I hear about you interfering with a duel, Amaryllis?"

They turned to see Lady Dreggins stumping into the room, her features crumpled and sour. "I told you it's unpardonable—that a man will never forgive such an insult even if it's a case of false identities. Ain't that right, Leighton?"

He opened his mouth to speak, but she cut him off with a wave of her cane.

"I suppose you'll be calling on the morrow to break the engagement. Well, for once, I can understand. What Amaryllis has done is beyond the pale, and should you cry off, it would be rightly so. Imagine such widgeon-like behavior, after all I've done for you, Amaryllis—"

Matthew cleared his throat. "If I might interrupt, Lady Dreggins."

He looked down at Amaryllis. The sweetness of his smile took her breath away, and the glimmering emotion in his eyes surely echoed the sentiment in her own heart.

Drawing her hand to his lips, his gaze caressing, he murmured, "Alas, I have fallen in love with your charge, my lady, and the engagement most certainly stands."

BONNIE BLYTHE

Bonnie Blythe is a homeschool mom of five and resides with her husband in Oregon's lush Willamette Valley. Her pastimes include being a part of her Ladies Bible Study at church, leading a literary book club, attempting to learn French and Latin, and one of these days she's really going to learn to play her fiddle better! She has always been an avid romance reader and believes God is the *true* author of romance. Visit www.bonnieblythe.com for more!

Moonlight Masquerade

by Pamela Marie Griffin

Dedication

With deep gratitude to all my critique partners, and especially to Professor Buddy Strittmatter and Ginny Aiken for your help with Spanish phrases.
Muchas gracias!

To my compassionate Lord, who helped me to step out from hiding behind a mask that concealed self-doubt and insecurity while showing me that I was precious in His sight.

Behold, I stand at the door, and knock:
if any man hear my voice, and open the door,
I will come in to him, and will sup with him, and he with me.
REVELATION 3:20

Chapter 1

London, England—1865

Dense, yellow fog shrouded the empty streets, causing Letitia to feel as lost as a soul in the tower's darkest dungeon. The night was wretched, unfit for man or beast. Yet for Letitia, her cousin's word was law.

Cautiously, she walked over the slick cobblestones, feeling as if she were nothing more than a fetching hound to a cruel mistress. A thankless slave. An unappreciated servant. It was a shame she didn't possess more than two feet on which to travel—like the cat that suddenly appeared out of nowhere with a screech that stopped her heart cold. It raced across her path toward the River Thames, which she assumed to still be on her left from the trickling of water she heard.

Shaking off the fright, Letitia drew the sack of pastries deeper within her cloak. She yearned to be soaking up the comfort of a warm coal fire. An uncomfortable tapping had begun just behind her left eye. Not quite an ache, as her hip was now aching, but a discomfort most certainly.

Through the fog, halos of light shone from the lamps along the streets, but not until she came upon them did their tall iron posts become apparent. Now and then, black hansom cabs rattled past, the creaks of their wheels and clacking of horses' hooves sounding far off. Head downward, Letitia pressed on, silently bemoaning her quandary.

A frantic whinny shrieked to her right followed by the jangling of harness. Hand flying up, as if to ward off an attacker, she twisted around. Her leg crumpled beneath her, and she fell. Heart frozen in terror, she watched a horse emerge from the fog like a phantom, rearing upward. Its lethal hooves crashed down within inches of her cowering form.

The driver cursed at Letitia, ordering her out of the street as he fought to regain control. The beast's hoof had landed on the edge of her cloak, trapping her.

Unexpectedly, someone stooped beside her. Large, warm hands covered her shoulders. "Are you hurt?" a masculine voice asked near her ear. The man looked down where the horse trapped her, and with slow grace, he stood. Speaking quietly to the horse, he took hold of its bridle. The beast calmed and eased backward off her cloak.

"You there!" the driver yelled. "Away from my horse. The fool wench has made me late as it is."

The man said nothing, only dropped his hands away and looked at the driver, whose heavy-jowled face could be discerned in the wagon's torchlight. Letitia wished she could see her rescuer's expression, also, for certainly it must be fierce. The driver averted his gaze as though cowed and drove away.

Letitia began to push herself off the cobblestones. Her

rescuer was again beside her, assisting her to stand.

"I was unaware that I'd wandered into the middle of the street." She felt the utmost fool. The fog had captured sound and tricked her into believing the wagon was farther away, but had she not been engaging in self-pity, she might have been more attentive.

His hands were gentle; she wondered why he wore no gloves. Surely this must be a man of distinction, as noble as his character appeared.

"This isn't fit weather for you to be out walking. Come. My driver will take you home."

Hesitant, Letitia looked up. She could see little of his face, since his hat was angled low over his forehead. "No, truly." She took a few steps backward. "I can manage."

He frowned. "You're hurt! See there—you're limping. I insist you allow my driver to take you home." He took firm hold of her elbow and began leading her to the other side of the street where a torchlight's glow pierced through the curtain of fog. A coach emerged. "I'll hear no more on the matter."

"Really, I—I shouldn't." Letitia stopped. "The pastries!"

He left her and returned with the parcel, smashed from where she'd fallen atop it. "I'm sorry. Your pastries appear to be ruined."

Letitia refused to think of her cousin Lady Marian's reaction when she discovered there would be no sweet cakes for her late night tea. The merchant had surely left with his cart once the fingers of fog thickened while the lamplighters had climbed their ladders and lit the streetlamps.

"Come, let us remove ourselves from this place," the stranger said, again steering her toward the coach.

In a daze, Letitia took scant note of her movements yet managed the awkward step up into his coach. He released her elbow, and she sank to the bench seat. "I'm grateful for your kindness, sir, but I've no wish to trouble you."

With stealthy grace, he moved to the opposite seat. "Nonsense. No trouble at all."

Letitia gazed fully at the countenance of her benefactor. In the flickering light of the globed torch near the window, his eyes appeared a soft bluish gray, the color of a storm-washed sky on a gentle dawning, when the earth stood quiet as it struggled to breathe again. If peace had a color, his eyes would be the bearer of it. She noted the coarse weave of his drab clothing and assumed him to be a servant such as she. Perhaps he was some fine lord's gentleman and a man of great worth. A servant whose master deigned important enough to send out into the night with proper transport. Indeed, the coach in which she sat with its crimson leather seats, gold fittings, and the intricate brocade lining its inside walls appeared that of a nobleman's.

His finely chiseled lips curled into a smile revealing even teeth. "One problem remains. For my driver to take you to your place of residence, you must tell me where you live."

"*Sí*—yes, of course." Letitia felt flustered that she should be caught so boldly staring. "I reside on the other side of Covent Garden, in Belgrave Square, at Lord Ackers's manor."

"A fair piece for you to be walking," he said in some surprise. "This district isn't safe."

"I was on an errand for my mistress while it was still

daylight. The fog thickened upon me unawares and evening came."

He alerted the driver of their destination, and then before she was aware of his intent, he shrugged out of his woolen cloak and wrapped it around her shoulders. "This may help to take the chill off. You're trembling, poor child."

The garment felt pleasantly warm from the heat of his body, and Letitia's cheeks blazed at the intimate gesture. She darted a glance his way, noting his fine breadth of shoulder and trim build in the simple clothes. Aware of her own unsightly appearance, with her fog-dampened hair plastered in clumps against her face and her skirt filthy with mud, she lowered her gaze.

"You're very kind, sir," she said as the coach jounced along the cobbled street. "I pray my fall won't be the cause of your finding trouble with your master. Will he mind your tardy return?"

A look of incomprehension crossed his features before a glimmer of realization entered his eyes. "Don't be concerned for my welfare. I shan't suffer at the hand of Lord Dalworth." He glanced toward the window, putting an end to their conversation.

Soon the carriage rolled to a stop. The driver opened the door to the familiar sight of the Ackers's four-story manor apparent through the veil of fog. Letitia shrugged out of his cloak to return it, but his hand on her arm stopped her. "Keep it. I'll send a messenger for it in the morning."

"Oh, but—"

"I insist. You're still shivering."

Not knowing the proper way to respond to such benevolence, she nodded. "*Vaya con Diós*—God go with you."

Drawing the man's cloak about her, Letitia hurried to the

side of the house. The lonely, hollow sound of hoofbeats trailed away on the cobblestones. Before taking the stairs down to the servants' entrance, she turned to watch what little she could see of the coach's slow retreat.

Edward pondered the encounter as the driver transported him home. Home. A far cry from India, to be sure. Already he missed the hot, sunny days and the glorious, royal sunsets above the perimeter of jungle that enclosed the plantation. England's weather was abominable compared to the exotic land of sunshine from which he'd come. True, India had its monsoon season, but it seemed as if rain made a permanent home over London. If it wasn't raining, fog as thick as treacle smothered the city. Days of clarity were few, and the countless coal fires belching black smoke into the air did little to help. Still, his place was not to disregard orders given him, and so he'd undertaken the journey to England alongside the man who'd proven to be a trial, the man to whom he must answer for the next few weeks.

As the coach rattled forward, his attention drifted to the slight indentation the girl had left on the leather cushion. Never had he seen such big brown eyes ringed by such thick lashes. Her skin had been pale from shock, but in normal circumstances he assumed the color to be as creamy and white as a dove's breast. Her slim jaw had been pronounced, her nose narrow, her cheekbones high, though without the usual rosiness he'd perceived on other girls of her youth.

From the little he could see of her face within its gray hood, she'd been a comely lass, and her Spanish accent gave her soft husky voice added delight. Still, it did no good to dwell on pleasures of which he could never partake. The duke had given him an order, and Edward must see it through, however taxing the mission might be.

Heaving a resigned sigh as the coach traveled alongside St. James's Park toward his destination of Mayfair, he directed his attention toward the upper story of Buckingham Palace appearing above the fog. His brief stay in London had brought him no closer to resolutions. Nor did the prospect of a week in the country assuage the guilt of taking on the challenging role he soon must play.

Chapter 2

"It was always said of Scrooge, that he knew how to keep Christmas well, if any man alive possessed the knowledge,' " Letitia read. " 'May that be truly said of us, and all of us! And so, as Tiny Tim observed, God Bless Us, Every One!' "

Little Sally lay on her mother's cot, looking up at Letitia with shadowed dark eyes. "Miss Ticia, why did God let ye get huwt like Tiny Tim?"

Letitia closed Dickens' story *A Christmas Carol.* With Michaelmas Term recently upon them, it just being October, the selection of the child's favorite story might seem odd to some. But the novel was the only one her mother possessed, a gift given to her by the Dowager Viscountess Ackers. The cook couldn't read but treasured the book, nonetheless.

Letitia brushed back limp flaxen strands from Sally's pinched face, thankful the child's eyes were no longer fever-bright. "God wasn't the cause of my injury, Sally. I chose not to heed wise counsel and was confident I could jump a wall though I'd learned such a maneuver mere weeks before." She didn't add that she still often had difficulty obeying those in authority.

"And they had to shoot the ho'se?" The little brow creased.

Letitia nodded. "His foreleg was broken. There was nothing left to be done. I was but three and ten, and the harrowing incident served to teach me a difficult lesson. We must listen to those older and wiser. Had I listened to my *papá*, I would walk without a limp today." Letitia smiled. "That said, it's time for you to rest."

Sally's eyelids were already drooping. The straw mattress rustled as Letitia rose and covered the child with a woolen blanket. She lowered the flame in the lamp and left the servant quarters, taking the stairs to her room.

Before her hand could touch the glass doorknob, quick footsteps padded toward her.

"Where have you been?" Cousin Marian asked, a bite to her words.

"I was reading to the cook's daughter."

Marian sniffed. "Why do you waste your time on that urchin each night when you could be attending me? I don't know why papa doesn't dismiss the cook; her pastries are horrid. Speaking of which, have you brought my cakes?"

Letitia silently counted to three to compose herself before answering. "I'm sorry. I had an accident. The cakes are ruined."

"Ruined, are they?" Marian's green eyes flashed sparks. "Can you not carry out even the simplest of tasks?"

"It was the fog; a horse nearly ran me over—"

"Never mind." Marian stalled her apology with an uplifted hand. "I don't wish to hear excuses. Really, Letitia, you shall need to improve on your serving skills if you're to accompany me to the country in two weeks and attend me there."

"The country?"

"Yes." Marian's chin rose in a patronizing manner. "My family received an invitation last week to the Duke of Steffordshire's estate. Father has said we shall accept. The duke is my father's second cousin, as you must know since he was discussed at Lady Filmore's tea three days past. Everyone of importance will be at the ball he'll hold. It's considered quite an honor and a privilege to attend one of his affairs. . . ."

With half an ear, she listened to Marian rave on. Letitia viewed the ladies' teas as an excuse for idle gossip, and she assumed she must have excused herself from the women's company prior to them discussing the duke. Though she couldn't partake in London's social season, having never been presented to the queen, once she turned seventeen, Grandmama had insisted Marian take Letitia on informal outings. Yet she often escaped any tedious gatherings to walk the grounds or visit the stables. Her absence never resulted in anyone's undue distress. She was only allowed to attend because of Grandmama's influence. No decent member of society would have her otherwise.

". . .And such a scandal it caused!" Marian's expression hinged between disgust and excitement. "Of course, no one dares speak of the matter in good society."

"What?" Letitia's attention became fully aroused. "What scandal?" Surely she wasn't rehashing the so-called folly of Letitia's mother once again.

"The duke's son—Lord Dalworth. Have you not been listening to a word I've said?" Marian frowned. "Really, Letitia. I was bringing up the fact that the marquis' intended, Lady Anne

Salinger, was discovered to have a lover whom she frequently met on the high moors. When she didn't return to the manor, her maid, who knew of their nighttime trysts, went in search of the lady and found her horse to have thrown her. Since that time, she's been destined for Bedlam, though her father will not relinquish her. She carries a china doll wherever she goes and speaks to it. The incident created a fine scandal, especially since Lord Dalworth had recently returned from abroad for the wedding. It's been said they quietly dissolved the engagement, and the marquis will be looking to take another wife. I'm confident that this is the reason for our weeklong hiatus to Hepplewith Manor."

Marian extracted a fan and cooled herself, as if what she'd just divulged had shocked her into vapors, though Letitia knew better. " 'Tis rumored the marquis will look for a wife from among those guests invited. He's destined to inherit a silk plantation in India and so much more."

"Poor Lady Salinger," Letitia murmured.

"Hardly! Letitia, do you not yet understand?" Marian looked put out. "Lady Anne Salinger was with child, unwed since she and the marquis were yet to be married. And she'll not give the name of the man whom she took as her lover."

"Oh!" Letitia felt the heat of embarrassment's blush. "But why should she do such a thing when she was promised to the marquis?"

"Oh, you truly are hopeless." Marian's gaze swept to the ceiling. "You might as well have lived on the other side of the moon than in Spain. And I'd heard the people were so passionate in your homeland. Never mind. I'm retiring to my room for the evening and won't require further assistance. But I'll want those tea cakes on the morrow!"

Marian whirled to go in a froth of ruffles and lilac scent. Before Letitia could retire to her own room, Lady Ackers's petite maid hurried her way. "Her ladyship'll be wanting a word with ye, miss."

"Thank you, Bertha." Letitia moved down the corridor to a bedchamber, the largest in Windham Hall.

Dowager Viscountess Regina Ackers stood in her sitting room, facing the fire, with her gnarled hand cupped over a mahogany cane and her back to Letitia. Dressed in a blue satin bed robe and white nightcap with lappets hanging down either side, she hardly looked intimidating. Yet appearances were deceptive.

The elderly matriarch had once dined with queens and princes and had lived a thoroughly fascinating life. It was said that Queen Victoria greatly admired this woman, who spoke her mind and did as she pleased, and in the days before age robbed her strength, Lady Ackers received many an invitation to the royal court. Everyone stood in awe—and many of those, in fear—of the great dowager viscountess.

She turned regally, her posture as erect as it must have been in her youth when she dazzled the courts with her beauty. The portrait hanging above the mantel claimed testimony to that.

"Tell me, Letitia, when will you desist in allowing my granddaughter to make a spectacle of you and speak to you in such a manner?"

"Perhaps when I'm crowned Queen of England," Letitia returned wryly. "Yet even then my coz will doubtless consider herself more lofty than I."

Lady Ackers's mouth twitched at the corners. "Come, sit by the fire. I have a matter of import to discuss with you."

Letitia did so, relaxed in her company. They shared a strange bond, one Letitia never fully understood. With Lady Ackers, she could be herself. She was allowed and encouraged to lapse into her native Spanish tongue, which Marian, who didn't know the language, forbade. Due to her fond feelings for Lady Ackers, who herself could converse in Spanish, Letitia had given in to the woman's desire to call her Grandmama, though they weren't related.

"You shall go to Steffordshire," the woman declared, sitting across from Letitia on her settee. "But not as a companion to Marian. No, indeed. You shall arrive as a lady, the lady you were meant to be. And you will be the one to win the heart of the handsome marquis."

Letitia laughed. "*¡Seguro que bromeas!*" The woman was dear to her heart, but Letitia presumed that senility often robbed her of sound reasoning.

"I? Jest? No, Letitia, I'm quite serious."

"I very much doubt a marquis would show interest in a poor relation of the Ackers, and a woman coming from a background of scandal at that." Especially after what Marian had divulged about the unfortunate marquis and his recent state of affairs.

The old woman harrumphed and banged her cane on the plush rug. "The earl was a fool to disown your mother. He would have had her wed to a cruel old codger destined for the casket. Indeed, Lord Rotsby died of old age not six months from the day

Kathryn eloped with your father."

Letitia remained silent, not wanting to speak about what the nobility viewed as her mother's fall into disgrace.

"I've decided. You shall go. I will write Beatrice, informing her of the need to prepare for an extra guest."

That she referred to the duchess in such familiar terms bespoke her close ties with the woman. "And will you also attend, Grandmama?"

"I?" The woman gave a shrug that might have been considered graceful if her expression weren't so dour. "Perhaps, if I'm well. Perhaps not. But you shall go, Letitia, and do not change the subject as I sense you are doing. You will be provided with adequate frocks, of course, and I shall send my abigail along to assist you."

Her lady's maid? "But who will serve Lady Marian?"

"Rose did before you came. She can do so again."

"What of my aunt? Who will dress her hair if not Rose?"

"Hester is indisposed. She cannot be seen in public until her time arrives."

"Sí, of course." Letitia's cheeks flamed at the reference to her aunt's delicate condition.

"No, Letitia. I've made up my mind. You shall go as a guest, not a servant. And I'll not hear another word on the matter." Lady Ackers banged her cane once more before she stood. "I am weary; the hour is late. We'll speak more of this another time."

Letitia rose and kissed the soft, wrinkled cheek. If she could have chosen a grandmother, this is the woman she would have chosen. Still, Letitia wondered what Marian would say to this new development, given that Lady Ackers's will was rarely crossed.

"Papa was a fool to give in to Grandmama's wishes," Marian fumed two weeks later as the coach in which they sat rattled along a lonely country road bordered with stately poplars. "You'll never pass as a lady of breeding; never mind that you were tutored alongside me. Our family shall be made a laughingstock, and all because of Grandmama's ludicrous directive."

Withholding a sigh, Letitia stared at her cousin. Marian had dispensed with the usual sober traveling dress and had clothed herself in a splendid brocade gown, wanting to make a lasting impression upon those at Heppelwith Manor, as she'd earlier told Letitia.

Beside Marian, Rose stared out the coach's window, as if to dissociate herself from her lady's ranting—which had gone on for the better part of half an hour—and Bertha sat quietly beside Letitia. Normally, Lord Ackers would have shared the coach with his daughter, but he'd chosen to ride astride his horse and given the lady's maids access to the interior.

Letitia envied him and was certain at this moment neither Rose nor Bertha counted it a blessing to ride within.

"If this change of plans distresses you so, I could attend in disguise," Letitia suggested lightly when Marian paused to breathe.

"In disguise?" Marian frowned.

"As a friend of the family. I could attend under a different name rather than be introduced as a relation."

Marian scoffed. "Really, Letitia. I should think you might

recognize the gravity of the situation rather than jest about it. 'Tis a shocking turn of affairs, and one that could well put an irreparable blotch on the Ackers's name—if you were to act in a manner unbefitting of the role you shall temporarily possess."

Letitia sighed. "I assure you, my lady, I, too, am not overly pleased with this arrangement." Most of her life she'd helped her family with farming, and then she'd lived three years in servitude as a companion to Marian. Now she was expected to take on the role of a lady of leisure? The prospect was daunting.

"You say you're not 'overly pleased,' which leads me to believe there is in fact some amount of pleasure involved." Marian's green eyes were calculating. "A word of caution, Letitia. Do not forget who you truly are. A pauper you were born, and a pauper you shall remain. And keep away from the marquis!" The last directive came out clipped.

Letitia had no interest in hooking a marquis' attention; the thought was absurd. Even if he were to show interest, such an emotion would wane once he realized her true state of affairs. Although her family could hardly be considered paupers, they did possess little. Yet if love had been a commodity by which to live, her parents would reign as king and queen, and she and her siblings as princesses and princes. For the measure of love, they possessed in abundance.

"Why do you smile so?" Marian's eyes narrowed in suspicion.

"I was thinking of my parents and my brothers and sisters. I miss them."

Marian gave a disdainful little huff and looked out the window.

Letitia relaxed against the seat. Minutes of blissful silence elapsed before a commotion erupted outside and galloping hoofbeats were heard.

"You there," a shout came. "Pull aside!" The jangling of harness and creaking of wood ceased as the coach jolted to an abrupt stop, almost sending Letitia into Marian's lap.

"Stand and deliver!" came another command.

Letitia's eyes went wide.

Highwaymen!

The door flew outward, revealing a man with a black kerchief tied around his jaw. In one black-gloved hand, he aimed the barrel of a pistol in their direction.

"Well, and what have we here?" he sneered. "Come out, my pretties."

Rose crossed herself while Bertha uttered a low moan of despair. Letitia's own heart seemed to have lurched to a stop.

Chapter 3

When no one made a move to alight, the highwayman grabbed Bertha's arm and heaved her from the coach. Shrieking, she went flying to the dirt and landed on her knees.

"Come out, and no trouble will befall you," he instructed Letitia and the others.

"Do as he says, Daughter," Lord Ackers's shaky voice came from without.

"Go on," Marian whispered to Letitia. "You first."

Bottling up her fear, seeking to be courageous, Letitia moved to step down. Marian assumed a stance behind her.

The late afternoon sun blinded as Letitia struggled to see who waylaid them. Three men, one on horseback, circled the carriage. One had his pistol trained on Lord Ackers and the driver, now absent from his box seat. The other bandit watched from his mount. All had black silk kerchiefs tied around their faces and wore broad-brimmed hats. Their manner of clothing appeared as if it had been pulled from a trunk of a bygone day.

"Come, hand it over," commanded the man who'd ordered them out. He held open a large drawstring pouch.

"What is it you wish from us?" Letitia asked.

"What, indeed?" he mocked, his glare cutting into her. "Your jewels, of course!"

Marian clapped a hand to her elaborate necklace. "No," she breathed. "You shan't have them."

"Do as he says, Marian," her father instructed, "and they'll let us go in peace. Their leader has given his word."

Letitia doubted the word of a highwayman but remained silent. The clink of metal and Marian's sniffle informed Letitia the girl had done as ordered. While one of the bandits tossed the luggage from the carriage's boot and began sorting through it for valuables, the first highwayman approached Letitia. "Your jewels, also, if you please."

"I have none."

"A lady traveling without gemstones to flaunt?" He stepped closer, and Letitia forced herself not to recoil. "Be warned, if you don't remove them from wherever you've hidden them on your person, I shall remove them myself."

"And I tell you, I have no jewels. Moreover, if you lay a hand on me, I can promise you it will be a decision sorely made and one you'll greatly lament."

He raised his hand to strike her. Letitia, having endured the sting of Marian's hand a number of times, was not cowed.

"Enough!" the mounted rider called, the first time he'd spoken. With languid grace, he dismounted and approached. The first highwayman stepped away.

"Have I your word you carry no valuables?" The leader

spoke almost in a whisper, as he took his stand in front of Letitia. His blue gray eyes above the kerchief gleamed with something akin to admiration, amusement, and more.

"Yes." Mesmerized by his stare, she could find no voice to protest when he lifted his fingers and stroked her neck. Something cold and rough rubbed against her skin—the feel of a gemstone—and she realized he must be wearing one of his ostentatious rings backwards.

"Ah, but what have we here?" His smooth fingers plucked from her high collar the thin silver chain upon which hung a cross. He held the minute symbol of her faith against one fingertip and rubbed the bottom half with his thumb.

Letitia swallowed. "A jewel such as you covet, this is not, as you can plainly see. It is but a token *mi madre* gave me. Worth little save for its sentiment."

He looked up into Letitia's eyes. A strange mix of fear and excitement made her blood pound in her temples. There was something strangely familiar about those eyes. . . .

At last, he released his hold on the cross.

"You speak rightly. 'Tis of no value to me. Keep your talisman, my lady." Swiftly he turned and addressed the others. "Come away. We've tarried too long."

He mounted his chestnut mare while his two lackeys did the same with their horses. As he settled on his saddle, his focus again went to Letitia. Removing his hat, he swept it over his breast and out to the side, effecting an elaborate bow. "And so, without further adieu, we bid you good day."

Spurring his horse, he took off in a cloud of dust, the other highwaymen trailing him into a distant copse of trees.

"Well, I never," Marian fumed. "Papa, why do you stand and stare? Are you not going in pursuit? Those were some of my most exquisite jewels."

Lord Ackers moved to his horse. "I shall report the matter once we reach Heppelwith Manor. Until then, there's little to be done."

Pouting, Marian ordered Letitia and the other servants to retrieve the remaining contents of the luggage strewn over the ground. Once they completed their task, the driver again secured the trunks in the boot.

The remainder of the journey passed in relative silence. By the time the coach reached its destination, it bore a somber party indeed.

Letitia stared at the multistoried, gabled structure of Heppelwith Manor. Welcoming light poured forth from tall windows along the ground floor and a few smaller arched windows on the floors above. Half full, the moon had arisen beyond the sprawling country manor, outlining the expansive rolling grounds and silvering a still pond flanked by trees.

Letitia sensed a shadow at a window and lifted her attention there. The broad-shouldered form of a man looked down upon them.

Edward watched the tardy guests alight from the carriage with the aid of the footmen. Four women stepped down, one wearing a splendid gown that appeared ill-suited for travel. Light from the lower windows illumined the face of another lady as she turned her attention upward. His breath mired in his throat, and he stood stock-still.

"Edward?" The voice of the duchess interrupted his thoughts. He turned from the window as her plump form filled the entryway. "There you are. Tell me, are you still determined to go through with this outlandish scheme of yours?"

He nodded once.

She sighed. "Very well. I've only just now learned that thieves accosted Lord Ackers and his party during their journey. This makes the second daylight robbery by highwaymen since you and William arrived from India two months past. See about fetching the constable, will you?"

"Of course. No one was hurt?"

"There's no need to summon a physician, though poor Lady Marian is beside herself with the loss of her jewels."

"I'll leave at once."

"Edward?"

He halted his rapid trek to the door.

"You are aware I don't approve?"

"Yes, well aware," he said quietly, not needing her to elaborate. "But as things stand, I see no other recourse."

Before she could detain him with yet another homily about trusting God, he left her presence.

Upon descending the curved stairway, he caught sight of the new arrivals near the foyer, one woman in particular. The same who'd looked up at him while he'd stood at the window.

She stood near twin oil lamps bracketed to the wall. Their muted glow brought out the shine of her dark curls within the beribboned gray bonnet. Her manner of dress was tasteful, simple. While a servant took their cloaks, she turned impossibly huge, dark eyes Edward's way.

A jolt of familiarity struck—he assumed that's what robbed him of breath—before she dropped her gaze to the black-and-white tiles. Hearing the duchess descend the stairs behind him to see to her guests, Edward continued to the servants' wing.

Yet all during his mission, the girl with the haunting brown eyes never left his thoughts.

Letitia was shown into the bedchamber she would share with Marian. Her cousin's disparaging gaze darted about the large room with its modicum of furniture. "The canopy is small." Placing her palm against the high mattress, Marian pushed down twice as though to judge its softness, then pulled at the braided cord holding back the bed curtain. The olive-green drape whooshed alongside the bed. "It will have to do, I suppose."

"It's a delightful room," Letitia said. "I'm well pleased."

"Yes, you would be." Marian's mouth compressed. "Really, Letitia, must you be so gauche? Your behavior downstairs was reprehensible. One would think you'd never viewed a fine estate with the way you gawked at the furnishings, yet you've resided at my father's estate for the better part of three years."

Letitia held her tongue. Windham Hall, with its slightly worn furnishings, could hardly compare to the splendor of Heppelwith Manor. For Marian to wed the wealthy marquis would benefit the Ackers. If her cousin was correct about their reason for being here, such a manner of choosing a bride—by inviting eligible women from all over the countryside and choosing from among them—seemed odd to Letitia. Yet she'd long ago learned of the eccentricities of the titled and wealthy.

Marian preened in front of a standing oval mirror, pinching cheeks already rosy. "Our dreadful encounter with those robbers delayed us from a prompt arrival, but it worked to my advantage. We're the talk of the evening." Her eyes gleamed as she turned from the cheval glass. "Mine will be a name the marquis shall not easily forget. Did you see him? Was he not dashing?"

Letitia recalled the tall, fashionable gentleman, a trifle brusque and loud, with wavy brown hair and long sideburns. He'd been standing surrounded by a bevy of fawning, chattering women.

"I saw him." She poured water from a widemouthed pitcher into a matching porcelain basin to wash her face and hands.

"He's so debonair." Marian clasped her hands beneath her chin and came close to swooning. "The duchess mentioned that except for those functions they've planned, we're free to do as we wish during our stay. I have no doubt the marquis will be keeping close watch over those women presently unattached so as to choose his bride. And I plan to be in his vicinity often. I will be the marchioness."

Weary of the incessant talk of the marquis, Letitia dried her hands on a linen towel.

"How do you plan to amuse yourself?" Marian's words bore a sharp edge.

"I noticed a maze in the gardens. Perhaps I shall also visit the stables."

Marian softly snorted. "One would think that your childhood fall would leave you wanting nothing more to do with the creatures. Very well. Ride the horses. I care little what you do as long as you stay away from the marquis." So saying, she flounced away and called for Rose to tend her.

Expelling a lengthy breath, Letitia touched her cross and its comforting ridges. At least Marian didn't require her presence throughout their stay. The thought made Letitia's lips curl upward. There might be something to be said for Grandmama's idea, after all.

Chapter 4

The next morning passed without much to distinguish it from any other and certainly without the excitement of the previous day. A prisoner to her cousin's never-ending monologue, Letitia spent her early hours in the bedchamber she shared with Marian. A servant brought them scones and thick cream at Marian's command. Letitia grabbed one from the platter and bit into it with delight.

"Really, Letitia," Marian scoffed. "I do hope you conduct yourself in a more suitable manner when we're in the company of the duchess. You eat like one of the hogs."

As always, Letitia chose not to respond. In the privacy of their room, she didn't consider her behavior so horrid, especially since she was quite ravenous. A creature of habit, Letitia had been dressed since dawn in a soft plum day gown with wide pagoda sleeves flaring out from the elbows. Marian rose much later and took extreme measures with her appearance—over an hour to have her hair styled by Rose. Yet Letitia was usually the one on the other end of the brush. With nothing to keep her hands occupied, the minutes seemed to drag by like aged souls tottering on the verge of eternal sleep. Marian had expressly forbidden Letitia to make an appearance downstairs without her. She supposed it didn't matter. Years ago, she'd learned of the habit of the nobility to break the fast late in the morning and assumed customs at this country estate would be no different.

Half past eleven, Marian declared herself presentable, and they made their appearance downstairs. A servant showed them the way to the breakfast room.

Silver chafing dishes lined the sideboard, and guests served themselves. Letitia filled her plate with kippers, sausages, and eggs. Throughout their meal, Marian scanned the entryway, and Letitia assumed she searched for the absent marquis. Except for one doddering old gentleman with a chain fastened to a monocle that had the habit of falling into his plate, all the men were absent. Likely, they'd taken their meal earlier and now gathered in the smoking room or were off on a pheasant shoot.

Across the table from Letitia, next to the posy-papered wall, a servant in dark livery stood surveying the room of frivolous females. Letitia observed him, experiencing a peculiar recognition. When a guest inquired something of him, his benevolent smile made Letitia catch her breath. Before she could collect her thoughts, he turned on his heel and quit the room.

Letitia took note of her surroundings. Each of the eleven breakfast patrons was engaged in conversation, including her cousin.

Silently Letitia rose from the table and advanced in the direction she'd seen the servant go. The room in which she found herself opened to a small room with a fireplace. Spotting the manservant standing with his arm against the overmantel, she relaxed. Unaware of her presence, he lifted his hand, frowning as he looked upon it, then closed it into a fist and stared into the fire. How odd. . .

The duchess suddenly appeared at the door in another part of the room.

"Edward," she said with authority. "I must speak with you."

So her rescuer's name was Edward, for Letitia was almost certain that this was the man who'd come to her aid on London's foggy streets. She watched him approach the duchess; then together they disappeared into the next room.

Disappointed that her query would have to wait, she pivoted to return to the breakfast room and almost collided with a man behind her. She jerked back to avoid contact, but her leg gave way. A gasp left her lips, as his strong arm wrapped about her back. She, in turn, grabbed his other arm to prevent her fall.

She blinked in astonishment as she met the marquis' dancing eyes. He held her close a moment longer than appropriate. A wave of heat rushed to her face. She made as if to move back, and he dropped his arms to his sides. Quickly, she retreated.

"Have a care," he said. "The flooring is slick."

"Sí, I will try to remember." She didn't look at him again. Surely, her mind must be playing tricks on her. "*Gracias*, my lord."

He made no move to go, and she couldn't leave since he blocked her path.

"Have we met?" he asked.

"I am Letitia Laslos. Viscountess Ackers is my aunt."

"Of course. You arrived with the unfortunate Lady Marian who lost her treasured emeralds and diamonds to thieves. Pray tell, did you suffer a similar fate at the highwaymen's hands?"

His words sounded glib, and curiosity compelled Letitia to lift her gaze. Was he truly so unfeeling? "I was happy to escape a similar misfortune. The jewels stolen from my cousin had been her great-grandmother's. It is a difficult trial for her to bear."

The marquis offered a little shrug, then tilted his head in a manner both indifferent and assessing. "You've given your report to the constable?"

"Yes. However, I'm distressed to say that the sun blinded me, and I couldn't see the men clearly."

"Ah well." His smile was tight. "Fear not, dear lady. I'm certain these blackguards will be caught in due course. I must take my leave, but I hope we shall have opportunity for further discussion in the future. If you require anything, you've only to ask. It is my humble wish that your stay here at Heppelwith be an enjoyable one." Before she knew what he was about, he reached for her hand and bowed over it, holding it a fraction from his lips.

Letitia watched him stride away, his head high. He seemed anything but humble. Handsome, surely. Charming, debonair. But he lacked character. Letitia had been able to perceive that in the few minutes she'd conversed with him.

She stepped from the room—and halted in shock.

Marian stood outside the door, her eyes murderous.

Edward left the private parlor, his conversation with the duchess concluded. He heard a woman's voice raised in anger.

"How dare you defy me? Did I not explicitly tell you to stay away from the marquis? Be warned, Letitia. I'll not be crossed. Grandmama may have had her say in the matter of allowing you to masquerade as a lady, but you're still my servant."

"Yes, m'lady." These words came quiet, meek.

Curious as to what poor soul was receiving such an undeserved diatribe, Edward rounded the corner. The lovely woman he'd glimpsed the previous night glanced at him, her eyes widening. Her stance haughty, the woman he remembered as Lady Marian Ackers looked over her shoulder at him, then turned her attention to the timid girl who evidently bore the brunt of her ire. He assumed his servant's attire had summarily dismissed him from the lady's mind.

"We will speak more on the matter later," Lady Marian said in dulcet tones. "I've other affairs to which I must attend." She flounced away, the bell skirts of her yellow gown swishing with her actions.

Edward did a quick study of the other woman. Her huge eyes had narrowed, and her rosy mouth was pinched as she looked after her departing mistress. Ah! What's this? Perhaps the fair maiden was not so timid after all.

Before he could walk past, her hand lighted upon his sleeve, and he halted in surprise.

"Please, sir." She dropped her hand away with a becoming flush. "If I may have a moment of your time? Two weeks past, on a foggy night in London, I had the good fortune to receive aid from a stranger whose nature was the epitome of benevolence. Are you that man?"

Edward started in surprise. "The girl with the tea cakes." But this was no child, as he'd thought her then!

She awarded him with a most beatific smile. "Sí, 'tis I. Your kindness is surpassed only by your consideration, sir, if they're not one and the same. When the servant came to Windham Hall to fetch the cloak you'd lent me, I was amazed to receive your gift of tea cakes as well."

Edward inclined his head. "I'm delighted to hear the act brought you pleasure."

"Such a word seems inadequate, given the circumstances. Your thoughtful deed spared me a second chastising, since I was unable to replace them the following morning due to the rain."

"After witnessing the behavior of Lady Marian Ackers, I don't doubt it."

Her long lashes swept downward, and Edward realized he'd intruded where he had no right. "Forgive my lack of decorum. My only defense is that I detest seeing anyone mistreated." In India especially, he'd been appalled by the manner in which Lord Hathaway's servants were dealt. Perhaps the man could run the silk plantation upon which Edward lived, but he was not a merciful lord.

"Please don't misunderstand me. Lady Marian isn't so dreadful. Not compared to some of the nobles I've met." Her eyes grew large at her gaffe, and she swept her gaze to the tiles once more.

Edward was delighted. Not only was she loyal, she was also sweetly naive. Not polished to a hard sophisticated sheen like most of the women he'd met. "And you're not one of those greatly esteemed?"

"Indeed not. Surely you heard what my lady spoke?" At his slight nod, she continued, "I'm but a poor relation and, except for this week, my cousin Marian's companion. But please don't reveal this. It's supposed to be kept secret."

"Indeed?"

She nodded. "The Dowager Viscountess Ackers arranged it."

Ah, that explained it. "Your secret is safe with me. But tell me, why the intrigue?"

"She expressed her desire that I be treated as a lady this week. I almost was a lady, you see—" Her words abruptly ceased, as though she'd just become aware of what she revealed. Shock dissolved, the small chin went up, the slim shoulders straightened, and Edward received a glimpse of her proud, indomitable spirit. "My *mamá* denied her father's choice of a husband and eloped with the youngest son of a Spanish count. My papá. Because he's the youngest son, according to law he received nothing when his papá died. All the land and monies went to his eldest brother."

"I see. So you traveled from Spain by invitation to become a companion to your cousin?"

"Yes. Three years ago." Her shoulders wilted. "Oh, but why do I tell you this? Marian is right to say I'm gauche."

"Nonsense. I see nothing amiss in your manner, but then, having lived in India for six years, I'm accustomed to a more straightforward approach in conversation than that which is employed here in England."

"Then you were with the marquis? You are his valet?"

Edward hesitated. "Yes, I was with him. And now, dear lady, I have matters to which I must attend. Fear not; I shall keep your family secret. Nor will I reveal your little masquerade." He chuckled, thinking how her predicament mirrored his own trial to a degree. "Indeed, I believe the Dowager Viscountess is correct. You should be treated as a lady. And so, I hope you'll not deny me the pleasure of addressing you as such during the remainder of your stay." He stopped short of taking her hand, instead giving her a deferential nod. "If there's any way in which I can be of service, anything you require, you have only to ask."

"I'm already indebted to you, sir."

"Edward, please. And it would be my pleasure."

"Edward, then."

The image of her smile stayed with him long after he entered the marquis' chambers.

Chapter 5

The ten-course evening meal proved to be a formal affair. Served *à la russe* with footmen in constant but discreet attendance at the guest's elbows, everyone was given their choice of whatever dish was at hand.

On Letitia's right, a rotund man with a mole dotting his nose spoke with a French accent so thick Letitia struggled to understand him. Feigning interest, she nodded at times that seemed appropriate but had little idea what was said. To her left, a gentleman with a bulldog jaw seemed more interested in tippling his glass of claret and viewing the lovely flaxen-haired dinner guest across the table than in trying to partake of conversation, though he did manage a few amiable words. In between continual nods toward the talkative French count and a brief response on the rare occasions the other gentleman spoke, Letitia managed to swallow her serving of lamb cutlets and buttered asparagus with peas.

Once dinner ended, the gentlemen left for the smoking room, the women for the drawing room. A piano sat near closed curtains. At the ladies' urging, the duchess's daughter,

Lady Eleanor, went to it and claimed the seat. Letitia found a chair near the open door, which was removed from the others. While listening to Lady Eleanor play, she was alerted to the noise of men talking in the corridor.

"His *lordship* requests our presence." The low words came with swift contempt.

"Now?" His companion sounded no happier. "Why now?"

"Ours is not to question, but to obey. Has he not told us that often enough?"

"Huh! Let him issue orders for the present. One day we shall exact vengeance."

The first man agreed, and Letitia heard their footsteps depart but could scarcely think.

Those voices. . .she'd heard one of those men before. When he'd ordered her to hand over her jewels.

Capturing a deep breath, she slipped out of her seat as quietly as her wide crinoline skirt would allow and hastened to the corridor—to find it empty.

She pondered her dilemma. She must find Edward. He would know what to do.

A servant stood in front of the doors to the men's smoking chamber, and she moved toward him. "I must speak with Edward. Can you tell me where to find him?"

The man's snow-white brows hitched upward. "Edward, m'lady?"

"The marquis' servant."

He motioned with his white-gloved hand down the corridor's left.

"Thank you." Letitia moved that direction, her hip again

aching, and soon found herself faced with three scrolled doors. Two were closed, one stood ajar. She chose the latter.

The room lay in darkness save for branched candelabra flickering on a table against an opposite wall. Birdsong lilted to her ears. A partition of the two-story outside wall had been removed and replaced with a hexagon of glass, against which a light rain pattered. Inside the aviary, trees grew to the ceiling, their trunks rail-thin. Lush foliage dotted with multicolored birds decorated the somber room with color. Flutterings of wings filled her ears as she exhaled in wonder and moved forward.

"You dare mock me?" came a booming voice from a shadowed corner.

Letitia spun in surprise. Her leg went out from beneath her. She grabbed the back of a curved settee to curb her fall. "Sir! You gave me a fright." Her heart slowed its frantic pace. "Why should you accuse me of such a thing? I don't even know you."

Her eyes now accustomed to the scant light, she noticed a bearded gentleman reclined in a wing chair, one leg outstretched and resting on a low stool. With his walking stick, he pointed to his bandaged foot. "Can you not see? Are you blind as well as impertinent?"

"Are you always so rude?"

"*What?*" he sputtered.

Letitia drew herself up, despising the tears that threatened. With Marian, she'd resigned herself to take the abuse and not strike back. Otherwise, she might be sent home to Spain, which would surely cause her parents distress. Yet she refused to bear anyone else's cruelty.

"To answer your query, sir, I could not see when I first

entered the room. But I assure you, I would *never* make sport of anyone with an infirmity." Shaken, Letitia turned to make her escape but trembled so that she could barely walk.

"Stay, girl," he said gruffly. "I meant no harm. 'Tis this accursed gout that sharpens my tongue." When Letitia made no move toward the settee, he barked, "Sit down, I say!"

Although she wanted nothing more to do with the rude guest, she found herself doing as he said. Three years she'd been in servitude; following orders came naturally.

He peered at her beneath thick winged brows. "You say you're not mocking me, so I presume you've injured yourself in some manner?" When she didn't answer, he bellowed, "Well, speak up! I know you've a tongue in your head."

Letitia dug her nails into her palms to prevent herself from responding in kind. "My limp is due to an affliction I suffered as a child."

"Indeed? And does your limb pain you? You walk with great difficulty."

"Only during foul weather or when I've walked overly much."

"How did you come by it?"

His questions hinged on boorishness, but an air of authority cloaked him, making it impossible to deny his request. "When I was a child, I was given a horse by my uncle, one he no longer wanted. My father farms for him. In Spain."

She ignored his raised brow and continued. "It wasn't an extraordinary horse by any means, but it was mine. One day, I raced her and tried to take a low fence but failed. My hip was injured due to my fall."

"I see," he said thoughtfully, then grimaced as he shifted and jarred his foot. "You say you're the daughter of a laborer. Yet you speak as one well educated."

Letitia thought about not answering his pointed statement but sensed he would bully it out of her if she remained silent. She chose to tell him as little as possible. "What my mamá did not teach me, I learned alongside my cousin."

"Indeed?" he raised his brows. "And your cousin is. . . ?"

"Lady Marian Ackers."

"Then your mother must be Lady Kathryn Bellamy."

"She was."

Further conversation halted as Edward entered the room. "I must speak with you. . . , Your Grace." His last words came vaguely when he caught sight of Letitia.

Blood froze in her veins. If the color of her face could be seen in the dim lighting, it must be the cast of death. *Your Grace?* Oh, let the floor rip open and swallow her whole! The rude stranger with gout was the Duke of Steffordshire. Her host.

Letitia opened her mouth but remained mute. Should she rise to her feet and attempt a curtsey, or should she apologize for her former argumentative behavior?

Edward seemed to discern the cause of her discomfort. His glance was sympathetic before he turned to the duke. "The marquis wishes to speak with you on a matter most urgent."

"Oh, he does, does he?" The duke gave Edward a measuring look. "Very well, you may inform my son that I shall see him presently. First I wish you to assist this young woman to her room. Have one of the servants give her something for the pain. Perhaps some of that laudanum the physician left on one of his infernal visits."

Edward swung his gaze to Letitia. "You're injured?"

"No. Please, Y–your Grace." She stumbled over the title. "I need no special favors."

"You'll do as I say, Edward. You may both go." The duke glanced her way, a gleam in his eye. "At present, my condition leaves me in a most foul temperament, and I'm not fit company. Depicted as rude even."

Humiliated by the entire episode, Letitia felt the need to redeem herself in whatever small way possible. "I would presume to say, Your Grace, that such is the trial of everyone at one time or another. At times, I've been described to have a most horrid temperament. Grandmama Ackers has taught me to count silently before I speak."

"Indeed?" His lips twitched.

She clamped her mouth shut, aware she was allowing her tongue to outrun her thoughts again. Thankfully, the warmth of Edward's touch as he helped her to stand reassured her, sending pleasant tingles through her arm as he solicitously moved his hand to her elbow and assisted her to the door.

"Gracias," she said a little breathlessly once they were in the corridor. "I can manage."

"Perhaps, my lady. But I've been given my orders. I'll locate a servant to help you to your room where you can rest."

"Really—no. 'Tis only a trivial discomfort. I don't wish to return to my room."

"Then I shall find you a comfortable location in one of the sitting rooms."

She agreed and walked with him to a room decorated in yellows and greens. Gold drapes of damask were partially drawn, exposing the cold drizzle, but a fire in the grate welcomed her.

"This is the duchess's favorite room," Edward said.

"Will she mind me being here?"

His countenance gentled. "She has expressed her desire that all rooms on the ground floor be open to the guests."

He settled Letitia comfortably on a plump brocade sofa, propped a tasseled pillow behind her back, and went in search of a servant to make a medicinal tea. She felt ridiculous but had to acknowledge her pleasure at being waited on for a change. She would be dishonest if she didn't admit to enjoying this bit of pampering and the concerned attention Edward gave her. Settling her head against the cushion, she listened to the soothing crackle of flames.

Soon Edward returned with a dark brew of bitters and made Letitia drink every sour drop. Once she handed him the empty glass, she remembered her reason for leaving the drawing room.

"The highwaymen—they've come," she said.

He started, taken aback. "What?"

"The highwaymen who accosted us. They've come to Heppelwith Manor. While I was listening to Lady Eleanor play, I heard two of them converse in the corridor and attempted to follow."

A black thundercloud crossed his face as he sank to the edge of the cushion beside her and gripped the curved back of the settee. "And is it they who harmed you?"

"N–no." She blinked, astonished at the change that came over him, grateful she wasn't the recipient of his ire. "No one harmed me. The injury is an old one."

The stony tautness left his features, but his eyes remained grave. "You were right to inform me of the matter. Be assured, I will tend to this. However you must tell no one what you've told me. If you're correct, and these are the men who waylaid you, you could be in grave danger if they suspect your knowledge of their presence here."

She stared.

"Do you understand, Letitia?"

Her name on his lips was enough to startle her into a nod. "Sí. I—I understand."

His shoulders relaxed. He studied her a moment, the look in his eyes indefinable, before rising to his feet. "I must leave you now and carry out the directive His Grace has given me."

Hand pressed to her bosom, she watched him go. It wasn't fear that caused her heart to race within her breast; from the little she knew of Edward, she sensed he would never strike a woman. Rather, it was the sense of believing she'd always known him. The strength of his manner, the warmth of his tone, the gentleness of his eyes. . .

Her breath caught as a pebble of truth smashed into her mental assessment of his character.

From a distance, his eyes appeared darker, but up close in the yellow light of the lamps, his eyes were blue gray. And now she understood why they'd seemed so familiar.

They were the eyes that belonged to the leader of the highwaymen.

Chapter 6

Perhaps she was mistaken; she must be mistaken. No two men could be one person.

Seeking solace, her mind a cacophony of conflicting opinions, Letitia strolled through the maze of tall yew hedges angling off in intricate bends and scrolls in the center of the garden. She mulled over her encounters with both the marquis and Edward the previous day. Each time, she had thought she was looking into the eyes of the highwayman. Now she realized such a concept was absurd. Likely, the strain of these past two days had led her to believe things that didn't exist.

Inhaling deeply, she pulled her mantle further about her shoulders and lifted her face to the brisk air, just washed with morning freshness. Whatever tea Edward gave her yesterday had helped, and this morning a servant girl had brought more of the same, along with a salve of goose grease melted with horseradish juice, turpentine, and mustard. Dreadfully odorous, but it had relieved the ache in her bone to a great degree.

A ladies' tea had been scheduled for the afternoon, but Marian forbade Letitia to attend. The intended punishment for yesterday's unexpected encounter with the marquis was actually a reprieve. Letitia didn't wish to sit among strangers in a stuffy room, sipping weak tea, eating iced cakes, and listening to gossip.

Coming upon a wall of yew, she rounded the corner and almost barreled into the marquis.

"Oh!" She stepped back, putting her hand to the bush to maintain balance.

He also started in surprise, then smiled, though it seemed a trifle forced.

"My dear Lady Letitia Laslos." He took her free hand and bowed over it. "This is indeed a pleasure."

Ill at ease, she pulled her hand away and used it to smooth the flounces of her skirt. "I thought to take a walk through the maze."

"You need not explain; you may go wherever you like." Instead of allowing her to pass, however, he took her elbow and turned her around the way she'd come. "However, areas toward the center are slippery with mud, and I wouldn't wish you to fall. Allow me to escort you back."

Letitia had no say in the matter as he moved with her toward the entrance. She thought she heard rustling from within the maze and wondered if he had been alone, but no one followed. Likely the stirring of bushes had come from a bird or small animal.

He asked personal questions, and though Letitia was not as forthcoming as she'd been with Edward and the duke, he learned of her love of horses.

"You must ride with me," he said. "I happen to know of a

gentle mare that would suit you well."

"No, Lord Dalworth, I cannot—"

"And you must call me by my given name, William."

"Again I must decline. Surely you realize that doing so would cast an aspersion on my character if someone were to overhear?" Even if that weren't the case, she didn't feel comfortable enough in his company to comply.

"Blasted nobility and its rules," he ground out before his face resumed a pleasant cast. "Nevertheless, I insist you ride with me. I'll not take no for an answer."

Letitia was flummoxed. She dared not further exasperate the marquis by refusing, yet at the same time she feared Marian might find out. But oh, to ride again. . .

Marian tolerated the sport only when social functions demanded it. Letitia hadn't been seated on a horse in months. Desire won out over wisdom, and she nodded.

She was hard-pressed to keep up with him as he accompanied her to the stable, his hand at her elbow as though he thought she might change her mind. Brain in a muddle, she forced her legs to move. This was madness! Apparently he wasn't going to give her opportunity to change into her riding habit. What if someone should see?

A short time later with the cold wind whisking her face, making her feel wholly alive, and the strength of the galloping mare's muscles bunched beneath her, Letitia forgot her former worries. Laughing, she agreed to his challenge of a race, and both horses flew across the waving fronds of a wide meadow. The hood of her mantle flew back, her hair bounced free from its loose chignon, but she didn't pause or care. Her horse reached the thicket first, and she gaily laughed her victory as she turned the mare's head around and reached down to pat its glossy neck.

"You're an accomplished horsewoman." Approval tinged the marquis' tone.

"I've not ridden much."

"Perhaps. But some are born to the saddle and need few lessons. I presume you are one of those gifted few. You must ride with me again."

His words knocked the exultant breath from her, and she shook her head. "I cannot, but I've enjoyed our outing. I must return before the ladies finish their tea."

In her delight to ride again, Letitia had lost track of time. She could see by the sun's position that afternoon was upon them.

"Of course," he said lightly. "We wouldn't want aspersions to be cast upon your character."

Discomfited by his wry words, Letitia glanced at him, but he'd already turned away. She prodded her horse to follow.

Upon reaching the stables, Letitia was surprised to see Edward outside, his face a mask of disapproval.

His smile wide, William dismounted and strode over to Edward, clapping him jovially on the back. "Edward, old man! What brings you to the stables?"

"His Grace wishes to speak with you, my lord. At once." Somehow Edward managed to keep a civil tone.

"Does he now?" He turned his attention to Letitia. "A more faithful manservant one cannot find in all of England or

India, I'll wager. Imagine. Standing out here in the muck and awaiting my return. What loyalty!"

William laughed, but Edward remained sober. His gaze shifted upward to Letitia, and his breath caught. She was lovely.

Her thick, glossy hair had broken free of its restraints and waterfalled down her shoulders and back in wavy abandon, while soft tendrils caressed her face. The healthy color, once absent, now bloomed from her cheeks, reminding him of blush-pink roses kissed by morning dew.

"Boy!" William addressed a stable hand. "Tend to my horse." He then affected a ridiculously flamboyant bow to Letitia. "Alas, I must leave you, dear lady. Duty calls. But I hope to again have the pleasure of your company."

Gratification thrummed through Edward to hear Letitia's noncommittal reply. Once they were alone, he held up his hand toward her.

"Permit me?"

Letitia hesitated before nodding. He placed his hands at her waist and helped her to alight. When her feet reached the ground, she stumbled into him.

"Oh! Forgive me." Her words a mere breath, she turned her face upward. "I'm unaccustomed to the saddle. That is—it's been a long time."

His own legs as shaky as a rice pudding, he nodded. His thoughts ebbed as he continued to stare into her luminous, wide eyes.

"Edward?" she whispered in quiet entreaty.

The dictates of propriety fled. Sound judgment escaped, hot on the heels of trained wisdom. Before he could change his mind and call them back, Edward lowered his head and brushed his lips against hers. No more than a feather's touch. The kiss of angel's wings. Of earthly sweetness encapsulated in what must resemble heaven.

The shrill call of a hawk sliced through the air and startled them apart.

Letitia's face flamed. "Oh." She pressed her fingers against her cheeks and stepped back. "Oh!"

Concern filled his eyes. "Letitia—"

"No." She retreated another step, backing into the mare. "What have I done?"

"Please, don't take this to heart so. The blame was entirely my own. You've done nothing of which to be ashamed."

Wanting, needing to escape his quiet words and gentle eyes, she abruptly turned. Familiar weakness shot through her hip. Edward caught her as she staggered and almost fell. "Letitia!" Worry colored his voice.

She pushed from his arms. "Please—don't." Being in his embrace caused her heartbeat to escalate. Caused her to evoke the soul-stirring touch of his lips against hers. . .and hope for another kiss as sweet as the last.

If news of this were to reach Lady Marian or any of the guests, she would be in disgrace, cast away from decent society as her mother had been. Perhaps even sent back to Spain. While she would cherish seeing her family, she didn't want to be a disappointment to them or add to their trials by giving them another mouth to feed. Her mother wrote that the crops had been bad this year.

Picking up her skirts, she made haste for the manor, ignoring Edward's plea to wait.

Thankfully, he didn't pursue her, nor did anyone waylay her as she took the stairs to her room. A housemaid dusted within the bedchamber, humming. She bobbed a curtsey. "La, miss. I didn't expect you." With downcast eyes, she moved toward the door.

"Please," Letitia said. "Don't go."

The girl halted, uncertain, and Letitia realized her request must seem strange. After all, the girl didn't know Letitia was a servant, too.

"I don't mind if you stay and finish your chores," Letitia explained, unable to bear the solitude of her thoughts another moment. "And please continue your song."

The girl's eyes brightened. A slight smile shone on her freckled face, and she nodded, again flicking her feather duster along the wardrobe while she resumed humming.

The door banged inward.

Dismay pierced Letitia's heart. Marian stormed into the room, then caught sight of the maid. "Leave us."

The girl bobbed a half curtsey and scurried out the door, closing it behind her.

Marian stormed toward Letitia and slapped her. "How dare you!"

Letitia raised a hand to her stinging cheek. "I—I didn't mean—the kiss happened before I was aware—"

"You *kissed* him?" Marian backhanded her across the other cheek. "You kissed the marquis? Spanish strumpet!" She grabbed handfuls of Letitia's hair and pulled hard.

"No, it was Edward! Not the marquis!"

Tears stinging her eyes from the pain, Letitia struggled with her cousin. She clamped her fingers around Marian's punishing ones, trying to break their tension and pull them away.

"You rode with him," Marian sputtered. "Did you think I wouldn't hear? You willfully disobeyed orders, you wretched girl. You're no better than your mother. She was a strumpet, too!"

"Marian," a voice roared from the doorway. The rapid thumping of a cane followed. "Desist such unseemly behavior this moment! Do you hear?"

Marian loosened her hold and turned, shock draining the color from her face. Gratitude streamed through Letitia.

The dowager viscountess stood in the doorway, her countenance formidable.

Chapter 7

What is the meaning of this?" Grandmama Ackers's voice brooked no refusal.

"She has disgraced us," Marian cried. "She defied all convention and rode with the marquis—alone—then kissed him!"

"Not the marquis," Letitia cut in. "Edward."

"Edward?" Lady Ackers's brows lifted.

"You rode with the marquis. Lady Sedgeworth saw you!"

"Sí, but I kissed Edward." Heat seared Letitia's face, and she swung her gaze to Grandmama. "But I did not mean to kiss him," she added in a whisper.

"Hmm." The dowager viscountess studied them both, a speculative gleam in her eye. "Marian, I will speak with you later. Letitia, come with me."

Fearing a well-deserved lecture, Letitia followed the woman to the bedchamber she'd been given. Lady Ackers sank to a chair, her hand wrapped around her cane, but no chastisement followed. She did, however, study Letitia with a discerning eye.

Letitia shifted, uncomfortable. "I'm happy to see that you changed your mind about coming, Grandmama."

"Yes, I presume you are." The woman's words were wry, but Letitia didn't miss the amused twitch of her lips. "The trunk at the foot of the bed. Open it."

Letitia knelt to do so and fell back on her knees, bedazzled. A mound of shimmering satin shot with silver and gauze of the same color met her eyes.

"It's the gown you're to wear to the masquerade ball at week's end, and below is the mask. Bring it to me."

Letitia retrieved a white silk mask. Tiny seed pearls had been sewn along the edge. White feathers winged upward from the top. She gave it into Lady Ackers's hand and sat on the floor beside her chair. The gnarled fingers brushed over the stiff mask while a softness touched her time-worn face.

"I was seventeen, your age, when I wore this to my first masquerade ball," she said wistfully. "It was the week of my coming out, and the night I met Phillip."

Letitia's mouth parted. Lady Ackers's husband had been named Gerard.

"Our love was forbidden. His social status was beneath mine—he, a mere scholar and poet—and my father had higher aspirations for me. Still, we couldn't deny our love and sought for moments together throughout London's social season. We spoke of eloping, but days later Phillip was killed in a duel by a brash and prideful count who was skilled with weaponry. Poor Phillip wasn't as well-versed with a pistol." She sadly shook her head as if lost in another time.

Letitia was stunned but finally understood why the dowager

viscountess had become her dearest ally. She must have seen traces of the girl she'd once been in Letitia's mother.

"My aunt gave me this mask," she continued, her attention drifting to its shimmering front. "Lady Leighton. She wore it to her first masquerade ball, where she saved her true love, my uncle, from his cousin's evil scheme. The man pretended to be my uncle, hoping to get him killed by instigating a duel, and thereby receiving the title and lands that were Lord Leighton's. Ah, yes. In truth, this mask has quite a history. It's needed to be mended due to age, but it was said to be worn the night a young couple escaped Paris during the revolution. And also at a masquerade when a mysterious woman in red attempted to wreak havoc between a couple. But these stories I shall tell you another time."

Awed by the little she'd already heard, Letitia dropped her gaze to the mask.

"I want you to have it, Letitia. For your first masquerade ball. Perhaps you, too, might find your true love there."

Caught up in its past, Letitia took the proffered mask.

"Now, tell me about this Edward."

The abrupt change of topic brought Letitia's head up. "He's the marquis' manservant. A good man, kind and gentle. He's come to my aid twice."

"Do you love him?"

Taken aback by the abrupt question, Letitia only stared.

"Come, come. Do you love him?"

"I. . .Sí." Amazement swept through Letitia to realize the truth. "I do love him. But there is a matter that disturbs me." She smoothed her skirt's flounces, uncertain how to proceed. "His eyes, they. . .remind me of one of the highwaymen."

"Indeed?" Lady Ackers's brow furrowed as if in deep thought. "Have you shared this with anyone else?"

"No, I—I could not be certain." Letitia felt foolish. "The sun was bright, and the marquis possesses eyes of the same color."

Lady Ackers steadily regarded her. "Perhaps the strain from the ordeal confused you."

"Perhaps." Relief cloaked Letitia to hear the assumption she'd reached stated as fact.

"As to the matter of my granddaughter. . ."

Letitia stiffened. The mere mention of Marian brought back the pain of the attack.

"You needn't tell me what I witnessed was a rare occurrence; I know otherwise. Mayhap I should have spoken sooner." Lady Ackers straightened. "Be that as it may, I've talked to Hester and have decided to give to you early what I'd planned to bequeath to you upon my death. One hundred pounds, to be used as a dowry, if you wish it, or to sustain you until you find another position. If such is your preference, I shall do all within my power to find you gainful employment upon our return to London. Lady Fillmore seeks a governess for her children, and that family is mild mannered. You'd do well to find a position there."

Tears clouded Letitia's eyes. "You're dismissing me?"

"There, child, don't cry." Lady Ackers stroked Letitia's head, as if she were a small girl. "I cannot bear to see you further mistreated. I only desire your happiness."

"But I shall miss you. How can I be happy without your presence in my life?"

In a rare display of emotion, the old woman let her cane drop to the floor and gathered Letitia into her arms. "There, there. You're the daughter of which I've dreamed. Your name comes from the Latin and means 'joy,' did you know? And you've brought such joy to me in my old age. In thought and in heart, we'll never be far removed, no matter the distance that separates us. We're kindred spirits, you and I."

Closing her eyes, Letitia laid her head against Grandmama's shoulder, allowing the woman's slow rocking to soothe her. Letitia could only hope that this was indeed God's will for her life, but that didn't ease the ache within.

Catching sight of Letitia, Edward strode into the sitting room the family used for times of private worship. She stood looking at a framed portrait above the mantel. Uneasy, Edward followed her gaze.

Letitia glanced over her shoulder. Her expression grew stunned. "Edward."

"My lady." Since their kiss, he'd thought of little else but her. Yet his best recourse would be to keep that moment buried and not air apologies again. "The family came by that painting years ago. William Holman Hunt is the artist. The duchess requisitioned him to paint it after having viewed the original. She highly favors it and paid five hundred guineas, though I venture to guess it's worth far less."

"Oh, but who could put a price on anything so splendid? I believe some possessions are worth more in value than any monies can provide." Letitia returned her gaze to the painting. "It gives me such warmth to see our Lord Jesus standing near the door and clothed with lantern light against the darkness, His face so entreating, His hand raised to knock. He's always there for us, is He not? Always waiting for us to open the door to Him, assuring us that He's there."

"I wouldn't know."

The saddest expression clouded her face as she faced him. "You don't know or believe in the Savior, Edward?"

"He's never done much for me."

"Oh, but that's simply not true." Her smooth brow creased. She lifted her hands to her sides in supplication, stepping forward, as if in an effort to make him understand. "He died for you and gave His all so that you might live with Him for eternity."

Her beautiful eyes begged him to grasp her words. Despite his resolve to remain rigid in his unbelief, he was moved. She'd endured a lot, but so had he. How could she hold onto such faith? Why should she care that he did not?

"Sadly, the artist made a mistake," Edward said. "Have you noticed there's no handle on the outside of that bramble-covered door?" He'd stared upon the painting enough times to know.

She looked back to see. "Perhaps Mr. Hunt did so on purpose, to convey that one must open the door from within. The Lord is too much of a gentleman to walk inside uninvited."

Her words disturbed him more than he cared to admit. He gave a little bow. "I must attend to my duties." Before she could further argue her point, he left her company. An important meeting awaited, and he could tarry no longer.

❧

"Lady Letitia, will you take a turn about the room with me?"

Letitia looked up from her book in surprise to see Lady Eleanor, the marquis' sister, smiling down at her. A bold jaw resulting in something of an underbite and small eyes did little to detract from the woman's gentle beauty.

As always, Letitia was amused by the English nobility's tradition of strolling about the room when one wished to speak in confidence to another. No one sat near her on the settee, and the room was large enough that the four playing whist in the far corner wouldn't overhear. But she didn't wish to injure Eleanor's feelings and kept her thoughts to herself, setting the book aside. "Of course."

As they began to walk, Eleanor pulled Letitia's hand through her arm, drawing her close as if they were sisters.

"Dear Letitia, I've grown quite fond of you over this past week. You speak little, but when you do, your words are a delight." They walked past the duchess, the dowager viscountess, and two other women, all engrossed in their card game, past the fire blazing within the shoulder-high grate, and on toward the window that overlooked the manicured lawns. "I would venture a guess that my brother feels the same. He appears quite besotted by your company."

"The marquis?" Dismay pricked Letitia as she recognized the truth of Eleanor's words. These past three days William had sought her company often enough that his behavior must be noticed. Strangely, Marian said little when they were alone, for the most part ignoring Letitia, but the frown between her eyes indicated her displeasure concerning the situation.

"You appear distressed. Tell me, I must know. Is it only my imaginings?"

Letitia hesitated. The marquis' sister had become a friend, and Letitia didn't feel comfortable continuing the charade with her. "Lady Eleanor, forgive me, but I've not been forthcoming with you."

"Oh?"

"My station in life isn't as grand as I've portrayed. I'm but a simple companion to my cousin. An English earl's and Spanish count's granddaughter by blood, yes, but my father holds no title."

Halting her steps, Eleanor studied her. The pressure on Letitia's arm didn't decrease. "You have one day left with us. You could have kept silent, and I would never have been the wiser." An intelligent light filled her hazel eyes. "You have a reason for telling me this."

"Yes, I. . ." Letitia faltered, averting her gaze to the window and the maze beyond. How she had twisted things. "I ask pardon for baring my heart to you in what must seem an inappropriate manner, but I don't love your brother and fear I should have spoken earlier so as to discourage his advances."

"Indeed." It was a moment before Eleanor spoke. "Your heart belongs to another?"

"Sí." Relief seeped through her to tell the truth. "I hold deep affection for the marquis' servant, Edward. I've made his acquaintance such a short time, but I feel as if I've known him all my life." The frequent occasions she'd come across his path were some of the most precious to Letitia.

"Really? Well then, poor William will just have to pine his loss, eh?" Eleanor slyly smiled and squeezed Letitia's arm as they again took up their stroll until they came full circle to the settee. "Edward's a fine man. You could do no better."

"Yet his refusal to acknowledge God troubles me."

Eleanor's features clouded. "I understand. . . . Yet with you and me to petition the Lord on his behalf, he'll have no choice but to succumb to the truth. Yes?"

Letitia smiled. "Yes."

Once Eleanor left her, movement outside the window attracted Letitia's attention. She watched, puzzled. Though the men were supposed to be off on a shoot, three had just entered the maze.

Chapter 8

Letitia stared in wonder at the vision in the full-length cheval glass. Around her neck, Lady Ackers had hung a silver chain with the most brilliant opal.

"It reminds me of the moon," Letitia whispered. "The entire costume resembles moonlight."

"Ah, behold the moon," Grandmama said from behind her. "A shy maiden benevolently tending the earth, she sheds her pale light; a beacon to the weary traveler, a gentle radiance to a world laden with darkness. Daily her sister, the sun, blinds with her brilliance those who gaze upon her countenance. Attracted to her fire and magnificence, many pay little heed to the moon's gentle comeliness and disregard her when she visits the earth. Only those with a discerning eye observe the moon's hidden splendor, the splendor which the Creator bestowed only to her."

Letitia's cheeks flamed. Doubtless, Marian was the sun; yet could Letitia really be compared to something so beautiful as moonlight?

"Phillip wrote that," Grandmama said with a sigh. "An eternity ago."

Sensing Lady Ackers wanted to reminisce, Letitia kept silent. The voluminous ball gown of palest lavender satin bore fine vertical lines of sparkling silver that caught the light through the gossamer gauze she wore as an overlay. Layers of ruffles frothed from the gown's sleeves at the elbows. For the occasion, her hair had been curled, coifed, and powdered and now matched the gown—a shimmering soft lavender with strings of pearls for a headdress. The effect made her appear almost ethereal.

Letitia lifted the mask to her face and fastened its satin ties at the back. Her thoughts going to her cousin, she pivoted to face Lady Ackers. "May I ask a question?"

"Of course."

"I know it's none of my affair, and instruct me to mind my own business if you'd rather, but what did you say to my lady Marian?"

A sly smile lifted Grandmama's lips. "Relations between you have improved?"

"Tremendously. Oh, she still dislikes me; I can see that in her eyes. But the occasion is rare when she insults me or raises her voice."

"I told her the truth, a truth I shall tell you now. But it must never leave this room, Letitia. I stated that had your father preferred her mother over yours, she might be the one whose family had been disgraced and farming in Spain."

"What?"

"My dear child, Hester loved your father from the moment she set eyes on him, and a more dashing man I've never seen. She was jealous that her young sister had so wholly captured his affections. It was for spite that Hester told the earl your mother eloped with Roberto to Gretna Green before Kathryn had a chance to return home and soften his heart. I have no doubt your mother would have succeeded; she was the earl's favorite. But Hester hardened him against her. I learned the details years ago; she confessed her faults to me, admitting that in time, she'd grown to love my son. It was then that she asked permission to send for you since she felt she must do what she could to make reparation to her sister."

Amazement numbed Letitia's mind; she couldn't respond.

"Let us speak no more of the matter. Tonight, you shall shine like the Maiden of Moonlight for which Phillip penned the poem. But remember this, Letitia." She clasped an edge of the filmy gossamer. "These are merely outward trappings; forget not what is of true worth."

Letitia vowed not to forget but anticipated the evening. For one final night she would masquerade as someone greater than herself.

Bejeweled ladies in richly hued gowns of satin, silk, and velvet flitted past, introducing themselves by such allegorical titles as "Frost," "Last Rose of Summer," and "Evening Star." Stately gentlemen had dispensed with their normal black frock coats to don colorful garb for their oftentimes garish costumes, depicting characters from books and plays. All the guests wore matching masks or carried them on long sticks.

Letitia swept into the ballroom with Marian, whose shimmering gown of cloth of gold turned heads. With hair of deepest auburn and creamy-rose skin, even without her jewels, Marian as "The Golden Lorelei" was a sight to behold.

Discreetly hidden behind a decorative curtain of evergreens, a band of musicians played while couples performed a quadrille across the oak floor polished to a mirror gleam. The cloying scent of beeswax hung heavy in the air. Tonight, the gentry had flocked from the surrounding countryside. More than a hundred people were packed into the huge ballroom lit with candelabra, massive chandeliers, and wall sconces.

A short man in a moss green costume approached Letitia, introducing himself as Puck from Shakespeare's *A Midsummer Night's Dream*. He asked her to dance, but she declined. His affronted eyes stared at her through the slits in his mask, yet he bowed and departed. If she could dance, she would. Such dances might be considered effortless due to their mere walking, but the constant figures would be difficult to maneuver, and she didn't wish her leg to give way on the ballroom floor.

She socialized with the marquis' sister—robed in flowing white, with a garland of leaves and flowers woven in a circlet round her hair and a chain crossed over her waist as Tennyson's tragic "Lady of Shalott"—and with her stood Lady Carolyn Vaneers, a shy, sweet girl dressed in the deep gold and brown of "Autumn."

Suddenly, the marquis stood at Letitia's elbow. Instead of holding his glittering green mask to his eyes, he held it down by his side. "Will you dance with me, fair maiden? Or are you a sprightly fairy, having visited the earth to capture my heart?" He surveyed her ensemble. His own costume of counterchanged dark green and black stockings and tunic resembled a character from the Middle Ages.

"Neither, my lord." Even though he was unaware of her identity, Letitia raised her fan to her lips, recalling her resolve to discourage him. "I am Moonlight, and I prefer not to dance."

"Indeed?" His mouth firmed, but he turned to Carolyn. "Perhaps you will do me the honor?"

She curtseyed and accompanied him to the dance floor.

French doors to the moonlit terrace stood open in the next room, beckoning Letitia. The press of bodies had raised the room's temperature, and tendrils of hair stuck damply to her forehead.

The night air felt cool. Grateful no one else stood outside, she looked upward to the full moon. Glowing like a great pearl in a misty dark gray sky, it hovered over a grove of oak trees.

Footsteps on the paving arrested her attention. Startled, she turned.

"My lady?" Edward asked. "You are unwell?"

In his full livery of dark blue trimmed with gold, he was handsome. A moment elapsed before she captured enough breath to answer.

"I am well."

He nodded and made as if to go.

"Please, wait." At his evident surprise, she explained, "I should like the company."

His brows sailed upward. "You would rather converse with a servant than mingle with the fine lords and ladies gathered in disguise?"

"If that servant is you, I would." The words were bold, but behind the costume she felt safe from discovery.

He stared at her a long moment. "Might I have the honor of knowing whom I address?"

An imp of mischief took over, and she briskly fanned herself. "This is a masked ball, sir. To reveal my identity would break convention."

"Ah, a pity." He appeared amused. "Still, I don't wish to break convention. Henceforth, I suppose I shall have to address you as 'The Lady of Moonlight' since I have no other name to go by."

Letitia inhaled deeply as though struck. "For tonight, sir, indeed, you may call me Lady Luna."

"Luna. . .the Spanish term for moon. Is it not?"

She gave a slight nod.

Dawning light entered his eyes and he stepped forward. "Letitia, is it you?"

"Yes, Edward." She gave up her pretense and lowered the fan, suddenly grateful that he knew her identity.

"How stunning you look. When I heard the lilt of your accent, I should have known. You have a beautiful voice."

Letitia felt the kiss of a blush touch her face.

"But stay, why aren't you dancing? Don't tell me it's from lack of partners."

"I cannot dance," she said simply. "But I love the music and watching the dancers. And I've found dressing up in costume to be most pleasurable." Indeed, she felt like a little girl again and giggled.

The softest expression drifted over his face. "There's much I wish to say, Letitia, so much I wish to share. . ." He blew out a frustrated breath. "Hang it all, I will speak. I've come to feel strongly about you. Dare I hope my feelings might be returned?"

"I. . ." Shock robbed her of words, but any reply was

eclipsed as the duchess swept onto the terrace. She seemed astonished to see Letitia, with Edward standing so close, but quickly regained her composure.

"His lordship requests your presence, Edward." The duchess lifted her beaded mask on its stick, casting a curious glance Letitia's way before she regally entered the ballroom again.

"I suppose our conversation must wait." Edward's words were tense, though he produced a smile. "Tomorrow, before you leave for London, may we speak further on this matter?"

"Of course."

To her shocked delight, he lifted her gloved hand to his mouth. The gentle pressure of his lips on her fingers caused her heart to palpitate madly, and the steady look in his eyes captured her breath. "Until tomorrow, dear lady, I am your servant." He inclined his head in a slight bow.

Long after he entered the manor, her gaze remained on the last place she'd seen him.

Their encounter adding an extra layer of warmth to her overheated skin, Letitia strolled in the coolness of the night. Flickers of torchlight caught her attention at the front of the manor where blazing flambeaux illuminated the walkway and couples gathered.

She could scarcely believe that Edward cherished her as much as she'd come to love him. Was it possible? Could he find her a position at Heppelwith so she could remain by his side forever? Lady Eleanor would surely speak for them.

Buoyant as a crested wave, she drifted toward the maze. A flicker glowed through the bushes. Curious, she moved toward the flame. Men's voices rose in furious whispers.

"We shall proceed with the robbery after dawn as planned."

"I don't like it. Since that Spanish wench opened her mouth, there's been nothing but trouble. Mark my words, it was her who alerted the duke to our presence here. We should have done away with her when we had the chance."

"And I told you, I don't condone murder. I've taken care of the matter. She's not as acquiescent as the dear Lady Salinger, but doubtless I'll win her over. Once I claim her heart and have brought his lordship to ruin, nothing will stop us. I'll have what I want, and you'll have your gold."

Pressing her fingers to her open mouth, Letitia retreated a step. The gauze of her dress caught the bushes. She tore it free.

"What was that?" one of the men asked.

Letitia spun around in alarm. The familiar weakness struck her hip, and she staggered, grabbing the yew wall. At the loud rustle she winced and attempted to hurry away.

"Stop her!"

An iron-muscled arm wrapped around her, stalling her escape and her breath. She blinked back fear as the leader of the highwaymen came to stand before her.

No. . . I—it cannot be.

He pulled the mask from her face. A pained but resolute expression firmed his jaw.

"Ah, Letitia. Why? Why could you not have made this simplest for everyone by merely accepting my advances and minding your own affairs? If you had, I wouldn't need to do what I'm forced to do now." He nodded to the men standing behind her.

Each of them grabbed one of her arms.

"No!" Letitia fought to get free, but she was no match for their strength. "What will you do with me?"

His hand lifted, and the backs of his fingers stroked her cheek. "That, my lovely Letitia, is up to you." His fingers traced down to her jaw.

Angry tears glazing her eyes, she wrenched her head away from his touch. She never should have trusted him. He possessed the power to do whatever he willed with her. There was no one to stop him, no one to save her. Save for one.

Sálvame, mi Diós. . .My God, save me.

Chapter 9

"Edward?"

Upon hearing Lady Ackers's voice, Edward turned and affected a slight bow as the dowager viscountess came to stand before him.

The woman harrumphed. "Now then, none of that. I seek Lady Letitia Laslos, who tonight bears the name of 'Moonlight.' No one has seen her for some time."

"I was with her more than an hour ago."

"Hmm. My abigail found this near the maze." Lady Ackers handed him a white mask that appeared to have been crumpled underfoot. His heart plummeted when he recognized the bent feathers and seed pearls.

Letitia.

"I will get to the bottom of this. I assure you, she will be found."

"With you in charge, I don't doubt it. Notify me the moment she's located, Edward."

"Very good." He inclined his head.

A wry look entered her eyes. "You do that too well."

He was saved a reply as she turned and made for the stairs. Recalling Letitia's talk of overhearing the highwaymen, he alerted the house servants, and the search for Letitia quietly commenced.

One hour passed.

Two.

Then three.

After the fourth hour, Edward was beyond concern. Had he acted sooner, had he dispensed with his foolish scheme of which few approved, she would be by his side now. He was certain she'd been taken—but where? Was she alive? She had to be! He couldn't endure it if he lost her, too, the only woman he'd ever come to love. Now he realized how immense that love was. Could it be possible to feel so strongly about another on such short acquaintance?

Once Edward was so confident, attributing his position in life to his hard work and little else; now he felt utterly lost. Earlier, he'd combed the maze and grounds. Unsuccessful, he took his search to the manor. Room after room. Nothing.

Entering the empty chamber with the painting, the last place he knew to look, he glanced toward it. He could envision her standing there, her dark eyes wide, her hands lifted in entreaty for him to recognize and share her faith.

Moisture rimmed his eyes. "She belongs to You!" His heated words addressed the silent figure in the painting. "Why has this happened? If You're a merciful God, as she says, help me to find her—if You truly care so much. I cannot lose her, too!"

The lone figure wavered before him, and Edward dashed the tears from his lashes until the portrait was steady again. The expression of Christ in the portrait was so understanding, tender, compassionate. . . . The eyes seemed to beckon to him. . .to assure him that God's hope was the anchor on which he must now rely.

Inside Edward, something broke.

His palms hit the mantel, his head bowed low, while great gulping sobs he couldn't contain bellowed forth from the depths of his soul.

Letitia awoke to darkness most foul. Her arms ached where they'd been roughly handled, and what felt like strips of leather sawed into her ankles and wrists. Her jaw smarted from the scratchy gag bound across her mouth. She struggled to collect her senses.

The odors of horseflesh and hay led her to believe she'd been secreted away in the stable; there was no light to see. As if in answer, a horse's soft whinny and snort ruffled the air close by. She lay upon dirt, the chill seeping into her bones. A shelter stood overhead; she could hear the rain's patter strike wood and trickle through a crack. Water dripped onto her skirt with frequent splats. Its uncomfortable wetness had seeped through her skirt and petticoats. Shifting her legs, she winced as they strained against the tether, which cut more deeply into her skin.

Her mind couldn't grasp the truth. It made no sense. Why should he consort with unsavory characters? There appeared to be no rational explanation.

Closing her eyes, she succumbed to weariness.

When next she awoke, darkness still pervaded, but she could hear someone shouting far away. Calling her name.

Against the gag, she cried out, then raised her bound feet and kicked the wood. But her shouts came muffled, her actions weak. Frustrated tears burned her lashes and ran into her ears.

Please, Diós mio, let them hear. Forgive my foolishness in desiring to be someone I'm not. I've harbored bitterness because I wasn't one of the peerage, because I'm considered an underling to my cousin, something only You've known, something I was too ashamed to confess even to Grandmama. If I could again be given opportunity to serve Marian—and be warm and safe—I would be content; I would be obedient. Never again would I complain about my lot in life. Deliver me from those who would harm me.

Time passed. The rain ceased. Again her mind drifted.

Light behind her eyelids woke her, and she opened them to see dim gray light filtering through the cracks. She weakly moved her head and saw that she was nailed into a crawl space smaller than a closet and couldn't lie straight without her feet or head touching the walls. Focusing on the light, she tried to form prayers.

Cheery whistling broke her concentration. Her limbs stiff with cold, her hip aching fiercely, she raised her legs and kicked the wall. The thump was hardly effectual, and she tried again. And again. The whistling stopped. Footsteps crunched closer.

Letitia kicked again, forcing her raw throat to emit grunts. She saw wide eyes peer through the crack.

"Blimey, I'll have you out in a jiffy, miss." More footsteps, then the creaking of wood being pried, and a rectangle of daylight appeared as a plank tore away. The young stable boy stooped to look. "You stay right there, miss. I'll fetch help."

Where would she go? Letitia closed her eyes, assured her rescue was at hand.

Soon she heard more boards being torn away with fury, and blissful light covered her. Pressure weighted her wrists and ankles as a knife sawed through the cords. The gag was unbound from her mouth. Strong arms lifted her with ease and held her with supreme gentleness. She laid her cheek against the muscled shoulder beneath a coat that felt like serge and forced herself to look at him.

The eyes of peace stared back at her.

"Edward," she rasped, her throat like fire. Weary, her eyelids fluttered closed again.

"Shh." His lips brushed her forehead. "You're safe."

She was barely aware of him carrying her to the manor or upstairs to the room she shared with Marian. But when Edward laid her upon the counterpane, she roused enough to grab his sleeve. "You must stop him."

"Who?"

"The marquis. He robs Lord Bellingham this morn." With that, she fell back, and her fatigued mind and body relinquished themselves to rest.

Chapter 10

Inside the carriage, alone, Edward grimly recounted the facts. How could he have been so blind? Despite the little information he'd gleaned, he hadn't wanted to believe the truth, had avoided it for weeks. But there it was, staring him in the face. He'd been a fool! And he'd almost lost the woman he loved because of his folly.

To find Letitia bound and gagged. So pale. . .at first he'd thought her dead. The sick feeling returned, the abject fear that he might have lost her, the terrible ache in the center of his being, but he forced such memories away. She was safe and warm, and he must keep his mind on the present situation.

Almighty Father, I'm new in my service to You. I humbly ask that You help me to be successful this day, to remember Your Son is the anchor to which I must hold. I cannot accomplish this in my own strength.

When the shouts of riders came, Edward was ready. Before Lord Bellingham's carriage rolled to a full stop, he withdrew his pistol and flung open the door. There was a scurry of surprise, but he aimed his weapon at William before he or his men could get a bead on Edward.

"It's over, *Lord Dalworth*," he stiffly addressed the kerchiefed rider on horseback, who wore a brace of pistols, one on each side. "Tell your men to throw down their weapons."

Instead, William made a frantic grab for one of his guns. Edward was saved shooting him when five riders burst through the trees on horseback, pistols aimed at the three.

The two highwaymen threw down their firearms. William lifted his hands in the air, his chuckle terse. "Bully for you, Edward. You win. This time."

Instead of rising to the bait as he'd done all his life, Edward walked toward him. "You possess something that doesn't belong to you. Allow me to relieve you of it."

William glared but pulled off the loose ring that had slipped around his finger and placed it in Edward's outstretched hand.

"You almost killed her!" Edward tightened his hold on the ring, attempting a calm he didn't feel. What he desired was to pull the man from his horse and knock him senseless.

"I was confident you'd find her in that storage area where we played as children. And you did, didn't you? Otherwise, you wouldn't be here. But if not for me, my men would have killed her."

As the constable led him away, hands bound, William called, "She's not the type to wink at lies and deceit as Lady Salinger did. She'll never forgive you, Edward."

He bit back a reply. In his heart, he prayed such wasn't the case.

❧

Letitia dressed, anxious as to why she was being summoned.

Three days she'd remained bedridden to regain her health and strength. Except for Grandmama, the Ackers party had returned home to London. Soon, Letitia must go, too. Yet she'd learned a hard lesson. Just as the marquis had hidden behind his title to do evil, she'd hidden behind her masquerade, desiring to be someone she wasn't. Well, no longer. From this day forward, she would accept her role in life, whatever that may be. She would be content and embrace each day cheerfully. Having almost lost the opportunity, Letitia was grateful to receive a new start.

She'd been shocked to discover Marian had imparted helpful information to Grandmama, telling how she'd observed three men with Letitia near the maze. Later, she'd recognized one of them by his fairy-like costume as Puck on the outside steps and had eavesdropped on their conversation. Both men were upset that William prevented them from killing Letitia, and they'd quietly discussed returning to end the deed, then blame it on William. Near dawn, Edward learned the information and met the stable boy running with news of finding her.

While Marian's farewell to Letitia days ago had been devoid of emotion, Letitia knew she had her cousin to thank for saving her life and told her so. Marian had flushed as if uncertain how to respond but hadn't pulled away when Letitia gently squeezed her hands in farewell.

Following a servant, Letitia entered the private parlor in which she'd glimpsed Edward walking with the duchess on her first morning at Heppelwith. The duke stood near a gold-veined marble fireplace, and Eleanor sat on a damask-covered chair. Edward stood near her. Seeing Letitia, the girl smiled and moved to embrace her.

"I'm pleased to see you fully recovered, Letitia, and I'm confident there are others here who share my sentiments." She glanced at Edward, whose face had reddened. "Alas, I must attend to my morning correspondence. We shall converse at tea, as we have much to discuss. Father?" She went to him and affectionately took hold of his arm.

The duke sternly eyed his daughter, though Letitia noted he patted the hand at his sleeve. "Very well, Eleanor. I'm not dim-witted. I'll leave you to it then, Edward. I must tend to my songbirds." The two left the room.

Puzzled, Letitia waited. Edward pulled at his cravat, looking ill at ease. For the first time, she noticed he wasn't in his livery. Had he been dismissed?

She sank to the cushion. "Edward?"

He moved to the opposite chair, looked at her, then shot to his feet and began to pace. "First, it's imperative you know I'm not a man who practices deceit. I had a sharp blow dealt me shortly after my arrival from India. My betrothed had proven to be a woman of immoral character."

Letitia swallowed over a dry throat. This had been the first she'd heard that his heart was attached to another.

"So as to avoid her further pain, the engagement, arranged by my father, was quietly dissolved, but the experience bred caution within me. I don't intend to return to India without a wife. No one of eligibility resides there—the few English women are married or are too young—and it's time I settle down."

Again he nervously pulled at his cravat, so hard, it went askew. "I devised a scheme to select a woman I could love who could love me in return. For such a plan to succeed, I had to take drastic measures. My family wasn't in favor of the idea, but neither did they prevent me from following through with it. The recent robberies aided in their acquiescence, due to the fact that the first victims who'd been robbed are dear family friends. In my role, I was able to investigate the matter, piece together facts. That's why I was in London."

"Oh," Letitia managed to breathe. She tightly clasped her hands in her lap. A sense of unreality teased her mind. Perhaps she was dreaming. This must be a dream.

He returned to his chair and brought it closer to hers. "My desire was to find a woman of virtue. One loyal and true. A woman who would bestow the same consideration to a servant that she would to a nobleman. However, in order to seek such a woman, it was imperative that I conceal my identity. How else would I know she wasn't playing me false for selfish gain? I'd been deceived once and couldn't let it happen again. Do you understand, Letitia?"

Face afire, she could only stare. Her spinning mind desperately rejected the words he had yet to say.

He leaned forward, covering her cold hands with his warm ones. "I am Lord Edward Dalworth. The marquis."

His face blurred. She desperately tried to force rational thought, to force any words to her lips at all.

Alarm lightened his eyes. Grasping her shoulders, he settled her back against the cushion and poured something into a glass. He put it under her nose, but she shook her head.

"Drink," he commanded.

One small sip of the bitter brew burning down her throat

was enough to revive her. Disgusted with herself, she pushed his hand holding the glass away. She wasn't one to swoon. She must still be weak from her ordeal.

"What of Lord Dal—I mean, Lord William? Or. . .whoever he is?"

"He's my cousin. We both work for our uncle in India. My father and my uncle, Lord Hathaway, own a silk plantation there. William's father also had a smaller share, but he died of malaria."

"He robbed us." The words were inane, but Letitia couldn't think of anything intelligent to say.

"I apologize for the harm William caused. While he masqueraded as me, I learned of his plan to implicate me in the robberies."

"But I'd seen him, heard their plans! I knew he was the one."

His eyes were grave. "It would have been your word against his. He knew of my feelings concerning you and could have easily turned your words around to suggest that you were protecting me."

Letitia dropped her gaze. He needn't elaborate; no English court would believe the word of a domestic over that of a nobleman.

"He desired to take everything I possessed. I learned quite recently that he was the one to rob me of my fiancée by wooing her. Poor Lady Salinger." Edward sighed, briefly looking to his hands clasped between his knees. Letitia could now see his ring with the family seal, the same ring William had worn all week. "I should have suspected his involvement, but he covered his tracks well and pretended to be a friend. Doubtless he hoped to rob me of my title by having me sent to prison and achieve a higher position with our uncle in managing the affairs of the plantation."

"Is that what you do?" she whispered.

He smiled. "I manage the accounts. You would love India."

"I?"

"Of course. Don't you understand what I'm saying?"

She shook her head.

"Dearest Letitia, I wish to marry you."

Again her mind grew vacant. She sought for words. "But I'm not. My mother—"

"Was a lady who committed no crime. I know all about your so-called family scandal. I've talked long with the dowager viscountess this past week. As have my parents. You've won my father over with your spirit; you're the only one besides family who's ever exhibited enough courage to stand up to his bluster." He grinned. "And my patient sister was forced to hear the workings of my heart these whole miserable ten days."

"But"—Letitia shook her head—"I cannot marry you. I've never been presented to the Queen."

He chuckled. "That can be arranged. Lady Ackers seemed confident you would be agreeable. She sent a letter to Her Majesty, Queen Victoria, three days past."

Letitia stared, hardly daring to believe what was happening.

"Yet perhaps the lady dowager erred, and you don't return my feelings?"

At the worry in his eyes, she was quick to speak. "No, Edward. I've had great affection for you since the night you rescued me in London and took me into your coach." Her cheeks warmed. "It was *your* coach?" Of course it was. The knowledge that Edward was the marquis and not William still bewildered her.

"Yes." He shifted his gaze, again looking ill at ease. "Letitia, can you possibly forgive me for deceiving you by letting you assume I was a servant?"

She gave a faint smile. "It seems we both engaged in a masquerade. You as a servant, and I as a lady of worth."

"Ah, but Letitia. . ." He took hold of her hands, bringing her up with him as he rose to his feet. "You are indeed a lady of great worth."

He gathered her close to his heart, and Letitia relaxed her head near his shoulder. There was much more to say, much more to learn, but for now she was content to be held by the man she loved.

Epilogue

Three years later

Clothed in a gown of silver, Letitia stood beside Edward on the plantation's open verandah and watched their guests dance. From behind, a night bird called out from somewhere beyond the fringe of mango trees. A monkey chattered, setting off a chain of jungle music as the strains of violins produced their own melody in the ballroom. The air was warm, the scents heady with nearby branches of frangipani. Letitia loved this beautiful, dangerous, exotic land, which no longer seemed foreign to her after having lived in it for almost three years.

"I would say that our first masquerade ball is a success, wouldn't you, my love?" Edward took hold of her gloved hand and kissed it.

"Oh, yes. Quite."

Childish giggling reached her ears, and Letitia looked to see their curly-headed daughter peering round the wall, bare toes peeking from beneath her white nightdress, a crumpled costume mask of the same color held to her eyes.

"Regina," Edward warned, "shouldn't you be in bed?"

"Don' wan' bed, Papa." The girl scampered to her father's arms, and he hoisted her up. She kissed his cheek with a loud smack.

"Memsahib!" A young native woman with copper skin and a colorful tunic rounded the corner, out of breath. "Little missy leave her bed. She play in *memsahib's* trunk with pretty dresses, then run away from her *ayah* when I was not watching."

"Never mind, Yanni," Letitia told the child's nurse. "I'll tend to her."

"And you will read to the servant children again about the miracles of Jesus? I like to hear them, too."

"Tomorrow. I promise." Letitia was happy that Yanni had recently accepted the Lord. After two years of difficult communication and improving on the servants' English, Letitia had finally gotten through to them with the message of the Gospel while learning their language, too.

"I will tell them." Before leaving, the girl smiled and pressed her palms together, bowing her head and bringing her fingers to her forehead in a respectful *namaste.*

"As for you, young lady, you're being very naughty." Letitia studied her two-year-old daughter.

Regina gave the sweetest pout, wrapping her plump little arms across her chest. "Don' wan' bed."

The all-day excitement of preparations for the ball had buoyed everyone's spirits, especially the children's.

"If Mamá tells you the stories behind the mask, will you try?"

"Sto'ies?" Interest lit Regina's big brown eyes. She laid her head against Edward's shoulder and yawned. The hand holding the white satin mask hung down by her side.

"Sí, mi niña. The mask is almost one hundred years old and has many wonderful stories of adventure, including mine and Papá's. But you must be a good girl and do as you're told. Then I'll tell you all its wonderful stories." She kissed the small dimpled hand.

Regina's eyes drooped, the long lashes sweeping over rosy cheeks. "Mamá tew sto'ies."

"Tomorrow you shall hear them," Edward promised then smiled at Letitia. "I'll put her to bed."

During his absence, Letitia again looked from her place on the verandah toward their thirty-eight costumed guests. Eleanor was visiting from England and was dancing with a British officer, a titled lord in whom she'd recently expressed interest. Judging from his unwavering attentions, Letitia felt certain the girl's affection was returned. Eleanor brought news from home, too, of Marian, who recently gave birth to her firstborn son, having married a wealthy viscount twice her age. And Grandmama Ackers, as feisty as ever, had sent word that she planned to visit India for her upcoming sixty-first birthday, bringing Letitia's parents with her.

Letitia smiled, eagerly anticipating the celebration she would hold. She hadn't seen her parents or the dowager viscountess since before Edward and she had left for India directly after their marriage. First, they'd visited Spain, and with Edward's consent, she'd given her parents the hundred pounds Grandmama had given to her.

Hearing strains of a waltz begin, Letitia swayed to the music while staring up at the huge moon on its velvet canvas of black sky, bigger and brighter than it had ever been in all of England.

Sensing Edward behind her, she smiled when his hand slid around her waist then gasped as his other hand went beneath her legs and he swung her up into his arms. Automatically her arms flew around his neck. Nearby torches caught the mischievous twinkle in his blue gray eyes.

"Edward, what are you doing?" She laughed. "What will the guests say if they see?"

"I don't care," he said. "Ever since I saw you that night three years ago on my father's terrace at the masquerade ball, I've wanted to dance with you. Conventions denied me the pleasure of holding you in my arms then. My one regret is that I waited this long."

She smoothed her hand along his lean jaw. "I've always wished I could dance," she admitted. "And to do so with my husband whom I dearly love would please me."

"Then, my Lady of the Moonlight, your wish is my command."

He brushed a tender kiss across her lips before beginning to waltz with expert grace. While in the starry skies above, the great disk of the moon bathed them in its gentle glow.

PAMELA GRIFFIN

Pamela Griffin loves stories of intrigue and mystery set in nineteenth-century Europe, both reading them and writing them (and watching them). A&E's *Pride and Prejudice* has long been one of her favorite Regency movies, and she's recently added the 2004 film musical release *Phantom of the Opera* to her list of favorite European historicals. She makes her home with her family in Texas and has contracted over thirty books in both contemporary and historical romance. Writing to her is more ministry than career, and it thrills her to hear evidence of God working in others' lives through her stories.

She loves to hear from her readers at words_of_honey@juno.com and readers can visit her Web site: http://users.waymark.net/words_of_honey.

A Letter to Our Readers

Dear Readers:

In order that we might better contribute to your reading enjoyment, we would appreciate your taking a few minutes to respond to the following questions. When completed, please return to the following: Fiction Editor, Barbour Publishing, Inc., P.O. Box 719, Uhrichsville, OH 44683.

1. Did you enjoy reading *Masquerade?*
   ❑ Very much—I would like to see more books like this.
   ❑ Moderately—I would have enjoyed it more if ______________
   ____
   ____

2. What influenced your decision to purchase this book? (Check those that apply.)
   ❑ Cover ❑ Back cover copy ❑ Title ❑ Price
   ❑ Friends ❑ Publicity ❑ Other

3. Which story was your favorite?
   ❑ *Liberty, Fidelity, Eternity* ❑ *Love's Unmasking*
   ❑ *A Duplicitous Façade* ❑ *Moonlight Masquerade*

4. Please check your age range:
   ❑ Under 18 ❑ 18–24 ❑ 25–34
   ❑ 35–45 ❑ 46–55 ❑ Over 55

5. How many hours per week do you read? ______________

Name ____

Occupation ____________________________________

Address _______________________________________

City ________________ State __________ Zip __________

E-mail ____